A
DISASTER

IN
THREE

ACTS

Also by Kelsey Rodkey:

Last Chance Books

A DISASTER IN THREE ACTS

KELSEY RODKEY

HARPER TEEN
An imprint of HarperCollinsPublishers

HarperTeen is an imprint of HarperCollins Publishers.

A Disaster in Three Acts

Library of Congress Cataloging-in-Publication Data

Names: Rodkey, Kelsey, author.
Title: A disaster in three acts / Kelsey Rodkey.
Description: First edition. | New York : HarperTeen, [2022] | Audience:
    Ages 13 up. | Audience: Grades 10-12. | Summary: Eighteen-year-
    old ex-friends, Saine and Holden, are forced to work together on
    a documentary that threatens to reveal their true feelings.
Identifiers: LCCN 2021053165 | ISBN 9780062994493 (hardcover)
Subjects: CYAC: Interpersonal relations—Fiction. | Love—Fiction. |
    Documentary films—Fiction. | Schools—Fiction. | LCGFT: Romance fiction.
Classification: LCC PZ7.1.R639526 Di 2022 | DDC [Fic]—dc23
LC record available at https://lccn.loc.gov/2021053165

Typography by Jessie Gang
22 23 24 25 26   PC/LSCH   10 9 8 7 6 5 4 3 2 1

First Edition

To my mother, Wendy,
Thank you for being my first fan.

A DISASTER IN THREE ACTS

ACT ONE

in which a bad idea is born

ONE

At 6:43 p.m. on Football Friday, Corrine Baker is right on schedule for a pregame meltdown, and you bet your ass I have my camera ready for the freshman cheerleaders' reactions. This is a moment they'll remember for the rest of their lives. Something they'll want to cherish, look back on *fondly*—

"Macy, a doctor's note means nothing to me," Corrine says to the sophomore newcomer. "Your mother is a doctor. You getting a doctor's note is as easy as a baby drooling on itself."

Four perfectly red-lined mouths pop open, jaws on the dirty locker room floor.

I'd feel bad about Macy's semipublic humiliation at the hands of Corrine, but Macy isn't actually sick, she's just hungover. We all know she was drinking last night, on a *Thursday*, because her Instagram stories didn't end until about two in the morning or whenever she and her friends drained her father's liquor cabinet dry. One or the other.

I zoom in to Macy's face, her squad of freckles smothered

under the blush creeping onto her cheeks. If Corrine makes her stand there any longer, Macy'll probably throw up on Corrine's perfectly white sneakers that she only wears for games, and then we'll see how annoyed my best friend can really get.

Corrine snatches the paper out of Macy's hand. "*Get well soon.*"

My other best friend, Kayla Kishbaugh, slides onto the bench next to me, her dark brown curls loose over her uniform. "Corrine's being kind of a b-i-t-c-h, right?"

I turn my camera in her direction. She has no bad angles. "No, it's just . . . a pregame ritual. We all have them. I dissociate, you miss that tiny patch of hair above your ankle when shaving, and Corrine makes someone cry."

I get a whiff of her vanilla perfume when she pulls her leg onto the bench to check out her shave job. Sure enough, little specks of hair dot her brown skin in the curve of her calf. "How did you know?" she asks. "And more importantly, why did you never tell me? Have other people noticed?"

She's so used to me shoving my camera in her face that she's just now seeing that I have it pointed at her. She pushes it away with practiced gentleness—it was a gift from my mom and grandma for my seventeenth birthday. "Saine, don't you dare show this to anyone."

"Let's get out there!" Corrine cheers to the buzzing room. Coach Hartl stands proudly behind her, arms crossed over her faded red polo. "We have losers to support."

"Save the trash-talking for the other team, Corrine," Coach Hartl says, motioning for the cheerleaders to leave the locker room with her.

The four girls Corrine stunned with her earlier dressing-down leap to their feet and fly out of the room. Kayla stands, catching Corrine's Intense Eyes™.

"Kayla," she says, marching up to us, "you're going to fly in Macy's spot tonight."

Kayla gestures to me. "What, you expect Saine to hold me up by herself?"

"No," she says. "I'll be your base, too."

"Please don't let me die," Kayla says to me with a groan in her voice.

"You'll be fine," Corrine says with a laugh. All the humor slides off her face when she turns my way. "You, on the other hand. What's that on your mouth?"

"A smile?"

Her own cherry-red lips frown. "Black is not a cute or school-sanctioned lip color." Lying is a waste of energy, she always says. Better to just get straight to the point.

"It's one of our school colors, though."

"She has a point," Kayla says, pulling her hair into a sloppy but passable ponytail.

"We wear red lipstick and you know this," Corrine says.

"She *also* has a point." Now Kayla slides her school-sanctioned, cherry-red bow from around her wrist and over her hair tie. This conversation feels ominously reminiscent of the one we had when Corrine convinced me to become a cheer-leader sophomore year. Resistance was futile, and not that I'd ever admit it to her, but I had been pretty excited to be part of a team anyway. She didn't need to put in so much effort to make me join with her. I'd follow her to the ends of the earth if she promised it would be a good time and I wouldn't be alone.

Corrine crosses her arms. "Thank you."

I've been trying to get black lipstick approved for two years now, but I guess this isn't the year either. "It's a lip stain. I'm sorry," I say, "but this sucker's not coming off until I'm cremated."

"Better start scrubbing." Corrine flips her strawberry-blonde ponytail over her shoulder and winks.

"Rude."

"There's lipstick in my bag if you need it!" she says before disappearing.

"It's just her *pregame ritual*," Kayla whispers before following Corrine out.

After some intense scrubbing and reapplying, I fix my long, dark hair into a higher ponytail and head toward the Cedar Heights High School football field, cursing Corrine's name. I'm a firm believer that it's better to ask forgiveness than permission and all that, so I can't fault her too much. I knew she wouldn't let it fly.

The wind whips at my bare legs, goose bumps appearing after one blow as I jog through the packed parking lot. To get to the front of the bleachers, I have to hustle around a bunch of people just standing around in useless clusters. The scent of fresh fries wafts toward me, stalling my progress just long enough for my stomach to growl—I had half a peanut butter and banana sandwich before the game, and it was filling enough, but it wasn't *fries*.

I'm about to swing onto the track where the rest of my team

cheers on our very unsuccessful football players as they enter the field, but there's a lanky pain in the ass in my way. I'm late, and not in the mood, but Holden Michaels, Corrine's ex-boyfriend as of about four months ago, either doesn't feel me tap him on the shoulder, or he doesn't care. Probably the latter.

I clear my throat.

"Oh, hi, Saine," he says in a bored voice, his face scrunched up behind his DSLR as he snaps at the players running in front of him. "I exist today?"

"You're in my way and I was trying to politely hint at that." And it's true, this is about as polite as I get with Holden since I don't have to be around him for Corrine's sake anymore. We occasionally spoke when they dated, with Corrine as a referee, but since the breakup, our communication has practically been on mute, and for good reason. Corrine never explicitly said she broke up with him because he was cheating, but when she said there was another girl, I put two and two together myself.

"Oh, of course. You just needed something from me." He drops his hands so I can see his face: red, wind-thrashed cheeks; bushy black eyebrows over icy blue eyes; deep pink lips in the shade of "First Kiss" forming an annoying, heartbreaking smirk. "That makes more sense."

Coach Hartl calls my name, so I shove past him. Despite his light coat, he still radiates heat, and I hate him for it as another ten thousand goose bumps invade my skin.

"What, no funny business?" he taunts. "Ran out of witty comebacks?"

I walk backward so I can face him when I say, "Sorry, but

I can't always be your source of amusement. Maybe invest in a mirror." I snap. "Look at that. I guess I *didn't* run out."

No amount of *rah-rah-rass, kick 'em in the ass* could encourage the Cedar Heights Hawks to complete any successful plays. We're speeding toward another loss when Corrine can sense I'm itching to film the team. She allows me to, as long as I capture her good side, which, like Kayla, is every side. She'd have at least seven good sides even if she were two-dimensional.

I run up the metal bleacher stairs to film the team front and center, but just as I'm positioning myself behind the guardrail, Holden appears and nudges me off-center.

"I'm taking photos for the yearbook," he says by way of explanation, not even bothering to look at me.

"I'm taking *video* for the yearbook." I try to nudge him back, but he's like a wall. A lean, skin-and-clothes-covered wall. I miss when he was shorter than me in elementary school.

"The *digital* yearbook. *TikTok* counts as the digital yearbook as long as you use the right hashtag. This is for the real yearbook." He lifts his camera, poised to take a photo of the girls mid-toe-touch, but I place my hand in front of the lens.

"I was here first."

He faces me. "Why aren't you down there with the other cheerleaders? I think there are some pom-poms missing your hands right about now."

"Well, they'll just have to wait so I can do this." I flick him off with a tight smile. "Don't think the girl who dumped you gave you permission to photograph her."

"Oh, please." He snaps a picture of me, my vision exploding into orbs and negatives. "Corrine loves having her picture taken." *I, on the other hand, do* not. "And this is a public, school event."

I reach for his camera, already imagining the terrible things he could do with a double-chinned photo of me in Photoshop. "Delete that."

He pulls a face at the display screen. "Don't worry. I will." He faces the field again and snaps a few photos in quick succession, each crunch of the shutter increasing my chances of a headache.

I film what I can, getting really dramatic close-ups and shifting the focus from girls in the front row to the whole way in the back, but my shots are fucking off-center, just because he's taller than me with bonier elbows. How does he expect me to get a filming gig one day with off-center footage in my reel?

With less than four minutes on the clock in the last quarter and no need for going into overtime, I abandon my shitty spot and deliver an acidic smile to Holden. "I hope all your files are corrupt when you transfer them."

"The ones with you in them will be," he says in the same sarcastic tone.

It's so weird to think we were ever friends. Like before he and Corrine got together. I was a naive seven-year-old and he was just the first kid to laugh at my extremely hilarious joke: *A guy walks into a bar. Ouch.* (My grandma taught me this crowd-pleaser.) He was also the only kid to even get it, so you have to understand that the bar was set pretty low. No pun intended.

But despite being inseparable until sixth grade, when we tried to maintain a friendship after starting different middle schools, an unspeakable and embarrassing spin the bottle mishap caused those five years of inseparable best friendship to dissolve like my hopes of wearing black lipstick to football games as soon as I laid eyes on Corrine Baker. I knew I needed to be her best friend. Sorry not sorry, Holden. He just didn't laugh as much or make his own tie-dyed T-shirts and banana nut muffins, didn't like happy music, didn't write me notes about each teacher that read like villain origin stories explaining why they chose to teach the subject they taught.

Holden Michaels simply could not compare to Corrine Baker.

The game wraps up in what the local newspaper will undoubtedly call a humiliating defeat—we're well past being humiliated— and Corrine takes me home. Even though the porch light is on, there's no one inside. I haven't seen my dad since I was ten and he moved to New York without so much as a goodbye—there was a note, sure, but no manning up and doing the hard work of a face-to-face. Monday through Friday, my mom works as a night manager at the local Amazon fulfillment center, and my grandma, whose house this is, died five months and one day ago from a completely random heart attack that never should have happened because she was in her early sixties, jogged every day, and drank gross green smoothies. But it's cool; if my therapist I saw precisely one time asks, I'm moving on, everything is fine, I'm *coping*, and I definitely don't need to pay my future life savings to sit in a stuffy office and say exactly that. Shit happens.

I could've taken Corrine up on her offer to hang out, but I have an early shift at the Penn State Harrisburg film department rental desk and I need to sleep. Hell hath no fury like film students on a deadline.

When I reach the front door, my backpack over my shoulders and my duffel bag in hand, I wave to Corrine, but I know she won't leave until I'm inside. I wave to the camera mounted by the porch light, knowing my mom's getting a video sent to her phone to show her I made it home, and unlock the door.

Bagel, aka Shame Bagel, aka Seamus Bagel when he's being bad, greets me in all his tan-and-white Pomeranian glory as I turn the living room lights on. He's named such because when my grandma found him digging through the trash a few years ago, it was for the remnants of a burned bagel. Next, I turn on the TV. I like feeling like I'm not alone, even when I am. Unless not feeling alone is because it feels like a stranger is in the house with me. My constant predicament.

I let Bagel out back to do his doggy deeds, a floodlight drenching the scene in yellow and shadows. I wave to the other security camera by the door before calling him back inside and heading to my room. I kiss my fingertips and press them against the mural my grandma painted on the living room wall of her, my mom, and me a few years ago. Some nights, when I can't sleep, I watch the time-lapse I took of her painting this. She was a brilliant artist, and each room in this house is a testament to that. She spent her days giving art lessons to amateurs (mostly little kids with a lot of energy) in our living room and dubbed herself the Easy Easel; she was a town favorite and was even asked to paint a mural on the steps of the capitol building before she died. My favorite of her work in the house—murals showing scenes from documentaries I love—fills the walls of my bedroom, where I go now and collapse face-first onto my bed.

I have a busy weekend ahead of me; the game was just the beginning. Tomorrow, I work an eight-hour shift at a school that I don't attend, *or plan to attend*, then I have to rent more equipment—another camera, microphones, lenses, everything—and make sure I'm ready for Sunday, when I start production on my very first documentary.

The butterflies in my stomach swirl to a new height.

I've been trying to keep my excitement to a minimum, because it feels like a betrayal to finally be doing this only now that my grandma, my biggest supporter, has passed, but I have no control over the timing. I've filmed this and that in the past, edited footage together in shorter narratives, but this is practically the big leagues, and it's not just for me and my friends to watch.

I pull my phone from the waistband of my skirt and open my emails to reread the words that are burned into my mind:

Dear Ms. Saine Sinclair,

Thank you for applying to the Fiona O'Malley Documentary Pilot Program at Temple University. We've received your primary application and eagerly await your portfolio, which should showcase your camerawork, directing, and knowledge of story structure, to be submitted by **December 16.** We hope you'll be one of the fifteen applicants accepted into our exciting first year of this program! Please find a list of the documentary's requirements attached to this email.

I open the list and scan it for anything I may have missed, even though I know there's nothing. I have it memorized by now. The documentary must be self-shot, local, and at least forty minutes long. All footage must be original. Content warnings should accompany the film if necessary.

The little *ding* of a notification sounds when a new email from Yvette Lacey, my documentary subject, lands in my inbox. I had asked her if she could pick me up Sunday night because my mom has to work an extra shift and, therefore, will be taking the car. I could order a Lyft, but I've had my eye on a new external microphone for my camera and every dollar counts. In her email, Yvette says she will gladly give me a ride to and from the event—though she's sad she won't have a chance to reconnect with my mom. Since I'm basically asking to stalk her and use her personal life for my personal gain, I had already decided to be understanding if she couldn't. Even if it meant her own obligations got in the way of this potentially life-changing event of mine. Though it could be life-changing for her, too.

Admittedly, I worked a bit backward on this documentary so far. A smarter person would find an interesting subject and create a documentary around them, but instead I found an interesting *plot* and searched for a person to throw in it. As a rule, nothing exciting ever happens in central Pennsylvania, so I was stressing over my documentary being too boring to stand out. But then my school did one of those alumni spotlight emails that are usually skim-worthy at best and highlighted James Heath, the young CEO of the virtual reality company, Vice and Virtual, who graduated almost ten years ago. The email said his company was just funded by some venture capitalist and was making the move to New York. To celebrate that move, Vice and Virtual announced the Create Your Own (Virtual) Reality contest.

Over the course of three video games "brought to life" into physical competitions, the contest offers one winner the Reality Now virtual reality headset prototype that convinced the VC to invest. The actual product isn't due to be released to the public for another year and is already rumored to cost over a grand. I'm not up to date with the latest technology outside of cameras and video editing software, so the "impressive" list of specs the Reality Now headset boasts reads more like an ingredient list for a recipe to burn down my house, but the tech community online is freaking out.

So why would Temple find their heartstrings pulled by a documentary that barely meets the minimum requirements for submission? Because James is holding his events at the local businesses he worked at as a teen, to highlight the commu- nity and all that stuff—my grandma would've loved it. He's a hometown hero, bringing buzz and sales to family-owned stores around town like Repairisburg and Anderson's Gadgets. In an ideal world, James Heath would have been available to be the star of my documentary, but apparently, he's really busy. I even mentioned I go to the same high school he went to and yet my email still went unanswered.

It ended up being fine, though, because as people were entering their submissions—videos, graphics, vision boards, essays, et cetera showing what the person's perfect virtual reality game would be—my mom stumbled across a frantic Facebook post from her high school best friend's little sister, Yvette, asking for help in creating her own submission. On paper, Yvette doesn't seem like an ideal documentary subject—she's a twenty-seven-year-old divorcée with a teething child and a full-time job in data entry, and her favorite color is beige—but she's accessible, presents as an untraditional gamer, and is super-duper-sign-me-up-for-the-chalky-candy-hearts-on-Valentine's-Day in love with James Heath.

Despite not actually being into video games or able to come up with her own virtual reality game idea—I introduced her to Fiverr and all the affordable freelancers there to solve that problem—she has more heart than I could hope for. Her goal is to get as far in the contest as she can, just so she can talk to her childhood crush again. Impress him. Make him really see her.

A perfect underdog story.

I don't know if James Heath will see her, but I know Temple Admissions will. And when they see her, they'll see me.

TWO

My mom gets home from work the next morning around the time I'm finishing up a chocolate Pop-Tart and washing it down with a glass of water. It used to be a glass of whole milk, but then she stopped buying dairy to prolong our lives or something annoying like that, and milk substitutes just aren't *milky* enough for me.

"I see you're still eating the devil's breakfast even though we have perfectly good bread and eggs here," she says, her eyes puffy with exhaustion. She slips out of her sneakers and takes the baking soda from the fridge, sprinkling some in each shoe.

"*Whole-grain bread*," I say with disgust. "You know, I have more of a chance of dying from undercooked eggs than a bag of pure sugar."

"I'd like to see the study on that."

I take my dishes to the dishwasher, practically tripping over Bagel as he begs for scraps, but can't find empty spaces to slot them. By the time I'm done loading a detergent tab into the dishwasher, my mom has moved from guzzling a bottle of water by the refrigerator to lying down on the couch in the living room.

"No," I say, jiggling her foot. "Don't lie down. You'll fall asleep."

"What's wrong with that?" she mumbles into the cushion.

"You're not in bed." I grab her other foot—noticing that her socks don't match—and shake her a little more. "Up. Mom. Seriously."

"You're so bossy."

"It's darker in your bedroom anyway."

She shuffles to the bathroom and starts washing her face with the door open.

I lean against the frame. "Did you talk to your boss?"

Water drips down her face when she looks at me. "I'm next in line for a switch back to day shift, but unless someone leaves, I'm probably stuck for a while. No one will switch from days to nights."

"You did. For the pay raise. Aren't there any suckers you can strong-arm into it?"

She pats her face dry and loads her toothbrush with toothpaste. "No, sadly, I was the only sucker." With white foam dripping over her bottom lip, she asks, "It's not that bad, right? If I switch, I'll lose the shift-difference and the promotion. I'll probably have to get a part-time job, and I'll see you even less then."

Just before my grandma died, my mom switched from day to

night shift for a raise. At the time, I wasn't alone and taking care of myself; I had my grandma and the switch made sense financially. Without my grandma selling her paintings or teaching art classes, we don't have enough income to pay the bills . . . not without scraping the bottom of the barrel. So now we share a car, having sold my grandma's last month, and I see her when I'm rushing out the door to school or to work and she's just getting in. Sometimes I see her for a little while after school, if I don't have cheerleading practice or plans with my friends, but those days are rare.

"Once cheerleading is over, I'll look for another job, work after school." There's no reason she should be the only one making the whole-grain dough. I spend money, so I should earn money.

"No, Saine, you don't have to do that." She gargles some water and spits. "We're fine."

I push away from the door frame to let her pass, knowing I'll just have to bring this up again when she's not about to pass out. "Okay. I'll see you later. Car keys?"

She closes the blackout curtains in her room and the little dust motes floating in the air vanish. "On the hook. Where I expect them to be when you come home later."

"I don't know, I think throwing them on the counter so they get lost under bills is more fun."

She settles into bed, putting a mask over her eyes. "Oh yeah, especially when I'm running late."

"Love you," I say, closing the door gently.

"Love you," she says back, nearly asleep already.

In fairness, it's a little weird that I work at a college while still in high school. Also weird is that Holden's dad is the one who helped get me the job. I applied online and my application only made it through to the second round because apparently Mr. Michaels, professor of public relations, recognized my name—hard not to—and suggested they give me a shot. He probably felt pretty stupid telling them to hire me when I showed up like: *Yeah, so, I can only work some weekends.*

It ended up being fine, though, because none of the actual students wanted to work weekends, especially not the 7:30 a.m. to 3:30 p.m. shift Saturday mornings, and I can rent out the equipment to myself. I was never explicitly told that I *could*, but to work here, I need a school ID, and to sign out the equipment, I need a school ID. I did the math.

Victor Okafor, a sophomore with flawless brown skin and a buzzed head, stomps down the steps leading to several computer labs and stops in front of my desk. "I need a camera."

I fight the urge to be prickly by rolling out my neck. "What kind?"

He leans against the desk. "One of the Panasonics."

"There are none left."

His eyes dart behind me to the Panasonic camera sitting atop its case, making me look like a lying liar. But that's mine. The one I rented, at least. It's surrounded by my microphones and battery packs, which I also rented.

He points. "I see one right there."

"It's checked out."

"Doesn't look like it."

"To me."

"Check out a Sony or something. I want the Panasonic."

I slide my chair a little to the right, blocking his view of the camera. "It's checked out. If you wanted a Panasonic, you should have gotten here before we ran out. *You* can use a Sony."

We stare at each other for several seconds that could span an eternity.

He scrunches up his face. "Are you even allowed to check out equipment?"

"Yes." I cross my arms on the desk, daring him to call me out.

"I need this for a project. And I'm an actual student. I take precedence."

"I'm sure your professor would say the same thing as me. If you needed a specific camera, you should have gotten here—"

"Fine, I'll take it."

I smile at him before selecting the Sony in the computer. "Go ahead and run your ID through the card reader."

"What do you even need the camera for?" he mumbles, putting his ID back in his wallet.

"I'm filming a documentary." It's been a long time since I was embarrassed to explain why I'm always filming things. Now I have an actual reason, one that's a little sounder than: video is more reliable than memory. "I'm applying for the pilot program at Temple."

I hand over his receipt with the camera information and the return deadline. He nods toward the camera cabinet as if he has some authority over me and I unlock it, fishing out the most banged-up-looking Sony I can find. If I didn't know he checked his equipment before taking it—like anyone with half a brain should or else risk paying a damage fee for something they didn't do—I'd give him the one that a group of journalism students broke last weekend when they took it to University Park for a football game.

I slide the camera and its case across the desk. "Have a great day."

"What's it about?" he asks, leaning on his elbows, settling in.

"What?"

"Your documentary." He pauses for such a short amount of time that I've barely processed his words. "Right now, I'm working on a contemporary retelling of *The Phantom of the Opera*."

"I know it's a waste of my energy to hope it's less creepy than the original since *you're* the one making it, but—" I cross my fingers. Then I start messing with my open Probability and Statistics textbook on the desk, giving him an opportunity to just go away, but he doesn't take the hint. Not sure he even sees me offering it. My homework will have to wait.

"Come on. What is it, *A Day in the Life of Someone Boring*?"

"No," I say, deflating, "I didn't think you'd agree to let me film you."

He narrows his eyes. "You're being protective of your idea. Maybe it's actually good." He rushes through the rest of his words. "Or maybe it's terrible and you're embarrassed. Either way, good luck. You'll need it. I heard there are only, like, twenty spots in that program."

I know he's trying to rile me up, but I can't let him have the last word, even when it's to his favor. "Fifteen, actually." Even tougher to get into. Anxiety clenches my gut.

"Have you heard of Vice and Virtual?" I ask.

"No, is that like an online gambling thing?"

"No, it's a virtual reality company that was founded in my hometown. It's, like, hot up-and-coming shit."

"Are you into that stuff?"

"Not really." And after hours of research into it, I didn't even understand the appeal.

"Why are you making a documentary about it, then? Are they corrupt? Who's your subject?"

"My—" I hesitate to say my mom's friend, because it just sounds so juvenile. It would sound even worse to call Yvette the woman my mother used to babysit. "A woman from Philly. She wants to profess her love for the CEO of the company, but she needs to get his attention."

His eyebrows rise in disapproval. "She's in love with someone she doesn't even have the attention of? Are you aiding a stalker?"

I wish I hadn't opened myself up to this conversation. It's too much to explain to someone I don't even want to be talking to. "She's not a stalker. They were childhood friends. It's romantic and high stakes and has a message of supporting local businesses in the background—it's a good documentary idea!"

He blows out a laugh at my frustration. "So, you're just filming her attempt to get into his pants?"

Eye. Roll. "Vice and Virtual is holding a contest where she'll do obstacle courses and brainteasers, like, video games, but in real life. The winner gets a prototype of the VR headset they're selling next year."

He blinks, placing the camera bag over his shoulder. "Video games in real life?"

"Like, you know how Mario goes down pipes? A contestant would go down a slide or something. It's all real, and physical."

He doesn't look impressed. "So, they don't have to be good at video games, they just have to be fit?"

I try not to have second thoughts, but then there's one thought and then there's another. I reach for the necklace I know isn't around my neck. My grandma gave it to me, but I gave it to Corrine after her breakup with Holden, to help her ground herself when she started to feel any certain way she didn't want to feel. I miss that necklace. The only thing grounding me right now is gravity.

"It'll be great," I say, my cheeks growing hot. I remind myself that the Temple people approved this idea—it can't be that bad. *I will not doubt myself, I will not doubt myself, I will doubt myself.* "It has heart, action, and a cause; it's like the perfect documentary."

He smirks. "Yeah, sure. Good luck."

And then he walks away and I'm stuck behind the desk for several more hours worrying that my documentary *isn't* as great as I think it'll be, that the GoPro footage will be too shaky to use, that Yvette will get her happy ending on day one and leave me with no story at all.

I wonder if there's an angle to film her at that will give me a guaranteed acceptance and if I can find it before my deadline.

THREE

I believe words—hell, even *thoughts*—have the ability to jinx something into oblivion. But with how awful things are going tonight, there's really no way around the very obvious facts that I'm screwed; my documentary, if made, will be shitty; and I, Saine Sinclair, can't have nice things.

Sunday night is crashing and burning right before my eyes and I have no clue how to save it—I don't know CPR, I would never volunteer to run into fire, and I am just wholly inadequate when it comes to anything that's not cheerleading, filming, and Netflix marathons when I should be doing homework.

The agreed-upon time when Yvette was supposed to pick me up has come and gone. I call her and get sent straight to voicemail. I text and am ignored. My fingers, to Corrine's future horror, are a bloody mess of hangnails and stress.

An hour before the contest is supposed to start, Yvette finally eases some of my panic by calling to apologize and then admits she can't pick me up because she has to drop her small human off at the small human's father's house before the event and wouldn't make it in time to compete if she swung by Mechanicsburg first—even though it was so convenient for her just two days ago.

So, I order a Lyft. I would rather be talking to the subject of my soon-to-be college-acceptance-earning documentary for half an hour instead of Santiago, who, despite not being Yvette, makes the ride entertaining with his five-star politeness and interest in the event at what he calls "a store too fun to be allowed."

Repairisburg is like something out of a movie. I've only ever been here once, with my dad before he skipped town, but even that can't taint my memory of it. It's one of those best-kept-secret type places, where word of mouth keeps it in business. They mostly do repairs, like fixing your computer when it's on the fritz or replacing a smashed cell phone screen, but they also offer one-of-a-kind eccentricities, devices that used to do one thing and now do another. Their website, which looks like it was made before the internet even existed, showcases one of these items every month, and this month's is one that James Heath himself helped make as a twentysomething. I personally just think it's something that Repairisburg couldn't sell: a standing lamp with speakers instead of lights.

Outside the store, I wait twenty-three minutes for Yvette to show up. This delay pushes us right against the start time for the event. Even now, in the final moments before she starts the contest, she stands next to me, staring at something on her phone with a blank expression. This is a pivotal moment for this documentary—she's mentally preparing to see her childhood crush, to play this ridiculous game in hopes of winning not the VR headset but his *heart*, and yes, I plan on using that line in the documentary narration because it's fucking good—but she's using this time, *my time*, to . . . check Facebook, apparently. I will never understand her generation's obsession with it.

The contest is being held *inside* Repairisburg, which I think is risky because of all the shelves and electronics and the fact that twenty people are going to be running around the store trying to kill each other.

In this first event, participants are playing Time Out, an online multiplayer first-person shooter in which staying alive means beating the clock and killing an opponent. Those are pretty much the only rules. Essentially, it's every person for themselves and you can't just hide to wait out the clock. You have to kill at least one other opponent—and survive until the end—to be considered a winner. Or so the YouTube play-throughs led me to believe during my research.

To play this game in real life, Vice and Virtual has set it up to be, essentially, laser tag around the store, and the time limit is just however long it takes until only half the contestants remain alive. Again, I'm concerned about the products lining the shelves, but I suppose the benefit of having the event here is to get the foot traffic and (hopefully) sales. An empty shelf is a safe shelf.

Yvette finally glances up, her shoulders back but eyes still blank. I begin filming. "Sorry," she says with a faltering smile.

"It's okay," I lie. "Thinking about your game strategy?"

She chews her lip. "The opposite, actually. My exit strategy."

A bomb goes off in my stomach. "What? Why?"

"He didn't accept my friend request."

I can see her motivation dissolving away through my view screen. "But that could mean a lot of things—"

"Like he doesn't remember me." Yvette glances around the packed store and lowers her voice. "Or that he does and doesn't want to make a connection."

"I'm sure that's not it." I struggle to find another reason he would have rejected her like that. Too scared to face his own feelings? Yvette went to James's tech events; she cheered him on from the stands when he did football for a season in middle school—she was supportive and totally charmed by him. She described such tension between them. Is it just that he's secretly taken and can't face his feelings for her for fear of screwing up something he has going on now?

"Well, I'm sure that I don't want to be the weirdo who gets rejected and then tries to win his contest to see him. He'll think I'm a creep."

"Or he'll think you're impressive and regret not accepting your request. Maybe it was an accident." I gesture around the store. "I haven't even seen him here. He might only be at the final event. All you have to worry about tonight is getting through to the next round. We'll come up with a game plan from there."

She nods stiffly.

Tonight's winners continue to the next event at the Harrisburg Mall. And it isn't until now, seeing her second-guessing her quest for love, that I realize there's a strong possibility that if she doesn't walk away intentionally, she still might be forced to. Was I really so foolish to think the power of love could propel this wholly unprepared woman to become one of the final ten? Five? The final *one*? She didn't even create her own (virtual) reality for the application process.

The contestants are called forward before I can get any more from her, something that might calm my own nerves. The good news is, she seems so panicked that her body decides to follow the pack. I trail after her, trying to capture her face, but bump into bystanders. An Asian woman who looks like she's in charge because of her black-and-gold Vice and Virtual shirt asks the contestants to show the IDs they received in the mail to verify who they are. Yvette shows hers, completing a circle of the contestants, and blocks me out.

I pause for a moment and then find a new spot in the crowd so I can see her face as she listens to the rules, which I can barely hear over the rumble of people impatiently waiting for the contest to start. I film as much as I can, but my hands get shaky. Maybe things will be fine. Yvette will move forward and we'll have a good interview after the contest that, combined with her win, will make her reconsider abandoning her mission. Then she'll take me home, where I can edit all the footage I have until the next event.

Assuming she gets to the next one.

Assuming she hasn't convinced herself this is a terrible idea.

Somehow *I'm* the one "blinded by love" right now.

The contestants break and Yvette's given a vest with attached gun, just like in laser tag. She stares at it in her hand like it's actually loaded.

"Contestants and fans," the Vice and Virtual employee says into a microphone. There are professional camerapeople on either side of her, one filming her and the other capturing the crowd, which is now being ushered to the second floor overlooking the bottom like a Roman arena. A sign outside the store said they would be filming for a web series and by entering, you were agreeing to have your face shown. Thankfully, mine will be behind my own camera, because I didn't cake on makeup for behind-the-scenes work. "Thank you for being here tonight at the fantastic Repairisburg, home of CEO James Heath's first job after college, as Vice and Virtual begins our contest to provide one lucky winner with an exclusive prototype of our Reality Now headset in New York City next month. I'm Chrissy Lo, head of communications at Vice and Virtual, and I'm so excited to be joined here tonight by the twenty Create Your Own (Virtual) Reality winners. Their submissions are available for viewing on the Vice and Virtual website, along with the just-announced timeline for the Reality Now headset release." The crowd cheers. "You can expect to purchase the headset by the third quarter next year, in time for the holiday shopping season, but you won't be getting just the headset." She smiles, and it's clearly for the camera more than the crowd. "Every purchase of our headset will come with the three games we've adapted for real-life play in this contest, for free."

More cheering. Go, capitalism. Yadda yadda. There's pretty much no indication that Yvette heard her, or cares. It was never about the headset, anyway. I hope she's not replaying the shock of being denied over and over. Maybe she just gets really in her head before big things. Kayla, who is the most vibrant person I know, will literally yell at people who try to talk to her before any kind of major test in school, or before her band's shows, so it's possible I'm just waiting for Yvette to explode out of her shell once she feels more confident, with the mental image of her in James's arms in New York City.

"Gamers," Chrissy Lo says with a cheeky grin, "you've heard the rules. So let's play!"

Loud music that I can't get the rights for starts pumping through the store, most likely to impede people from shouting helpful remarks to players. As they head into the designated area to play, their initials pop up on a few screens hanging around. The screens tally their kills and keep them in order of who has the most even though it doesn't matter. Yvette is the last one to enter the area, only taking one step past the threshold. I watch the scene unfold in slow motion. She takes one step back, out of the arena. Her gun drops from her hand and bounces by the cable attached to her vest. She shakes her head.

And then it's over.

She steps fully out and takes off the vest, shoving it into the hands of the first person she can find, and she flees through the crowd.

"Yvette." I follow her, my heart hiccuping in my chest. "Yvette, wait!"

"I can't do this." I barely hear her over the noise.

Had we had a chance before the contest began, I would have

put a microphone on her, but I'll just have to add in subtitles for this scene. Please let this be a scene and not the climax.

She exits the store even though I'm no longer the only one calling her name. Some Vice and Virtual grunt—an intern, if his age means anything—is trying to wave her down, but he must catch the panic on her face when she turns to me because he lets us go.

"What's going on?" I can hear my heart beating, the blood rushing to my head. "I don't know if they'll let you back in to play."

"I don't care about playing," she says through clenched teeth. Tears are brimming in her eyes. She glances at my camera and then back to me. "Please don't film this."

"I—I mean, you agreed—what's going on?" I lower the camera but keep it recording.

"I can't do this. He didn't even want me through a phone screen; why did I think I could get his attention playing a stupid game? No one doing this contest is over twenty-two. I'm not old, but I'm not *that* young either. I don't stand a chance. And even if I did, what difference would it make?"

"How can you say that?" I try to beg with my eyes, make her see reason. "You want to do something so romantic and so strong—"

"We weren't friends."

My whole body droops. "What?"

"It's not romantic. It's pathetic. We were just classmates, not friends. He didn't know I existed then and he doesn't now. He doesn't care."

"But—" So, it was unrequited love. Was Victor right? I'm helping Yvette get up close and personal with this guy who didn't even know her?

"Saine, you're a sweet girl. I'm sorry. Please tell your mom I'm sorry. I can't do this. I'd embarrass myself, and if it's recorded and shown to people, then I can't pretend it never happened."

Without another word, she crosses the fire lane and slides inside her black Toyota.

I don't know what else to do in this moment, so I film her as she backs up and then pulls onto the main road.

"What the *hell*?" I whisper into the parking lot. I'm screwed. I knew it when the night began. This was the topic I prepared for—*the one Temple preapproved*. This is the topic I have to submit. I took off work for the events. I researched the games and already screen captured videos of people playing them online. I have the first ten minutes of the documentary rough cut including Yvette talking about James for, like, five fucking minutes with big heart eyes. She lied—or did I just hear what I wanted to? She never described things he did for her, only things she did for him—things that didn't involve them interacting.

"Who are you talking to?" a small voice asks behind me.

I spin around, agony making my face ache, to lock eyes with a girl, maybe thirteen years old, sitting on the curb with a phone in her hand. A golden braid lies over a black pleather jacket that can't be doing much to keep her warm because her little stick legs are bare under her dress, save for some knee socks she has tucked into her boots.

"Myself. Where's your person?" I step closer, resisting the

urge to bend down so we're eye level because it's so conde-scending. "Your adult?"

"Playing the game. He probably doesn't even notice that I'm gone." She scuffs her boot against the gravel. "I don't like big crowds."

"And yet he brought you along? Your dad's kind of an ass-hole." I glance around the parking lot. It's pretty dark despite the streetlights. Anyone could just snatch her up. "You know, you shouldn't talk to strangers, kid."

"You're doing it, *kid*."

"Touché."

"I'm Mara."

"You shouldn't tell strangers your name, either." I offer her my free hand. "I'm Saine."

She smiles at me, taking it with her smaller hand. "You're pretty. Do you have a boyfriend or girlfriend?"

"Your dad is probably old enough to be *my* dad."

"I'm not here with my dad. I'm with my brother. And as you can tell, he's quite the dork to be doing this." She points to herself. "He needs all the help he can get."

"We should return you to him." And I need to get back in there.

I can kiss even the chance of *applying* to the pilot program goodbye if I don't lock down one of these contestants tonight. My grandma was so excited when I told her about it. She researched new cameras, brainstormed topics, suggested sub-jects from the community, and queued up documentaries for us to watch in our own version of a film festival every weekend for a month. It was important to me, so it was important to her. After my mom decided she had no interest in art, I think my grandma felt this was her second chance at raising someone with an artistic passion. I can't let her down.

Inside, I count thirteen players left "alive" on the scoreboard. Mara and I inch as close as we can, but the people on the ground floor are too tall, packed too thickly to move through. Mara latches onto my arm and starts squeezing through, able to bend under their arms and slither around their sides. Bless her for thinking my much larger body can melt down to the same size as hers. It seems impossible that I was ever as small as she is. I somehow manage to get through, though, just in time for one contestant to get straight-up murdered.

"Only ten spots are open for the next event, yet twelve players remain," Chrissy Lo says into the microphone from somewhere I can't see. "Who will end this game?"

"Is your brother still in?" I ask Mara offhandedly. Maybe she sees him on the outskirts of the arena and can meet up with him without my help. Or maybe he's still in play and I can use her to introduce me so I can beg him to be in my documentary. It makes me all upside-down smiley face to know my future could very shortly be at the mercy of some random white dude.

"I don't know. I don't see him." She stands on her tiptoes but doesn't even come up to the shoulders of the man in front of her.

I aim my camera at the contestants still in play, trying to capture the winning moment, but it's pretty impossible with this new, shitty vantage point I have and the fact that if they're not running for a flag, they're hiding behind or below shelves. The optimal place for filming is definitely in the center of the second floor.

A chorus of yeses and nos fills the room simultaneously as a buzzer goes off, ending the loud music and making me nearly drop my camera. I panic, unsure if I should film the scoreboard or try to get the victors' glory. I shove the camera over a guy's shoulder just in time to film the winners running out of the arena with raised hands. The last person out does a conceited spin to see the crowd cheering him on. Everyone but me.

Because it's Holden Michaels.

FOUR

"That's my brother," Mara says, pointing at him with a red-chipped fingernail.

I blink. "Uh, no, it's not."

Her entire sweet face crumples into a frown. "Yeah, it is."

"Holden Michaels doesn't have a little sister. He has a little brother, Trevor."

Around us, the crowd slowly disperses into smaller groups around the store, people taking photos with items from the shelves and heading to the registers or exit.

"You know them?" she asks.

"Saine?" Holden comes up behind Mara, placing his hands on her shoulders. His cheeks are red and sweat clings to the hair by his face.

"You know her?" Mara asks.

"You know each other?" he asks, glancing down at her.

"Yes, we all know each other. That's Mara. You're Holden. I'm Saine. What the hell is going on here?" I bend to Mara's eye level. "Blink twice if you're being kidnapped."

Her eyes widen. "Now all I want to do is blink!"

"What are you talking about?" Holden directs Mara—and by extension, me—to the side of the store where there are fewer people. Vice and Virtual employees help Repairisburg employees move the shelves at the back of the store to their proper places, and a few winners are being interviewed for the web series. I wonder if Holden knows he's wasting an opportunity to get his smarmy face out there by glaring at me.

"What else am I supposed to think when a little girl says she's your sister and I know you don't have a sister?"

"He has two," Mara chimes in.

"You honestly thought I kidnapped a kid instead of, I don't know, I now have stepsisters?" Holden grinds his teeth. "You know what? Now that I've said it out loud, your idea makes much more sense."

I don't know why I feel guilty, and *betrayed*, for not knowing his parents split and one—or both—remarried, but I do. It's not like we've been friends the last few years, and this isn't exactly something you put on social media, but still. Even when Corrine dated him, she didn't talk about him much—not his personal life, at least. She definitely never mentioned a sister.

"Who's the other?"

"Taylor," Mara says. "She's in college and now Holden gets to watch me all the time. He loooooooves it."

"I won, by the way," he says to her. "Not that you'd know because you walked away and could have been kidnapped. I told you not to move. You'd never have done that if Taylor was watching you."

"Because she would have been *watching* me." She offers a

high five. "But you won, so it's all good?"

I snort, looking away when Holden glares at me.

"No. If something had happened to you—"

"She's okay," I cut in. "I found her and she's fine."

"*If something had happened to you*," he repeats, "that would be on me."

She rolls her eyes but sighs. "Sorry that my kidnapping and eventual murder would have reflected poorly on you, Holden." She points to me. "But she has a point. Someone much worse could have found me."

"I don't know about that." Holden glances at the camera in my hand. "What are you even doing here?"

I adjust my grip. "I was filming one of the players, but she . . . I don't really know."

"Oh, the lady that bailed?" He smirks. "What, did you scare her away?"

"No, thank you, she did that herself." And now I'm screwed.

The crowd around us thins. Holden grabs his jacket from a guarded area and starts moving Mara to the exit.

"Well, it was *great* seeing you, but we have to get home," he says without looking at me.

"What about your interview?" Mara asks him. "You're a winner and the world needs to know!"

"I'll do it next time. I told them I had to return you to the zoo."

"Wait." My body moves in their direction without my permission.

To my surprise, Holden actually stops. Mara peeks around

him, her eyebrows raised. They could be *less* interesting to watch, that's for sure. But it's *Holden*, and just liking video games and wanting to win a VR headset isn't enough to make anyone care about this documentary.

"What?" Holden asks, impatience tainting his words. Like he has any right to be mad at me for anything.

"I was making a documentary about someone trying to win this thing and—" Well, he doesn't need to know the profession-of-unrequited-love bit. "I need it for my Temple app, but, as you know, my subject bailed." Holden's here, he's local, I know him, he's going to the next round. This is my only option. It makes sense and is way more convenient than it would have been with Yvette—I lose the angle of an "older" Black woman competing in what is seen as a contest mostly for young white men, while balancing love and video games, but I can work around this. I can fabricate a story if I need to; it wouldn't be the first time I've managed it. I once edited random clips of Corrine and Kayla together to make it seem like they were having a heated argument about broccoli—and they both assumed they just forgot having that conversation. That it had really happened. *The power of storytelling.*

"That sucks," he says, not sounding at all sympathetic. "Well, it's already past this one's bedtime—"

"He means himself," Mara says.

"So—"

"Since you're already doing the contest," I say quickly, not letting him dismiss me, "and it makes so much sense to team up, maybe I could just, I don't know, use you as my subject?" I barely dare to breathe. It would literally be his honor to reject me.

His eyebrows crinkle. "Why?"

God, what a great question. "Why what?" I ask, turning it back on him and giving myself a moment to come up with something, anything.

"Why should I?"

Mara shoves her elbow into his gut, but he barely flinches.

"Because I could potentially get into my dream major?"

"I asked why *I* should. What do I get out of this?"

"Your ego stroked, I don't know. What do you want out of this?" I shift my weight to the opposite foot, trying to convince myself this would be better to work on with him than with a stranger. Maybe. "You're charismatic. Not terrible on the eyes. Please just help me."

"Not terrible, huh? I should add that to my Tinder profile."

"Your mom says you're not allowed on Tinder," Mara says.

"It was a joke—"

I steal Mara's focus. "Help me out here, kid."

"Do it!" Mara says, yanking on his arm. "You love hearing yourself talk. This is the perfect opportunity."

He pulls a face. "I'm not doing it for free. This isn't a friendly favor."

"That's a relief, because we aren't friends."

His gaze darkens. "Thanks for the reminder. I would have never remembered." He exhales all his annoyance with me in one long breath. "I have a portfolio due at the end of photography this semester, so if I do this for you, you have to model for me."

My heart kicks into an unpredictable rhythm. "Excuse me?"

"We're supposed to, like, photograph seniors in the wild, really get to the essence of their soul. And nobody wants to do it—well, except Taj, but I've already used him for other assignments."

"I'll save you the time. I have no soul. In here?" I point to my chest. "It's just a hamster in a wheel, running running running—"

"You have to agree or I'm out."

"Fine. Deal." I feel like I can't breathe. Am I really going to give Holden another chance to let me down?

He latches onto Mara's arm and walks out of the store. I follow, collecting my nerves from where they've spilled all over the ground. "Okay, well, we need to discuss a schedule for this whole thing."

"Saine," he says with a sigh, stopping next to his mom's beat-up minivan. "I have to get home. It's a school night and a long drive."

Thirty minutes isn't long, but I guess . . . "Longer than you'd like in this hunk of junk, I imagine." There's a vicious scratch along the side from when it got keyed in the school parking lot last year. Corrine went on a crusade with campus security to find the culprit but turned up empty-handed. And no, it wasn't me.

"Says the girl without a car."

"You don't have a car?" Mara asks, jumping into the back seat when Holden slides the door open for her. "How did you get here?"

"Shit." I pull out my phone. "Yvette was supposed to take me home."

"Can't we give her a ride?" Mara asks in a quiet voice.

I'm opening my Lyft app to request a driver when Holden puts his hand over my screen.

"Want a ride?" he asks in a voice that clearly says he is only asking so Mara doesn't throw a fit the entire journey home.

"No," I say like a lying liar. I do want a ride, but I definitely don't want one with Holden. He's . . . him, and Corrine wouldn't like it and *I* wouldn't like it. I'm not even sure I trust him to drive me after the car accident post-prom that's left me jumpy when other people are behind the wheel.

Holden shrugs toward Mara and opens the driver door.

"*Holden.*"

"She said no," he whisper-screams to Mara. "When someone says no, it means no."

As unappealing as a short drive with Holden seems, it would be a good way to get extra footage, to discuss a schedule. Plus, if he still lives where he used to, he'll pass by my house anyway.

"Okay."

"Okay what?" Holden says, his door nearly shut.

"I'll take a ride."

"Yes!" Mara pumps her fist. "Thank god, Holden likes to listen to NPR or whatever and I'll die if I have no one to talk to and have to hear about *taxes*."

I round to the front passenger door and slip inside, steeling myself.

"I'm trying to educate you," he mumbles.

"I have school for that."

He starts the car and clears his throat, looking at me from the corner of his eye. "You still live on Ambrose?"

"Yep."

"Okay."

Maybe thirty minutes is long.

"Saine?" Mara breaks the thick, awkward silence. I hadn't been able to work up the courage to start actually planning this thing aloud yet.

I angle toward the back of the van, my camera in hand, thankful for her saying something. I had been filming B-roll of the highway while keeping myself alert, but this could end up being more useful, and even though I'm not usually bothered or deterred by silences, I couldn't seem to form any words this close to my former best friend and his brand-new (to be determined?) stepsister. "Yes?"

"Can I ask you for advice?"

"No," Holden answers for me.

I raise an eyebrow. "Excuse you. Yes, she can. I'm great with kids. Kids love me. They have no filter and I have no filter."

"That's exactly why I don't trust you to give her good advice," he says. "Don't you remember your tooth fairy scam?"

Of all the things he could have said, I was not expecting *that*. A little bit of tension falls to the cutting room floor.

"What tooth fairy scam?" Mara asks.

"Saine convinced me to tie floss around my teeth so she could pull them out."

"It's not my fault you went along with it." There was so much blood.

"I went along with everything you said," he says, grip tightening on the wheel. "You nearly pulled out one of my permanent teeth. I still have nightmares about it wiggling."

"Okay, well, in my defense, I thought that teeth were like fingernails. Like, I thought your teeth would just keep growing in, and that we could keep getting money from the tooth fairy and never have to get jobs." I glance between him and Mara. "I thought it was a genius idea! I was looking out for us."

"This is why I don't want you giving her advice."

I wave away his comment and turn back to his sister, hating the tingle of familiarity that story gave me. I can feel it, like I'm standing on the edge of an abyss, how easy it would be to fall into old habits. To not have to speak to each other through this concrete wall we've built.

"What's up?"

She latches onto the end of her braid, brushing her hair over her palm. "Well. See. This girl in my classes, Rose? Rose is really pretty and she dresses super cool, and whenever she has white chocolate macadamia nut cookies, she splits them with me and *only* me at lunch, and she knows everything about stars, like black holes and moons with smaller moons—they're unofficially called moonmoons. The other day, she grabbed my hand—like held it—during lunch—under the table, but still—but then I saw her hugging Delilah by her locker, and I'm not sure if I should like her anymore because liking her now makes me feel awful."

I blink. "Rose sounds like a real bitch if she did that to you."

"Saine," Holden hisses. "She's twelve."

"But seriously."

"Where was this conviction with Elijah?" he asks gruffly.

I glare at him, but he keeps his eyes on the road. "I didn't have a chance to use it before you punched him."

God, it was so embarrassing. Everyone saw it and everyone knew what it was about. I could have punched him myself if that's what I wanted to happen. But nooooo, Holden had to go all alpha male.

"Corrine told me to!"

"Oh, and you do everything she tells you? No! Or else you would have fucked yourself by now." I mumble the last part, but—

"*Saine.*"

"Who's Elijah?" Mara asks quietly. "What did he do?"

More like *who* did Elijah do. And the answer to that is everyone. It's been almost six months and my anger still does a back handspring in my gut at the thought.

"She's twelve," Holden reminds me in a low voice.

"I'm nearly thirteen," she interjects.

"He was my . . ." I try to think of an appropriate metaphor or whatever, even though twelve-nearly-thirteen is old enough to know about sex; I mean, she's had to have had the same subpar sex education that Holden and I struggled through in, like, fifth grade by now. Twelve-nearly-thirteen is middle-school-aged. "He was my singing partner. We used to . . . duet."

Holden must pull a muscle with how fast he turns his head to stare at me wide-eyed.

"*Duet,*" I enunciate. "We sang together." We never sang a

full song together, though, if you catch my meaning.

"And then he started singing with a choir," Holden adds. "Without auto-tune."

The irony of Holden being pissed off about someone cheating is almost too sweet to point out. I'm about to say something when Mara says, "We're talking about sex, aren't we?"

Holden chokes on his spit.

"I think you should just talk to Rose," I say, changing the subject as my cheeks heat. "Tell her how you feel." I face forward. "Maybe she was just being friendly with that other girl. I hug my friends all the time, but I only share food with people I'm into."

"Okay," Mara says heavily.

"Topic change." Holden points at me. "Did you know your name means 'healthy' in French?"

For a second, I'm too confused to speak. "What? No, why would I know that? Why do you know that?"

"I like looking up people's name meanings."

"That's new." I watch him out of the corner of my eye, my hands sweating around the camera, as if I could spot all this newness on him, like a shirt with the price tag still on it. I fight the urge to film him so I can replay this later and dissect him.

"What's my name mean?" Mara asks.

"What? Why would I know that?" He stretches up in his seat to meet her eyes in the rearview mirror.

"Eyes on the road." I reach for my necklace, hot panic flaring in my gut, but of course it isn't there. I must look as nervous as I feel, because Holden turns to stare.

"Hey," he says. "You good?"

I let my hand drop and take a deep breath. "Yes."

"Are you having trouble breathing?" he asks.

"No, I'm fine," I say evenly. I count in my head, *five-six-seven-eight*. Let out another breath.

"You hyperventilating or something? You reached for your throat."

"Your eyes are supposed to be on the road." *One-two-three-four-five-six-seven-eight.*

"They are," he says with exasperation. "Forget I said anything."

I close my eyes. "I was reaching for my necklace, but it's not there."

"Did you lose it?" Mara asks. "We should go back to the store."

"No, it's okay." I try to smile at Mara. "My best friend has it. I gave it to her after—" I pause to consider Holden. "When she broke up with you," I finish in a softer voice. "It was my grandma's and it helped when I got stressed or whatever. I thought it could do the same for her." I'm not sure who I'm talking to anymore.

"A necklace isn't really going to help you in a car accident," Holden says.

"Well, I wouldn't need it right now if you hadn't rear-ended someone last year." I take a deep breath. "I have, like, PTSD or something."

I'm being dramatic and, truthfully, really insensitive. I know this. I just don't think I can trust Holden's driving even though he technically does everything he should. Last year, Corrine and I were drinking at prom, Holden was sober and he was driving, but we still hit the car in front of us. I'll never forget what metal crunching against metal sounds like ricocheting in my ears. Never forget the feel of the airbag dust on my skin as Corrine shrieked from the front seat about how her vintage dress was ruined.

"I'm sorry," he says tightly. "You know that wasn't my fault, though. That guy from prom—"

"Was an asshole white guy in a Porsche who didn't need any more handouts in life, and yet you let him in front of you and then he slammed on his brakes to make a turn."

I stop recording. "We'll discuss the documentary and stuff later. I don't want to talk anymore."

He makes a sound like he wants to protest, but he clamps his mouth shut. The silence leaves a lot of space for me to think about what a mistake this has already turned out to be.

FIVE

The only time throughout the school day that I see Corrine is during lunch. All morning, I try to mentally prepare what I'm going to say to her about the Holden situation, but nothing sounds nonchalant enough.

I visualize it: *Hey, Corrine, so, funny story: I'm gonna be working with Holden, like, all the time for the next few weeks. I thought maybe it wasn't that big of a deal since we* both *hate him? Plus, I kind of don't have a choice. I'm sorry?*

She punches me.

In my imagination.

But it still hurts, even if my imagination played it in slow motion at a few ideal angles.

My gut won't stop screaming, the butterflies having turned into vultures. And the worst part is that I think, if Holden and I can get past the awkwardness and the unfriendliness, we could maybe make a better documentary than I would have with Yvette. I'm still wrestling with the less-than-ideal perspective switch—I really didn't set out to make a documentary about a privileged boy—but it's what I've got to work with; at least this way, I can get more footage and won't feel as bad about yelling at him to just *be better* when I'm filming.

In the noisy cafeteria, I throw myself into a seat at our usual round table next to Kayla, who's hunched over her beat-up notebook. It looks like it's seen some shit—edges frayed and bent, pages torn out and distorted from water, the white color of the paper just slightly off.

She tenses for a second, eyes me, then slams her notebook closed. She drops a Ziploc bag of baby carrots on top for good measure.

"Working on a new song?" I ask, while looking around for Corrine. Students are settling into tables, in line for an appetizing lunch of lukewarm turkey burgers and soggy sweet potato fries, but I don't see her. Maybe it's a fundraiser day. She's in at least a million clubs, leading most of them because she wants to work at a nonprofit after college, and rarely has any downtime, even for lunch. Her guidance counselor actually made the school create a maximum number of clubs one person is allowed to participate in just for the sake of Corrine's mental and physical health. Today might be a chess club day, or a mathletes day, or maybe it's an environmental club day.

"Yeah," Kayla says, crunching into a carrot.

"Can I hear it when it's done?" We've played this game before. Kayla doesn't share her songs with anyone and, at this point in our friendship, I don't even feel offended.

"Sure," she lies.

"You'll be waiting a long time." Devon Miles Smith, the guitarist in Kayla's band, Nope.—yes, with the period—joins us with his girlfriend, Juniper Kim, like they do every day for lunch. I don't really care for Devon Miles Smith, even though his full name is fun to say. I've been told I have one of those names, too, but it doesn't make us kindred spirits. I only tolerate him for the sake of others.

While Kayla clams up when it comes to sharing her own material, she sings the shit out of other people's. Nope. does amazing covers and has an almost-almost-famous local EP of original songs written by Devon Miles Smith, like my favorite, "Wasted Youth Starter Kit." This past summer, they opened for Solo and the Wookiee at their reunion show, which isn't that impressive when you consider there were three other opening acts, too, but still. There were about two hundred people present, way past the standing capacity of the venue, which is a huge deal for them. Kayla's dream is to tour with her favorite band, Free Puppies!—yes, with the exclamation point. I suggested they call it The Punctuation Tour, but Devon Miles Smith didn't laugh. I think he didn't get it.

"I'd wait forever," I say with a biting grin.

"I'm not sure anything Kayla has written would be worth that, but okay," he mumbles into a cup of lime-green Jell-O. "Your life to waste."

God, what a dick.

Juniper nudges him and then faces Kayla. "I'm sure it's going to be great. You could sing random Google searches and it would sound amazing."

"Thanks," Kayla says with a smile. "Anybody do anything fun this weekend?" She glances at me. "I know some of us were too busy to even text."

"I had to work on my documentary." And, boy, does it need work. I don't know why I thought this would be easy. I *watch* documentaries; I don't make them. Maybe I would have benefited from fewer "you can do anything" speeches as a kid.

"Hey," Corrine says, breathless, slamming into the seat next to me and freeing a tuna sandwich from a crumpled brown paper bag. She's the only person who could make tuna seem appetizing. "How *did* filming go?"

I freeze, all eyes on me. Corrine doesn't look pissed, so it's unlikely she knows. I mean, who would have told her, Holden? They don't talk anymore.

"It was eventful." Tell her. Tell her tell her tell her. "Actually, my subject freaked out and then she left."

"She came back, though, right?" Juniper asks, eyes wide. "She's your mom's friend."

"No, I wish. I got another contestant to agree to let me film them, actually. So, it might be okay."

Here it is. My moment. I swear the cafeteria mutes itself, all attention on me. I can hear my heart thumping.

Corrine smiles wide, her teeth so perfectly white in contrast to her red lips. "That's good. Who? What's their story?"

"Uh, it's kind of funny." *No, Brain, we decided it was* not *funny.*

She waits with an eager smile, like all those times in seventh grade when she texted me something in the middle of class and couldn't stand waiting to see my reaction. I'm not ready to see her composure shatter, but I have to say it.

"My new subject is—"

"Logan Jiménez," she gasps. Her hand latches onto my thigh in a velociraptor-tight grip as her eyes lock onto something in the distance behind me. She's gone full predator. I follow her gaze until it lands on Logan in the lunch line, smiling his toothpaste-ad grin at something his friend says.

For a moment—just one tiny second—I forget what I was going to tell Corrine. Then panic settles in my gut again, knowing I'll just have to work up the nerve to say it one more time. But she cut me off; I *was* going to say it. I was.

"I'm obsessed with him," she whispers loudly enough for our entire table to hear. "My pen rolled off my desk in study hall last week and he ran the whole way across the room to pick it up, and you guys know that I have Ms. Greenwald and she's a total stickler when it comes to 'fraternizing with other students during a study period.' That's, like, the beginnings of true love, right?"

There are things Corrine won't talk about: sadness, uncomfortable and awkward things; and things she will talk about: love, stress, her feelings about Shaker-style cabinets. Sometimes, it's a minefield trying to navigate conversations with her—like, when does talking about a crush turn into something uncomfortable? How do you talk about stress without the sadness it can bring?

Juniper says, "Yeah, it totally is. Don't forget to invite me to your wedding."

"Can we all agree that if anyone else had made that joke, Corrine would be about to bitch-slap them?" Devon says, sounding like he's *mad* that his girlfriend isn't getting Corrine Baker's signature I Know You Didn't Just Use Sarcasm on My Feelings moment.

"Juniper has a charm no one else can replicate," Kayla says sweetly. "Especially you."

Corrine leans in, letting them fall into a conversation without us. She chews on her lip, like she's debating saying what's on her mind. "I haven't felt this way since the beginning with Holden."

Now! Is! The! Time! Tell her! Tell her tell her tell her. She's thinking back to her relationship with Holden wistfully, not with raging regret. Catch her while she's happy and distracted!

"That's great." I don't tell her. I can't. I don't want to ruin her happiness. I'll tell her later. Hell, I'll tell her once she's finished her food and we've moved on from her bliss. "Do you think he likes you?"

"We don't get much time to talk, but, like, my pen fell down three feet and he catapulted over seven desks to pick it up, so."

"Definitely sounds like true love. He's my partner in Prob/Stat. We do all our classwork together. I could mention you."

"Saine!" She shoves me with a smile. "Don't be too obvious, okay? Maybe just mention one of my fundraisers or something."

"But how will I choose just one?" We share a laugh before my eyes land on Valentina Fernández rushing to our table. "Oh, speaking of fundraisers."

Valentina, one of Corrine's environmental club lackeys, plants her palms on the available table with a gasp, startling Devon Miles Smith. "The money is gone. I don't know—it's just not there anymore."

"Slow down." Corrine snatches up her belongings and stands, all business and serenity, her crush forgotten, my new subject not even a blip in her memories. "Who saw it last and when? We really can't afford to lose that money. Literally."

Corrine's clubs, all eight million of them, are constantly on the verge of being shut down either for lack of participation or for lack of funding. She gets stress hives when her fundraisers sync up, but in her entire history of club racketeering, she's only ever said goodbye to one: the Free Compliments Club.

She walks with Valentina out of the cafeteria and I hate myself for being relieved. I turn back to my friends to join whatever conversation they were having, but they stop. And stare.

"So, what happened with your documentary?" Kayla asks. I could curse her for not having as short of an attention span as Corrine. None of them would tell her, but that might be even worse. That I told other people before I told Corrine.

Someone taps on my shoulder and I'm thankful for another— a third? fourth?—interruption, except . . . it's Holden and his best friend, Taj Chakrabarti.

"Got a few minutes for photos?" he asks, nearly monotone, holding his camera up. It's clear this pains him, and I'm too panicked to enjoy it.

That photo assignment.

I stare at him, unsure how to navigate this situation with all the witnesses around us. It's not like I'm in his photography class, where I could have been forced to work on something with him.

"Like, yearbook photos?" Kayla asks, wiping the corners of her mouth. She throws her arm around my shoulder and behind me, Juniper and Devon Miles Smith lean over the table, striking poses. I'm sure whatever Devon Miles Smith is doing wouldn't be allowed in the yearbook; he thinks he personally invented the shocker sign.

Taj throws himself into the seat beside me. "We look like a college brochure with all this posed diversity."

"Uh . . ." Holden laughs stiffly. "Yeah. I'd apply."

He raises his camera and takes a few photos. I can barely work up even a fake smile, my insides frozen. He lets his camera fall against his chest and directs Taj away from the table.

"I guess we'll just go?" He frowns at me unmoving in my seat.

"I thought Saine was coming," Taj says. "You said she was the model."

"Uh," he says quietly. "She's busy."

They walk away without another word, leaving me with my confused friends and Devon Miles Smith. How to explain this . . .

"Oh my god." Kayla says to herself, like she found a hair in her food. "No. No? Yes?" She locks onto my eyes, waiting, and I honestly don't know how to respond. I'm certainly not going to be the one to admit Kayla possibly connected the dots, because there's also a possibility she *didn't*.

"What's happening here?" Juniper asks quietly.

"I never know," Devon Miles Smith says in an equally low voice as he picks through his food. "I'm just here to be entertained."

"Saine." Kayla places her hand gently on my arm. "Do I need to be clearer?"

"No," I say with a sigh. "I know what you're asking; I've had years of practice in understanding you."

I should test the waters with them, to see if I'll sink or swim with Corrine. They know the tense and vague history between Holden, Corrine, and me, so they can tell me straight up if this is a horrible idea that I should abandon before I even need to tell Corrine. I'll use this as the rehearsal before the first take.

I suck in a deep breath and mentally call *Action!* "I haven't gotten to tell Corrine yet. It was a clusterfuck yesterday and it wasn't my choice and, I don't know, it just made sense. Don't say anything. I'm going to tell her."

At this, Juniper frowns. She's the newest addition to our friend group and can't always keep up. "I don't speak Kayla yet. What's going on?"

"Holden is my new documentary subject. And even though he's definitely evil and I still hate him, I have to hate him just a little less right now so that I can work with him and get into Temple." I look from one face to the other, holding my breath. "Do you think she'll be really mad?"

Juniper taps electric-yellow nails against the table. She'll tell me what I want to hear, even though I know it might not be right. "No," she says sympathetically, "you're probably just thinking it'll be worse than it will be. She's over him and you're just doing what you have to." She smiles. "There was no other choice."

I find the strength to force a smile back. "Yeah, I had no other choice."

But is that the truth, or just what I want to be the truth to make up for the fact that I jumped a little too eagerly into the easy way out of this documentary mess?

I know something's up when my mom takes the night off work, but she doesn't let on any problems, any impending sex talks that will leave me in tears from laughter, so I wait to question her. I let her night unfurl as planned and go along for the ride.

"We just passed the exit." I point out the passenger window, but the sign is behind us by now, my body moving a few seconds too slow for my mind's liking thanks to the food coma I'm slipping into. She knew just how to butter me up with breakfast for dinner at the Around the Clock diner a few minutes from home. "Where are we going?"

"I'm kidnapping you."

"By that logic, you're kidnapping me every time we go anywhere together."

"That's not true. Sometimes you *want* to go with me." She flicks her turn signal on and merges into the exit lane.

"That's what you think."

We turn onto a residential road and pull up in front of a large tan brick building with old air conditioners stuffed in the windows every few feet. It's an apartment building with a sign reading: "Now Leasing!"

"Uh, what's going on?" If we're visiting someone, I'd like some heads-up. And a say in the matter. For a fleeting moment, I wonder if I'm about to have my dad sprung on me. I haven't seen him in years, since he first moved to Brooklyn, and now is not the time for a reunion.

My mom parks the car in an empty spot and unbuckles her

seat belt. "I have an appointment to see an apartment. I wanted you to see it, too."

"Why are you looking at apartments?" I ask, unbuckling. "Are you moving out? Is this because I keep trying to summon Beetlejuice? Because that seems unfair considering you were the one who showed me the movie."

She laughs, but it's not funny. "You know we can't stay at Grandma's forever."

"Why not?" I was under the impression that it was exactly what we were going to do.

"You're going to be away at school the next few years, for most of the year, and then you'll move out, and what am I supposed to do with a three-bedroom home with a huge backyard, finished basement, and a swimming pool? It'll sell, and it'll sell quick, if I get a move on it."

I blink. "I don't understand why you'd want to sell the house, though."

Sure, it'll be a bit big for just her, but she grew up in it. After my parents parted ways, *I* grew up in it. I can't imagine living somewhere else. How can she?

"It's not that I *want to* necessarily. I need to." She sighs. "It just makes sense, financially and emotionally."

"Emotionally, it does not make sense. Not to me."

She avoids my eyes. "It's hard being in that house without her."

"I agree, but wouldn't it be harder to never be able to go back to that house again? What about her murals?" No one will get them. They're us. They're for us.

"Well, they'd be painted over, baby."

I whip my head toward her, heart racing. *"What?"*

She watches me for a second, pity in her eyes. *Pity.* "It's okay."

"No, it's not."

"It's expensive to have a big house. We could make some money, spend less each month. Afford your tuition." She sighs again, then checks her watch, because she's the type that wears those outdated things. It's not even a pedometer or anything, it just tells time—and it makes you work for it, too, without any digital display. "I have to get in there to meet the, uh, I don't know, the person."

"The Realtor?" I cross my arms over my chest, fully intending to wait this out in the car. Maybe she'll change her mind if she has to go alone. I would.

"No, she works at the front office." She opens her door and slides out. "Are you coming?"

I don't want to. I don't want to participate in this, see a new potential home, have the traitorous feeling of excitement at another room to decorate. But I can't let her do this on her own, either. Not after she admitted it was hard living in her mother's house without her there. I can't imagine growing up in that house and not having both of them, not having my mom. I guess I can see her point. The ghost of all the good times would haunt me every day, reminding me just how lonely I am.

"Do they accept dogs?" I ask without getting out of the car.

She walks around and pulls my door open. "Of course they do."

"All dogs?" I ask, slowly getting out. "I don't want to live at a place that excludes because of breeds."

"Bagel will have tons of non-Pomeranian friends here. There's even a dog park area in the courtyard." She pulls me to her side and squeezes. "Thank you."

"I'm not doing this for you. I'm doing this for Bagel. He needs friends or he's going to grow up into a dog that eats its owners."

"We can't have that."

We walk into the building and meet Bev, the office manager, who shows us into the most disgusting place I've ever seen, and I've seen every episode of *Kitchen Nightmares*. You'd think if they're trying to rent out this apartment, they might consider, I don't know, cleaning it? Spraying some Febreze? Cracking a window and throwing out all the shit left from previous owners?

Bev flicks on the light switch, which only illuminates how terrible the place is even more than the dying sunlight creeping through the broken blinds did.

"Here we are." She tries to subtly nudge aside an abandoned shoe, but I can't look away from it. "The family left in a hurry, so we're trying to get some new occupants as soon as possible to recoup the rent."

My mom steps inside, but I'd rather stay out here. I'm not even being stubborn anymore. I'm pretty sure if I enter, I will drop dead from at least twenty diseases. There is literal trash spread across the dirty gray carpet, pieces of paint chipped off the walls, a few flies buzzing over dirty baking sheets on top of the stove, and a pungent wall of odor. I don't care how cheap this apartment is; no amount of savings is worth this. No one should have to live like this.

With a voice that can't hide she's refusing to breathe through her nose, my mom asks, "And the utilities are included in the eight twenty a month?"

"Just the trash," Bev says, pointing over her shoulder in the general direction where I saw an overflowing dumpster.

"Do you mind if we look around?" my mom asks, pulling me to her side with force. I stumble over the shoe Bev tried to hide.

"Feel free. I'll be outside. If you have any questions, just shout."

"Do you think shouting for help did any good for the family that was one hundred percent murdered here?" I ask quietly, even though Bev shut the door behind her.

My mom breaks free and spins slowly in the small living room. "Total mess aside, what are your thoughts?"

"That it stinks."

"Stink aside." She stills, raising an eyebrow. "You meant the actual smell, right?"

"How is this nearly a thousand bucks a month?" I step toward the small—everything is small here—kitchen and recoil from the tapioca linoleum floor when I see a trail of ants making their way to the refrigerator that I'm definitely not opening. "Are they serious?"

"It's in our budget and it'll be cleaned before move-in."

"Will it?" I venture down the short hallway, the carpet

shifting under my feet because it's torn and pulled up from the wall. "This bedroom is definitely the scene of the crime. What—is that—mold?"

My mom leans over my shoulder. "Oh. Yes."

I gesture around. "Are things this bad for us?"

It wouldn't be the first time she's kept things from me. After my grandma died, my mom stopped treating me like an adult, even though the situation called for it even more. Sure, she lets me basically take care of myself because we have to and she says things like *our budget*, but she hides final notices, refuses to talk finances, won't let me help her cut coupons or accept any money I offer.

"There's a lot of upkeep with the house." She's about to lean against the wall when she second-guesses herself, crossing her arms. "It'll need a new roof soon."

"There have to be other places that are within our budget." I pass her and head toward the front door. I'm not living here. I'm not letting my mom live here, either. "Like, the house. Where we already live. We should try to make that work, not move into a shithole like this."

She follows me. "*Saine*—"

"No. Let me help you. I am half the reason we're struggling, so I should be half the reason we're not."

She frowns, latching onto my arm and squeezing. "It's not your responsibility. Plus, with more money, we'd have chances to do more things, like . . . Like, you could go back to Adhira—"

"I don't need to go to therapy. I'm fine." I pause on the way to the doorknob. "I mean, I might need some after this place.

This is the stuff of nightmares."

"Okay, we haven't always been the most secure financially, I'll give you that, but if you think it's not a privilege to have any roof over your head, you've got another think coming. This would be heaven for some people. All it takes is some cleaning. We're moving. Maybe not here, but we are, so deal with it. This would be a much easier process if you lost the 'tude, kid."

"Maybe if I knew this was even up for consideration before five minutes ago, I wouldn't have the attitude."

She pushes past me and out the door to tell Bev thanks, but we're going to consider other options. The only option I see is staying at home. Our home. My grandma's home.

Unknown

Today 3:17 PM

Hey

3:17 PM

It's Holden

3:17 PM

I know.

3:17 PM

How

3:17 PM

You just told me.

3:18 PM

Ha

3:18 PM

You can come over now

3:18 PM

I have to watch Mara though

3:18 PM

That's fine. I like her better than you anyway.

3:18 PM

SIX

Holden still lives a few streets over. It's so close that, when I was a kid, my mom used to let me walk there by myself during the day because there are sidewalks and the world wanted to make it as easy as possible for me to see my best friend.

But now it just makes me feel weird. It's been so long that I forgot the one slab of concrete that tips like a seesaw when you walk over it and I stumble in front of an old man walking his golden retriever.

Corrine was out of school today for a college visit, so I didn't tell her that I'm using her ex-boyfriend as my documentary subject, but I will. Soon. It's not something to say over text or when she's busy with fundraisers or considering the next four years of her life. It's not even that big of a deal, so for me to make it seem like it is when she's clearly exploding with all her to-do lists is just selfish of me.

When I turn onto Brasher Street, I spot Holden's house down the block as easily as my mom finds crumbs on the table after I clean it. I haven't seen this house for so long that I almost think I missed it. It's a white two-story in the same design as its neighbors, with black shutters, a huge tree in the front, a matching one in the back, and a white fence around the yard. I always loved that yard. It was like you had a little section of the world to yourself. Holden always loved my house because of the pool, but I burn easily so it didn't take long for me to resent everyone's desire to spend hours pruning in the sun. Corrine doesn't know how to swim, so.

I adjust my camera bag on my shoulder. It would have been nice if Holden had offered to pick me and all my equipment up, but, then again, I wouldn't have accepted the ride. It doesn't feel right to do unnecessary things with him when Corrine still doesn't know he's my subject.

My heart rate kicks into overdrive as I step onto the stone walkway leading up to his front door. I wipe my hand along my jeans and then ring the doorbell like I have so many times before his mom lied to me and said it was broken so I should just walk in whenever I got here. She also used to lie about other things, like she was too tired to get me a drink so I should just help myself. That she didn't care what movie we watched, so I should just pick it. That she hated hearing the word *bathroom*, so I should just feel free to use it whenever I needed to. It wasn't until I was friends with Corrine and did these things naturally with her that I realized Holden's mom was just letting me know I should be comfortable here.

There's no chance of that happening today.

The door swings open and Mara's smiling face greets me. "It's a stranger!" she calls over her shoulder, her chin rubbing against a puffy baby-pink vest. "Hope it's okay that I let them in!"

"Can't they just take you and leave?" Holden steps into view wearing the same jeans from school that aren't necessarily skinny jeans, but might as well be, with a white long-sleeved shirt underneath a vintage—and practically decaying—black The Commercials T-shirt. Corrine hates this shirt more than she hates the band's music. She says it's old and too sad. I have to agree.

"*Holden*," his mother says somewhere deeper in the house. "Who is it?"

I step inside when Mara and Holden give me the space to. "Hey, Mama Michaels," I say.

Holden cringes next to me. So maybe it's weird that I'm referring to her so familiarly, but she always insisted I call her that and I'm not going to draw attention to how awkward it is between Holden and me by *not* calling her that. Or am I doing just that by trying to be familiar?

"Oh my god," she says, leaning over the banister in a pair of violet scrubs with cracked eggs and chicks running all over. "Saine Sinclair."

"Her last name is Davis now," Holden says to me quietly.

Mara skips up the stairs and disappears into the living room, where the TV plays something with a lot of orchestral swelling.

"Oh. Sorry—" My words are choked off as she rushes down the stairs and pulls me into a tight hug. "I forgot," I squeak out.

"It's okay." She rubs my back like she's comforting me, and she speaks in a soothing tone. "I'm so happy to see you. It's been too long, sweetie."

She pulls away, holding me by my shoulders to get a good look. "You're so grown up. I can't believe it. I had a hard enough time accepting that Holden shot up like a weed, but seeing you is just making me feel like the Crypt Keeper."

"I don't know what that is."

"Oh god, even my references are old." She lets go of me and smiles at Holden. "What are you two up to? I didn't realize you still—" She cuts herself off, but her statement didn't need to be finished for us to know what she was going to say.

"She's helping me with the contest," he says.

"Yeah, actually, I was wondering if I could have a few minutes with you." I shift the camera bag on my shoulder again. It continues to dig into me, heavy. "I'm making a documentary about it."

"That sounds so cool, but I'm on my way to the hospital for a C-section. Can we make it work another time?"

I drop my jaw, knowing she'll love this one. "You're *pregnant*?" When she laughs, I nod to her scrubs. "Another time would be *egg*-cellent."

She snorts, putting on her jacket and grabbing her keys from the hook by the door. "That's cute." She kisses Holden's cheek. "I'll see you later, hopefully.

"Mara," she calls toward the living room, "Holden's in charge, sweetie!"

"Got it!" comes the distracted response.

She opens the door and then leans in to squeeze my cheek. "Good to see you. Bye."

"Bye," Holden and I say at the same time.

Holden shuts the door and we move up the stairs and into

the living room. I start unpacking my equipment so I don't focus on how much it's changed in here. Obviously, the layout of the house is the same, but the walls, which were a cream color before, are bolder now in a deep red. The couch is no longer a plaid monstrosity that left lines in your skin when you sat too long, but a sleek black-velvet sectional. The floors are still hardwood, but even they look rejuvenated somehow. It still smells the same, though, like warm sugar cookies. If only I could capture the smell on camera.

"Hey, Mara, can I interview you for the documentary?"

"I thought you'd never ask," she says, turning the TV off with the remote and angling toward me. She flattens her skirt over her gray-and-white striped tights, then clasps her hands in her lap.

Holden frowns. "She can't consent to this. You need my mom or her dad."

"Where's her dad?"

"He works until like eight o'clock," Mara chimes in. "We can ask for his permission after we film. Where's my key light?"

"How do you know what a key light is?" I set up the tripod in front of her on the couch.

"We're making video diaries for school. Like a time capsule thing for when we're old like you guys."

"We're not old," Holden says indignantly.

"Kids these days," I say. "No respect."

I finish setting up my equipment, which sadly does not include a key light because I'm just one person and I can't carry an entire film studio with me, check the memory card and the battery life, and when I'm about to hit record, Holden stops me.

"What am *I* supposed to do?" His tone clearly indicates that *this is supposed to be about me.*

"How about you get your submission ready? I got the copy you emailed me earlier, but I'd like to get your play-by-play of it on film." I shoo him away with a flick of my hand and turn back to Mara. He reluctantly leaves.

I press record. "Hi, Mara. Can you tell me your full name, your age, your relationship to Holden, and if you consent to be filmed?"

"Hi, world. My name is Mara Alicia Davis. I'm twelve and three-quarters years old, Holden is my stepbrother, and I consent to being filmed." She bats her mascara-free eyelashes with a smile.

I go through a series of introduction questions with Mara:

What's Holden like?

What's your relationship like?

Do you think he has a chance of winning?

What makes him suited to win?

What's your favorite moment with him?

To her credit, Mara answers like a champ. Like she's been waiting her entire life for this interview. She's articulate, funny, and gives me a ton of footage to work with—not to mention blackmail material when she says her favorite moment with Holden is the time she bet him a month of chores that she could eat more wasabi than him—and then proceeded to eat avocado while Holden struggled. I wrap up in about fifteen minutes and only then realize that Holden's sitting behind us on the ottoman.

"I'm all set up." He jabs a thumb toward the hallway.

"I'm having ice cream for dinner since you're being negligent and not feeding me," Mara says, halfway to the kitchen already.

"If you get it on anything, I'll kill you."

"Great babysitting," I say, pulling my camera off the tripod.

"So we agree." He stands. "Mara, if you don't wash your bowl, I'm going to put it on your head while you sleep and cut your hair around it."

"Yeah, I got it, I got it," she mumbles. She opens drawers and cabinets, setting a spoon and bowl down on the counter.

"Hey, Holden had a bowl cut around your age and he turned out—" I glance at him. He raises an eyebrow. "Make sure you get that bowl clean, kid."

"I said I got it, *kid*," she says.

We head to Holden's bedroom and I record everything. The artfully displayed succulents, the hallway runner, the family photos that now include a beautiful blonde girl I've yet to meet. But when we reach Holden's room, we don't enter. In fact, that room is very much Mara's now, by the looks of it. The walls are a bright yellow in the spots there aren't any Lulu Nex posters. Pillows are piled three feet high on her bed and there's a record player collecting dust on her sticker-covered dresser.

The room across the hall from it used to be Trevor's. Maybe still is. The door is shut, though, so I can't see inside to confirm.

"Is Trevor home?" It strikes me as odd that he wasn't at the first competition with Holden and Mara. Video games was the first language these brothers learned to speak to each other.

"With his friend," Holden grunts before starting down the stairs to what used to be the finished basement. I follow, filming how his hand slides down the railing the entire way down; the stairs aren't steep, so I don't know why he's bracing himself. At the bottom, two doors close off the basement. Holden opens the one on the right and, inside, band posters cover the walls so heavily it looks like some kind of Hot Topic–brand wallpaper. Empty picture frames Corrine bought are hung over the poster-wallpaper in a large triangle shape. I don't know if he picked up in here while I was interviewing Mara or if he's changed his ways, but there are no clothes on the floor like there used to be, and the top of his dresser is bare, save for the TV perched atop it and angled toward his queen-sized bed. He sits at his desk and wakes up the ancient MacBook Pro he got before entering middle school.

I didn't bother to watch the file he emailed me earlier because it seemed like a waste of time if I was going to see it now. But it's . . . wow. I film his computer, his hands, and his face in various close-ups as he explains his kind of genius—not that I'd admit it to him—submission. He shows me aesthetics, commercial examples, live videos of bands playing, first-person perspectives of being onstage and crowd-surfing, all the things that add up to his own virtual reality: a concert experience. In his submission, he explained that he wants to create a world where people can have the ultimate time at a show; he wants people to be able to enjoy it from the crowd, surf up to the front and get onstage, play the instruments, run into celebrities back-stage, the whole deal. He used to say he wanted to be a band photographer, or work for those dying music magazines, and it's evident in every second of his submission. I wonder how much time he put into this.

I sit on his bed, the camera trained on his face. "So, why did you want to do this contest?"

He stiffens for a half second, spinning his computer chair toward me. "Seems fun."

"I know, but—"

"And I want the headset, obviously."

"That's it?"

"Do I need more of a reason?"

"Kind of." *Where's the heart?* "Don't you think it's weird to put that much effort into something you're not more passionate about?"

He shrugs. "I've always liked video games."

"Yeah. That part makes sense, but this isn't even playing video games."

"Maybe I'll come up with a better reason later."

I try to keep the irritation out of my voice, but I fail. "Can you speak in full sentences that incorporate my questions, please?"

"Maybe I'll come up with a reason for why I wanted to do this contest aside from *it's fun and I want the headset* later," he says slowly.

"Too busy right now to do it?" He stares at me in response. I sigh. "So, when did your parents get divorced?"

"Are *you* asking or the camera?"

"Both." I try to hide my warming cheeks behind the view screen.

"My parents got divorced several years ago."

"When, though?"

"My parents got divorced when I was in the seventh grade."
So, just after our friendship ended. He's monotone by this point.
Shutting down. I don't know why he'd agree to help me out if
he's . . . not going to help me out.

"What happened?"

"They got divorced."

I cock my head to the side, not expecting him to air out the
dirty details, but *come on*. I guess if one or both of them cheated,
he wouldn't be the one to talk about it anyway. And, I guess,
it's not like I'm his friend, or someone he feels he can even trust
with something that personal.

Thinking I was waiting for the full phrasing, he says, "What
happened was my parents got a divorce—"

"Holden."

"What does that have to do with anything?" he asks, his
brows scrunching together. His cheeks pinken. "What does this
have to do with the contest? I thought you just wanted to film
someone playing the games."

"People need to care about you. Get invested in your story,
so if you win or lose, they feel something." And maybe I'm a
little nosy. Corrine never mentioned a little sister to tip me off
to these big life changes. I guess this is what happens when you
stop being friends with someone; you lose the privilege of really
knowing them.

"My home life has nothing to do with this story." He delivers a sardonic smile.

"Of course it does. It affects you, and you're the documentary."

He sighs, spinning his chair back to his laptop. The screen saver has come on, a photo of Holden and Trevor bouncing across the screen.

I zoom into the photo, but Holden wakes the computer. "How does Trevor feel about you doing this contest?" I ask.

"He wishes he could compete."

"What's stopping him?"

"He's not old enough, for starters."

"Shouldn't he be a freshman this year? I haven't seen him at school."

"He lives in Harrisburg."

It's implied that he lives with Holden's dad, but the fact that he didn't say it makes me question how things ended between Holden's parents, and how a sweet kid like Trevor, who was so close with his mom and brother, would decide to go with his dad. It . . . doesn't make sense. I hate when things don't make sense. He wasn't a bad parent, Holden's dad, but he never exactly seemed like #1 Dad material. He just did the job. The job and not much else.

"Do you see him often?" Harrisburg is only fifteen minutes away, but it's a different city, a different school district, across a gaping river. It feels far.

I shove my foot against his chair, turning him toward me.

"Yeah." He's not really giving me anything to work with here. He doesn't want to talk about personal things, and I don't know if it's me, the camera, the topic, or any combination of the three. "I don't want to talk about it. I don't think my family has anything to do with the contest."

Fantastic. This again.

Maybe over time, he'll open up. Or maybe I'll have to pry myself into his life the way I used to wish he had tried to pry into mine after I told him he wasn't my best friend anymore. But it's fine. I can work with this. If Holden's story doesn't have a heart, I'll *give* it one.

"So, the next event," Holden says with a smirk, "is based off *Extreme Racing*. So, should be a piece of cake."

Says the guy who got pulled over for going too slow. Mara couldn't stop at naming just one of her favorite Holden moments earlier. I have an arsenal of them now.

Taj is dating Nita López, who works at the Carlisle Sports Emporium, which is how Mara, Holden, and I end up there for "practice." Historically, the place is deserted on Tuesday nights in autumn. It's too cold to race around the outside track, the wind lashing at your face, the darkness heavy in your eyes despite the outside lighting. Not exactly convenient practice weather, but it's the best Holden is going to get, apparently.

Nita sets us up with two go-karts and two baskets full of the fuzzy dice no one ever wants to buy with their ticket earnings in the arcade, smiles at my camera with slightly crooked pearly whites, and then leaves to operate the front desk, insisting that Taj knows what he's doing.

I, on the other hand, do not have that much faith in him.

"I got this for Mar-Mar," he says, shoving a helmet on her head. He offers up a second one to me. It looks too small for my head and has a flower sticker on it. I have no clue where he got these from, so I can only assume they're from his personal collection. "Saine Sinclair?"

"No thanks, Taj Chakrabarti." But I kind of wonder if I'll need it when he takes the go-kart for a test drive and hits the bumper walls a few times, his dark hair blowing into his eyes.

Holden sits in his go-kart with Mara beside him, the basket of plush dice snug between them. He practices taking his hand off the steering wheel, grabbing a die, and fake-throwing it.

I try to rig my phone to record him in selfie mode, but I can't get it secure enough that I feel comfortable with him driving around.

"That would have been a flattering angle," he says sarcastically as I untie my phone from the wheel.

"Aren't they all?" I ask sweetly, batting my eyelashes.

He grins back, all teeth and squinted eyes, and a little warmth beats back the cold on my cheeks. "Thank you for noticing."

I cross to Mara's side as Taj lets out a whoop and comes to an abrupt stop next to us.

"Film Holden?" I offer her my phone with a shaky hand. If she drops it, I don't have over a month's rent at that shitty apartment to buy a new one outright and I'd want to be mad at Mara, but it wouldn't really be her fault. So then I'd just repress my anger and have no phone, and that sounds fucking miserable. But it's better than her dropping my camera or the rental.

"Don't drop it or I'll kill you." The words slip out, but thankfully Mara laughs.

Holden glares, but Mara misses it while starting to record.

"She's not joking," he says to her, way too close to the lens.

"Yes, she is." Mara points the phone at me. "You're funny."

"I'm glad you think so, because"—I drop my voice—"if you break that phone, I'll kill you."

She holds it with two hands.

"Are we ready to go?" Taj asks over the loud puttering of his go-kart's motor. A bit of exhaust creeps up my nostrils and I cough. "I want to throw some shit. Poop. Things." He smiles sheepishly at Mara.

"Does Nita find your swearing attractive? Because I said damn in front of Rose and she—"

Holden speeds off, taking Mara's question with him.

"Come on!" Taj revs his engine and I slide into the empty spot next to him, our legs cramped together, our hips and arms touching. At least I won't get too cold.

We spend the next thirty minutes with Holden and Taj racing all over the course and throwing dice at each other. Taj reaches the finish line first only one of the five times we do it. Holden's aim is pretty impressive. He only hits me instead of Taj twice, and I'm pretty sure only one of the times was on purpose.

Around eight o'clock, Nita comes out to tell us we have to wrap it up and drive the go-karts into the storage shed. As soon as Mara's feet touch solid ground, she lets loose all the ice cream she ate beforehand. Then, Taj bails, saying something about puking when others puke, leaving Nita and Holden to clean up the mess while I get Mara water. She leans against my shoulder as we replay the footage from my phone and the camera.

Holden definitely hit me on purpose that time.

Corrine

Today 10:21 AM

I have to pull out of the game this afternoon

10:21 AM

What's up? Are you okay?

10:23 AM

Been making out with the toilet all morning

10:24 AM

JEALOUS

10:24 AM

Need me to bring you some saltines? Walk bagel?

10:24 AM

Please don't be mad

10:24 AM

Of course I'm not mad!

10:25 AM

Let me know if you need anything

10:25 AM

You're the best

10:26 AM

SEVEN

Okay, okay, so I haven't told Corrine about the documentary and, sure, I pulled the biggest dick move by telling her I was too sick to cheer today, all so Holden and I could get to the Harrisburg Mall early to film, but in my defense, she hasn't asked about the documentary since that first time either.

Then again, yesterday, she did bring me a leather jacket from the thrift shop she works at—something she does a lot without ever wanting to be repaid, but I keep a running total—just because she saw it and thought of me. Which made it harder to bring this up.

We came inside about ten minutes ago, after Holden completed an interview for Vice and Virtual's web series. I filmed as much as I could, trying to be sneaky about it, but eventually had to stop when someone from the company asked me to. It's not like it was easy for me to pick up audio over the sounds of setup anyway.

"How do you think you'll do tonight?" I ask Holden now.

The mall, a sad dying dinosaur of a place, isn't that busy today and the Muzak isn't too loud, so I don't bother to put a microphone on Holden just yet.

"I'm great at multitasking, so I think I'll do well tonight." He abandons a carton of soggy steak fries he got at the food court in the nearest trash can and heads toward Kay Jewelers.

I smirk at the fact that he used a complete sentence for me. "Really? You couldn't drive and answer questions on the way here."

"I could. I chose not to." He thrusts his hands into his pockets. "Just like you chose not to let me take photos earlier this week."

"Look, Corrine doesn't know yet. I'm going to tell her, but you showing up like that just put me on edge."

"Why does it matter if she knows? We're not doing anything wrong." He surprises me by making a beeline into the store.

"Well, no, but she should know." I glance around. "Did you mean to come in here?"

He ignores my question. "Don't you think it's pretty telling that you haven't told her yet? You must feel like you're doing something wrong." He pulls his phone from his pocket and leans on the counter. "I'll just text her now."

"No!" I put my hand over his phone. "Not today. I told her I was sick. I missed an away game."

"You chose me over a game?" He places his hand against his chest. "I don't know if flattered is the right word, or maybe chuffed—"

"I chose the *documentary* over a game."

"I thought you said I was the documentary?" He spins toward the counter and places two hands over the glass, like an asshole. A salesman walks up, but Holden waves him away with a confident smile. "Just looking, thank you."

"Why are we looking at jewelry instead of, I don't know, doing something related to this contest?" I point the camera at his face. "Forget your mom's birthday?"

He glances up. "No one said you had to be here."

"You're my subject. You know—and *love*—that I have to follow you."

He ignores me. "What kind of jewelry do girls like?"

"Well, *Corrine* doesn't like jewelry from her ex-boyfriends, so . . ."

Pulling a face, he says, "It's not for Corrine. Or my mom."

Doubtful. He probably heard about Logan and wants to win her back. He's been single ever since Corrine ended things and, sure, she's been single too, but she has less to prove. She's busy 24-7. "Mara?"

"No."

"Your other sister, though, kind of weird."

"It's maybe for a teenage girl."

"You don't know her age?"

"No—" He rolls his eyes. "If I find something she'd like, *maybe* I'll buy it."

The full weight of this moment hits me. Is he finally going to make a move on the girl Corrine mentioned? It's been months, but I guess Holden's never been brave, or speedy. He does things at his own pace, and I used to find it endearing when we were kids—like when he'd stand at the end of the diving board just to backtrack and use the ladder into the pool, or when he'd read only one chapter of a book before bed even though we were reading it together and I could never discuss the ending with him because it took a hundred years for him to get there—but this is something I will not let him waste my time with. I already feel bad doing this behind Corrine's back; if she knew I was here—helping him—she'd for sure be pissed.

I point to the first piece I see, a small circular pendant with diamonds embedded into it. Unfortunately, it's not hideous. "It's not cliché like a heart, but it's still small and dainty, and silver goes with more clothes than gold does."

"Really? Just like that?" He motions to the salesman. "Could I see this one out of the case, please?"

The man smiles at me after placing it in front of us. "This would look great on you."

My entire body bursts into flames, right there, on the spot. Spontaneous combustion. "Oh, it's not for me," I say with a nervous laugh. "His ex-girlfriend is publicly moving on, so I assume he's gonna try to bribe some poor girl into dating him with this to make her jealous."

"No, it's— No. Thank you." He inspects it under normal lighting. "Still this one?"

"It's pretty, if you like that kind of thing." Pretty *expensive*. Holy shit, three hundred dollars for that? It's so small and the chain is so thin. It's gorgeous, still sparkling even though it's not under super bright lights, but damn. Pretty sure Ocean's Eight stole cheaper necklaces from the Met.

Holden clears his throat. "Do you, uh, do some kind of, like, payment plan–type thing? Like, could I make two or three payments at different times?"

"No, but if you're eighteen, you can sign up for our credit card." The salesman doesn't even bother pretending Holden's a real customer, placing the necklace back in the glass case before he says he's done looking at it.

"Okay, thanks." Holden takes a pamphlet on the credit card but doesn't make a move to start applying. The salesman walks away and Holden takes a photo of the necklace.

I get it all on film. Or memory card. A financial struggle is something I can relate to—something so many people can relate to. And, sure, no one expects a teenager to be able to afford some million-dollar necklace, and he has a MacBook even if it's nearly ten years old, a car—even if it's a hand-me-down that's been in accidents and has half a penis carved into the side. He's well-off in many ways, but people watching my documentary will see what I show them. I can flesh out the fake heart of my documentary later—a Gen Z financial struggle that will hopefully counteract his perfect, or at least average, life—but for now, I can't get distracted by this idea.

"Can we go outside now? I want some clips of you in front of the track." I turn toward the exit but stop, my heart in my throat. "Oh my god. Hi, Corrine."

Holden knocks into my arm, stopping at the sight of her. Maybe if I tell her he's here looking at jewelry for her, it'll soften the blow. Even if it's a lie.

"Hi." She stands awkwardly outside the confines of the store and flattens her uniform over her stomach, further reminding me that I bailed on my entire team to be here, not even filming what we're supposed to be filming. An A+ Health bag dangles in her hand. "Are you two here together?"

I say no just as Holden says yes.

I glance at him, eyes wide, then to her. "Physically, but not, like, *emotionally*."

"She wasn't asking that," Holden says in a quiet voice. "Hey."

They exchange that weird head nod greeting and the space between us, maybe six feet, feels like an entire ocean. My heart hammers in my chest, sweat forms just about everywhere, and I see my life flash before my eyes, Corrine-less.

"I'm going to head outside while you two talk," he says, moving swiftly past us.

I clear my throat. "Don't you, uh, need to be getting to the game?"

"I was on my way, but I stopped here to get some vitamins." She raises the bag, surveying me from head to toe. "For you, but you don't look very sick."

"I certainly feel it," I say more to myself than her.

"That makes two of us, then." She frowns, her mouth missing the usual red lipstick. She takes a moment to grind out her next question. "Are you two, like . . . dating?"

"No! God, *no*." I take a deep breath and step forward. "I had told you my original documentary subject bailed. Holden happened to be in the contest, too, and he moved on to this next round, the one happening in a few minutes outside, and it just seemed the most convenient? My documentary was already approved and I already did all this research on the contest . . . I . . . I'm sorry. I was going to tell you and then you were busy and I was, I don't know, scared? There's nothing going on besides the documentary, but I know we don't really talk about your breakup, and I didn't want to make things weird or harsh the vibe on the whole Logan thing. . . ."

She crosses her arms. Corrine's always preferred actions over words—hence the vitamins, the leather jacket, doing meal prep for an entire week after my grandma died—so I know it takes a lot for her to say, "It feels strange that you didn't tell me. Like you have something to hide. I don't know why you wouldn't just tell me you needed to film today instead of lying."

"I'm sorry, I—"

"Didn't want to open up the floor for a conversation about this?"

"Not through texts, at least," I mumble. "Would you have even *let* me talk about this?"

Her mouth opens to respond to my slight jab, but then a loud announcement tone plays throughout the mall, startling the elderly couple walking by us with huge, boxy shopping bags.

"*The Vice and Virtual Create Your Own (Virtual) Reality contest is beginning in ten minutes for anyone who wishes to watch. Please make your way to the parking lot outside the food court,*" the Mall God says.

"I'm sorry. I have to—" I raise my camera with arms that weigh fifteen tons. "I have to go film."

She nods, watching me hurry past her. "Saine? Please don't lie again."

"Of course not." I run out of the store and hope that I'm not also running out of Corrine's life over something that could end up being so stupid, so not worth it.

I find Holden waiting near the food court exit, looking a little smug—like he wants to say something but knows better.

"At least now you don't have to worry about sneaking around."

Or maybe he doesn't.

"Shut up." I grind my teeth together, forcing down the queasiness in my gut. At least that wasn't a lie back there; I really do feel sick now.

He holds the door open. "Oh, come on. That would have been a pain for both of us."

"Why? Because you have so many interactions with Corrine now that you're literally nothing but a memory to her?"

"You don't have to be a bitch about it," he says quietly to my back.

I whirl on him, just outside a huge crowd of people surrounding the makeshift race track. "Excuse me?"

"Why do you rub that in my face? I'm fine. You're the one who makes it a big deal. You keep assuming everything I do is for Corrine like I'm a sad puppy begging to be kicked."

"Why wouldn't you be upset that you don't have her anymore? *I'm* upset that she's potentially pissed at me and doesn't trust me. She left *you* and you didn't care."

"Of course I cared."

"But you cared about that other girl more, huh? What a shame you lost Corrine and then this secret girl didn't want you, either."

He frowns, face scrunching up as he chews on his next words. But then feedback from a microphone causes the crowd around us to hush.

"How the hell am I supposed to get through these people?" he mutters to himself. He tries maneuvering around a giant man in a Steelers jacket, but doesn't get far.

"Get low and crawl." I demonstrate, moving where there's fewer shoulders to block my way. Something I learned from his stepsister, actually.

"Aren't you worried about your face getting stepped on?" he asks, right behind me.

"I've had it eighteen years. Time for a new one."

Eventually people are so shocked and offended that we're squirming past their privates that they start letting us through. Holden breaks free to where the other players stand, shows his Vice and Virtual ID, and listens as they explain the rules: each player gets a go-kart and a series of soft balls to launch at other players, along with a confetti cannon and a squirt gun full of water. The course before us is extreme, as the game's name would indicate, with man-made hills and valleys, obstacles that move, and 360-degree viewing angles for the crowd. Anderson's Gadgets, the store James Heath worked at as a teen, his first "official" foray into the tech world, hasn't been at the mall in a few years. It went out of business, as many things do, but he wanted to pay respect to what it was by still hosting the second event here. And in the continued spirit of giving back to the community slash supporting local businesses, James Heath wanted to bring in a crowd of people to patronize the remaining stores at the mall.

My grandma once rented a little stand at the Capital City Mall where she sold her art, before I was born and before she started giving lessons and needed her own space. It seems like a terrible job to have—I mean, I've never once bought something from those vendors—but she always looked back on it fondly. Probably because she, in her own words, had a lot of eye candy to keep her busy during the long, boring hours.

Before the official announcement and start of the game, I latch onto Holden and pull out my lav mic, running it up the inside of his shirt and taping it to his collar, my freezing knuckles sliding up the warm skin of his chest.

"Wow, how about you buy me dinner first?" he hisses.

I ignore my blush. "How are you still hungry? Those fries equaled like three potatoes."

"Can someone really have too many potatoes, though?" He taps the microphone gently. "Is this a mic?"

"Yes."

"What if it gets wet?"

"It'll be fine."

"But will I be? Unlike potatoes, I'm not so good when I'm fried." He wets his lips. It's clear nerves are getting the best of him now. "Why are you putting a microphone on me?"

"Because you won't be within range of my camera to hear you."

"Okay," he says on a shaky breath. "Wish me luck?"

His cheeky smile doesn't fool me.

"Good luck." I actually mean it, too. I feel like I need to take a walk to calm down myself.

I zoom out with my camera, placing him in the center of the

frame. In my free hand, I've got the GoPro I rented from PSH, ready to be attached to whichever go-kart he's assigned.

"That almost sounded nice," he says genuinely.

"You need to advance for my documentary to continue, so. Yeah."

"I said almost."

The likelihood of running into Corrine here, on this day, in these circumstances, was slim. The likelihood of Holden being one of only *five* winners of this event is only slightly less slim.

Three more laps stand in the way of him potentially being first, second, third, fourth, fifth, or loser, loser, loser, loser, loser. He's been holding steady in third place, not really caring that his opponents loft balls at him and squirt water into his eyes or that he rammed into an obstacle full force thirty seconds into the first lap. He keeps a handle on the go-kart with expert skills that some of the other players seem to lack. Like the two who ran off the track and into the crowd when they tried to avoid collision, Holden narrowly escaping between them. I'm not sure this Holden would even know how to speak the same language as the Holden who got pulled over for driving too slow.

I try my best to properly convey the action and the tension of the event with well-timed zooms and shifting the focus, but I'm still only getting one angle. I wish Mara was here to film from the other side. Or Corrine. I wish I had told her from the moment I made the deal with Holden. I wish she approved and supported me.

When Holden starts his last lap, I notice something weird about the player behind him. The guy is practically driving on top of him, his front wheels hitting Holden's back wheels. Holden tries to shake him off, but the guy sticks close. They drive under a little bridge with swinging obstacles and Holden drives out rubbing his head, turning behind him to yell something. He says it again and I hear it in my own headphones attached to the camera synced to his microphone.

"—fucking hitting me, dude!"

I zoom in closer and see the guy pull up next to Holden, whack him in the head with his squirt gun, and then ram his go-kart off the track. Holden flies over the little track edge and tips over. The crowd around me groans and cheers, as if they really care about the outcome instead of the chance to see some bloodshed.

I rush over to the side of the track Holden's on, stuck behind the caution tape roping off the viewing area, my heart hammering. He flips his go-kart over as Vice and Virtual people run to help him.

"I'm fine," he tells them, rubbing his neck. His eyes latch onto each of the remaining players as they speed past him and toward the finish line. He tries to get into the go-kart, but the people stop him. I just barely hear one of them say he needs to be checked by an EMT. He argues with them and in the time it takes for them to let him go, everyone eligible to pass the finish line does.

This can't keep happening. This is going to be the worst documentary ever. What school, with only fifteen spots for the program, would accept me with *this*?

Holden gets escorted toward the exit, where they've begun announcing the top five winners, the Vice and Virtual cameras in their faces, and I duck under the caution tape to meet them.

"What the fuck?" I say to him.

The woman leading Holden off points behind me. "You can't be in here."

"What's it matter now?" I pan my camera to her. "He lost and the race is over." It pains me to say it aloud. My eyes sting and my throat clogs.

Holden shakes his head and a few drops of water fall from his hair to the ground. "Sorry, she's with me. We're getting off the track."

The asshole who knocked Holden off the track accepts *second place* as we join the crowd around a Vice and Virtual–designed winners' podium. This is such bullshit, for Holden *and* me.

"That guy sabotaged you." He sabotaged me. I can kiss my chance of going to Temple, of pursuing a career bringing stories to life, goodbye because of some shithead in a big-titty-anime shirt. And, sure, someone—like maybe Adhira, my one-time therapist—might point out that I shouldn't have gotten into the position of having my entire documentary hinge on something I couldn't guarantee, but it's too late! I did the thing! And now I'm fucked!

"He fucking clocked me," he says, massaging the back of his head. "And none of these people so concerned with our safety saw a thing."

We pass through people clambering to see the winners and

reach a bubble of space near a trash can. Holden exhales and then kicks it.

"Hey." I place my hand on his shoulder but pull it away when I feel how tense he is. "Chill."

If anyone should be pissed, panicking, or being a total sour-puss, it's me. But you don't see me going all Toxic Masculinity on inanimate objects. All he lost was something he could even-tually save up to buy in a year's time. I lost my future.

"No. That was bullshit." He kicks it again. Some people start to stare at him.

"Holden Henry Michaels, I'll show this to your mom and she'll be so disappointed in you. *Relax*."

He turns around slowly. "You wouldn't do that, *Saine Lau-ren Sinclair*, or I'll tell *your* mom that you spent prom last year drinking and making out with anyone with lips."

"I made out with *one person,* Drama Queen. And if it had been more, by your logic, I would have made out with *you*—" I lift my camera, pause the recording, and ignore the mental image I con-jured, one that has haunted me since I was twelve. It took almost a year for me to think or hear Holden's name and not cringe over his revulsion and refusal to kiss me during our immature game of spin the bottle. "I have it. I have him on camera hitting you and ramming into you. That has to be against the rules, right?"

"It was assault, so it better be." He takes a deep breath and then looks over the crowd to where the winners are congregat-ing. I'm sure someone is going to track down Holden for some kind of loser closure speech for the web series. "But how would I even—"

I latch onto his arm and start marching him into the crowd and don't stop pushing until I'm standing face-to-face with the lady who led us off the track a moment ago.

"Your number two, that guy with the spiky hair and ugly shirt, is a real number two. He hit my friend in the head with his squirt gun while the race was happening."

She raises a pencil-thin eyebrow behind her glasses. "Excuse me?"

"I was filming. You can clearly see for yourself that he was hit over the head and then rammed off the track. That's not okay. Did your rules account for people physically attacking each other with anything other than confetti, water, and plushies?" I cock my head to the side, waiting. Holden stands next to me, silent. Would it kill him to help me out here? This benefits him, too.

The woman taps her foot for a second, looking between us with a tight grimace. "Cue up the footage."

I navigate back and back and back, stop rewinding, and let the action play out for Holden and her to see. It's perfectly clear that the guy hit him and then shoved him off the track.

"So?" I ask, holding my breath.

She sighs, then pulls a walkie-talkie from her belt. "John, we have an issue with one of the winners."

Holden and I spend an hour after the event waiting for and then talking to Vice and Virtual representatives, showing them the footage, showing The Douche the footage. He gets disqualified and his win handed over to Holden since Holden was in second place when turning the last corner and would have easily made the top five. I film everything, from Vice and Virtual telling the crowd they're naming a new winner because of foul play—I bet they'll love putting this part in their little web series—to the end of the night when mostly everyone has disappeared and Holden claims his spot on the winners' platform, atop the big number two.

EIGHT

When we arrive back at Holden's house, his mom intercepts me when I step out of the minivan.

"Sweetie, are you going to stay for dinner?" She stands in silhouette in the doorway, darkness stretched out between us.

I really need to talk to Corrine, and the thought of awkwardly eating dinner with Holden's family certainly has me leaning toward that form of torture over the small talk kind, but then Mama Michaels says it's taco night and I haven't had a taco in months because I don't know how to brown the meat without it drying out and my mom's as bad as me at cooking and this is how I end up squeezed between Holden and Mara with Mama Michaels and Holden's stepdad on the other side of the table. It's all the tacos' fault.

"So," I say, cringing before the words even come out of my mouth, "what do you do, Mr. . . ." I swear Holden told me his last name. It's Mara's last name. It's—

"Davis. You can call me Darren," he says with a wide smile.

There's some taco sauce on his upper lip. "I'm a social worker."

"Oh, that sounds, um . . ."

"Depressing," Mara and Holden say at the same time, giving me that nice surround sound quality. Mara snorts into her taco, some of her hair sticking in the sour cream.

"Selfless," I finish, pushing some meat back into the hard shell with my fork.

"It's not always easy," he says, nodding. Mama Michaels gives him a shy smile.

"So, you both work with kids? Couldn't get enough of these goofballs at home?" I tilt my head in Mara's direction to make her laugh again.

"You don't have to fill the silence, you know," Holden says, his elbow brushing against mine as he reaches for his glass of water. As a lefty, he should be on my other side—we always had it worked out when we were kids, but it appears that Mara is also a lefty, so their usual seating arrangement typically works. "You can abort interrogator mode."

"No, it's okay." Darren laughs, wiping his mouth with a napkin. "Taryn warned me about Saine's inquisitive nature."

"Wait," I choke out. "Taryn and Darren. A coincidence?"

Mama Michaels laughs. "Well, it definitely wasn't intentional."

Darren's pinkie grazes the side of her hand. "We met under unfortunate circumstances at the hospital, but we hit it off and I think things are going pretty well, all things considered."

Mama Michaels's smile falters for only a second. "I know you're heading to the next round," she says to Holden, "but how did the competition actually go?"

"Can I go next time?" Mara interjects, crunching into the taco. I notice she covered her hard shell with a soft shell, so I do the same when I assemble my next one. It helps to keep the broken bits contained.

"No, the next one is in New York," Mama Michaels says. "You're going with Taj, right?"

Holden pinches my leg underneath the table, because despite our years apart, he *knows* me and I was totally going to ask when he planned on telling me this.

"Are you sure you don't want me to go with you?" she asks. "I can probably take off work."

"Yeah, it's fine. You booked the hotel?"

"Did it as soon as I got your text that you're advancing." She smiles fondly at him, her hand tucked around her glass. "Will you be there, too? To film?" she asks me.

"Uh, yeah." I glance at Holden, then back to her. "I'll be staying with my dad that weekend." Holden and I hadn't gotten this far in our discussion, which was a major oversight on my part and only semi-blamable on my belief in jinxing things.

I've never actually gone to see my dad despite him sending money for train tickets along with his child support. My mom doesn't know that, though. I get on the train and she just assumes I'm going to see him. She doesn't ask specific questions because she doesn't want to know. She asks things like: how was your trip, did you have a good time, did you do anything fun? And I can answer those without lying, without mentioning that I have never once stepped foot in my dad's Park Slope apartment and I have never once done anything but explore the city by myself, filming whatever struck my fancy. Even though I turned eighteen and he's not legally bound to send child support, he still does. It almost makes me feel guilty for using his money to go to his city and not see him. Almost. It's better than spending *my* money.

I really don't want to spend that money on a hotel, though. Not with the way things are going at home. Shit's expensive in the city, so maybe I can crash on the boys' floor or sucker one of them into letting me sleep in his bed because Chivalry.

"Oh, great. Will you tell him I say hello?" Mama Michaels asks.

"Sure thing," I lie like a lying liar. My mom has never asked me to say hello to my dad for her, so I think this lie has just been a long time coming.

"You know, Saine, I've been curious as to when I'd meet you," Darren says. "It's kind of funny to live in a house with photos on the wall of a person you've never met."

A particularly hard bit of shell stabs my esophagus. "What?"

Mama Michaels grins. "We have so many cute baby pictures of you and Holden. They're just too good not to keep hanging."

"We didn't know each other when we were babies." I raise an eyebrow at Holden.

"Well, you're *still* babies in the grand scheme of things," she says, sliding out of her chair and rushing from the dining room.

"Here we go!" She comes back with a black picture frame and shoves it into my hands. "Look at how cute you two were!"

My stomach drops. I hope Corrine didn't see this when she came over.

In the photo, a little version of me—definitely around the

time when Holden and I became friends, so maybe I'm eight—kisses a little version of him on the cheek. He's smiling like an idiot, his oversized backpack slung on both shoulders, the slack tucked in his tiny fists. I'm wearing a baby doll dress that Corrine would die to get her hands on, if she could somehow manage to fit into a child's clothes.

Holden huffs out a laugh, his warped eyebrows only showing a bit of annoyance. "What was this, third grade?"

"First day," his mom says, sitting down and placing her chin in her hands. "I remember how Trevor cried and cried, because you two were going to school all day, but he had afternoon kindergarten and had to wait to leave."

"He didn't know what was waiting for him," I say, handing the picture back to Mama Michaels with care. She doesn't seem to be resentful when she talks about her other son. "Growing up is a nightmare."

"I want to grow up more," Mara says, crinkling her napkin between her palms. She wiggles her eyebrows at Mama Michaels. "I want some real boobs—"

"*Okay*," Holden says abruptly.

"Boobs aren't that great." I say while Holden shakes his head. "Sometimes they get in the way of things."

"Well, yeah, I don't want *huge* ones like yours, just, like, the size of Corrine's maybe."

Now things get even more awkward. Holden tenses beside me.

"Who's Corrine? Someone you go to school with?" Mr. Davis asks, frowning at his daughter, though half of it is hidden by his bristly brown mustache.

Mara looks at Holden and then to her dad. "No, Holden's ex-girlfriend."

"She means my prom date," Holden says in a clipped tone.

"Oh yeah," Mama Michaels says, gathering our plates. "She was so cute. Whatever happened to her?"

I sit there, mouth clamped shut, with my hands clenched. They don't know Holden and Corrine dated? They were together for *months*. Their relationship lasted longer than the loose McDonald's French fries I lost somewhere in my mom's car, and neither of them bothered to delete their photos together off Instagram; like, it was legit. I was worried about my trace in the house and Corrine's never even been here? Maybe she *didn't* know Holden had sisters. Maybe she didn't know much about him at all. Maybe *I* didn't know much about them as a couple.

That's too much not-knowing for me. I want to *scream*.

"Things just didn't work out." He shrugs. "I already had a girlfriend anyway."

Now I'm just reeling, teeth gritted. Is he referring to the other girl Corrine mentioned? Was he bringing *her* around here instead of my best friend? How am I supposed to keep my mouth shut when there are so many lies, so many questions that need asking. I am a question asker! I must—

"I know *you* didn't respect the fact that I was your boyfriend, but I stayed loyal." Holden nudges me with his elbow.

"Excuse me?" There's not a word strong enough to articulate my confusion, or my anger. Is he making a joke about being loyal in a relationship? When he's *him* and I was literally cheated on? I'm all for a bit of story editing when necessary, but this is just a plot twist that's come out of nowhere.

Mama Michaels coos. "Aw, that's right. You two were each other's first love."

"Excuse me?" It's not like she knew about the incident at the party, the reason we stopped being friends. Holden wouldn't have told her that. Or would he? It's starting to become quite apparent that while I knew Holden of yesteryear, I do not know the one sitting next to me. It's terrifyingly possible that he told her all about when our friendship started to change, when I started caring about how my hair looked in front of him, or if my legs were shaved before we hung out. All the little things that I tried to be subtle about but added up into a huge crush. They probably had a ball, laughing at me.

"I asked you to be my girlfriend when I was, like, ten and you accepted." Holden rests his arm on the back of his chair, facing me. "Remember? You liked my light-up sneakers and sharing my Hershey's Kisses at lunch."

A laugh bubbles out of me, partly in relief and partly because I do finally remember it. "I had bad judgment as a kid. We know this." I whisper, "Tooth fairy."

He rolls his eyes, a smirk on his mouth. "You never did break up with me."

"Should we do that now?"

"If you were ten," Mara says, "it doesn't count. I barely remember anything from when I was ten, and that was two years ago." She slides away from the table. "Dad, can we play *Extreme Racing: Dubai?*"

"I don't know," he says good-naturedly, "can you handle getting your butt kicked by an old man in bifocals?"

They leave the table and, in the kitchen, Mama Michaels starts washing dishes, the water running full force as pots and pans clank together.

"Can I help you with the dishes, Mama Mic—Mrs. Davis?" I ask, standing.

"No, but thank you, Saine. I wish one of my *children* had offered!"

"You always end up rewashing the dishes I wash anyway, so I'm saving water!" Holden calls, standing.

"Thanks for dinner," I say loud enough for her to hear. "It was great."

"You're welcome any time. I'll see you soon for an interview, right?"

"Hopefully next week, please!" I can ask about the divorce, the marriage, Trevor's separation from the family, and how expensive it must be to have the prospect of sending four kids to college now. A financial struggle gold mine. I will give this documentary some kind of heart if it's the last thing I do. The magic of editing will save me.

I push my hair behind my ear and head to the front door, where the leather jacket Corrine got me hangs. Holden follows, quiet in his sock-covered feet.

"Good job with your driving tonight." I grab the jacket and it feels cold to the touch even though it's stifling in this house.

"I can't tell if you're being sarcastic or not," he says, scratching his eyebrow. "But thanks. I was pretty great."

"I'm being serious. Good job. We'll need to discuss the logistics of New York and everything, but it was a good night."

"Corrine stuff aside," he says.

I drop the volume of my voice. "What's up with that, anyway? Were you, like, embarrassed of Corrine? Why didn't they know you were dating her?"

He sighs. "She didn't want me to tell them because I said they'd want to meet her. You know how she is meeting parents and stuff. She doesn't just mesh with people immediately like you do." He pauses to think. "At least, not unless she's in the power position."

He's not wrong. The first time she met my mom, Corrine completely froze up, so yeah, I know how she is with parents and stuff. I guess this explains why she was drinking before we even got our hair done for prom last year. She had to meet Holden's family for photos and she was nervous. His siblings must not have been around—Mara seems to have a standing date every Saturday with a piano she's fated to battle to the death, and Trevor, well, he's got a life with his dad now.

"But the relationship is over," I say like it's breaking news. "Why haven't you said anything to them? Mara knows."

He leans against the door frame, crossing his arms. "That's because Mara knows everything somehow. She's scary intuitive."

"Or she has an Instagram account you don't know about." I pull my jacket on. "Don't use me as a distraction from the truth next time."

He pulls an exaggerated frown. "Are you breaking up with me?"

I pat him on the cheek, a little roughly. He winces but

doesn't stop me. "No light-up sneakers? No girlfriend."

"Have fun walking home, then," he says with a shit-eating grin.

I roll my eyes and zip up my jacket. "Don't pretend like you cared enough to even offer a ride."

Nope. and friends

Today 9:03 PM

Kayla
NEW MUSIC VIDEO COMING ATCHA
9:03 PM

Kayla sent a link.

DMS
Starring my hot girlfriend
9:04 PM

Juniper Kim
It was so fun!!
9:05 PM

Kayla
Really? Nothing?
9:27 PM

Saine are you mad that I didn't let you film it?
9:28 PM

It's a cool concept to do it entirely on FaceTime, you said so yourself!

9:28 PM

Juniper Kim
SAINE!!! CORRINE!!! Helloooooo!!!

9:30 PM

Blink twice if you guys need help

9:30 PM

DMS
I don't care

9:31 PM

It's not like she showed up last night to help film it

9:31 PM

Kayla
Corrine?

9:40 PM

Are they still in the chat?

9:40 PM

ACT TWO

in which mistakes are made

NINE

According to Kayla, Corrine had a "thing" during lunch and that's why she wasn't eating with us. I saw her a few tables over, talking to people I know she's in clubs with, so maybe she wasn't just avoiding me. Regardless, she can't avoid me at cheerleading practice since she's the captain and I am a dutiful minion who really needs to make up for the fact that I missed a game to spend the night with her ex-boyfriend—and then his family.

In the gym, Kayla and I stretch next to each other in our practice clothes while others talk and goof off, waiting for Corrine and Coach Hartl to show up.

"I have a joke for you," Kayla says, stretching her arm across her chest. She's been lobbing them my way all day because she can tell I'm nervous about something. "Do Christian schools play football?"

"Yeah?" I mimic her motion with the opposite arm.

"What's their mascot?"

"It depends on the school—"

She cuts me off with an excited smile. "The Devil's Advocate."

"I'm not sure that one makes sense, but A for effort."

"Okay." She switches arms. A light brown scar wraps around her elbow from a nasty fall off Corrine's trampoline freshman year. "What about 'The White Savior'?"

I drop my arm. "I'll see you in hell."

"Thanks. You know how nervous I get when I have to go places alone."

"Hey," Corrine says, walking up to us with a smile, almost like things are normal. Coach Hartl is nowhere in sight. "Can I talk to you, Saine?"

Here it is. The longer version of what should have occurred on Saturday—or even Sunday, but I carefully avoided my phone by spending the day transferring footage and hacking together what I've got so far. I knew things weren't good between us. I was stupidly optimistic earlier.

I stand.

"Good luck," Kayla says quietly, but not quietly enough that Corrine doesn't hear.

She looks between Kayla and me. "Does she know?"

"I want to answer truthfully, but I'm not one hundred percent sure what we're talking about here."

"The documentary." The smile has slipped off her face, replaced by a thin line of unhappiness.

"Then, yes."

"Did she know before me?"

Kayla looks like she's ready to get away from this conversation, even if she has to crab-walk to do so.

I lower my voice. "Yes, but not because I wanted to tell everyone before you—"

"*Everyone?* Who else knew before me?" She crosses her arms, and I know it's taking everything in her not to tap tap tap her tightly tied sneakers against the gym floor. This awful conversation needs to happen quick, before she reaches too-high levels of sad, mad, and uncomfortable.

"Just Devon Miles Smith and Juniper. You left the cafeteria for some club-related crisis and Holden came up, and it just came out." I shrug, trying to relieve the tension in my shoulders. "It wasn't intentional. I wanted to tell you."

"So why didn't you tell me at any point before or after other people knew?"

"Because you didn't bring it up and then the longer I went without saying it, the more I felt like not having said it was going to make it worse when I *did* say it. I worried you'd be mad."

She drops her arms with a sigh. "But why would I be mad?"

"Well, not mad, but upset? We're just doing this documentary, and I'm helping him with a small photography assignment, and then things will go back to normal." I try not to cringe when I add in the part about his photography assignment. I hadn't even thought about it before, but I might as well get it all out in the open now.

Corrine's eyes flick to the ceiling and then slowly meet mine, like she's trying not to cry. I didn't want it to be this way. I wanted Yvette's story! Holden and I basically can't stand each other and Corrine has new prospects in Logan. He nearly jumped for joy when I gave him Corrine's phone number in class the other day. I thought she was moving on.

Somehow, her gaze gets even more Intense. "I don't understand why you wouldn't tell me unless there's something you're hiding." She drops to a whisper. "Other people knew before me. This makes me look . . ."

After a moment, she shrugs, working her jaw.

I latch onto her arms, shaking her a little. "I'm sorry. I said I wouldn't lie again and I haven't and I won't. I just knew from the beginning that it was a weird situation to get in, and I need to do this documentary, to get into the program. I had to do what was best and, unfortunately, it's this. I didn't mean to hurt you or make you think I was sneaking behind your back."

"You were, though. I would have understood if you had told me as soon as it happened."

God, I feel like a real asshole. Holden was probably sneaking around with another girl behind Corrine's back, and now I was doing it . . . with *him*. I'm terrible.

I scuff my shoe against the floor, checking that no one else is listening. Kayla disappeared at some point and I wish I could join her. "I'm so sorry. I really should have thought about how this would look, because of how you two broke up." I reach for my necklace, but it's not there. Corrine doesn't even have it on. "I didn't mean to bring up those feelings again," I add quietly. "I was trying to avoid doing that by not telling you, actually. I know I'd be upset if you had to work with my cheater ex on something."

She frowns. "He didn't cheat on me."

"You said there was another girl," I say, but I'm really saying *You don't have to lie.*

"I just meant that he liked another girl." She avoids my gaze and I can tell we're tiptoeing the line of What Corrine Will Talk About and What She Won't. The line reads: *Will it make Corrine cry?*

"He didn't date anyone after you, so . . . I mean, do you regret breaking up with him? Did he *say* there was another girl—"

"Saine, he didn't cheat and I don't regret breaking up with him." She gives me a look like I should leave this alone, so I go back into apology mode, storing the fact that Holden's not a cheater in the previously dusty Holden file I've been opening in my mind lately.

"All of this to say that I guess I did everything I didn't want to do by trying to avoid telling you. I suck."

She releases a breathy laugh. "You do."

"I'm sorry."

She delivers a wavering but genuine smile. "I believe you."

"Are you okay with him and me working together for a little?" I can't imagine she'll say no, but I swear my heart stops while I wait for her answer. If she says she's not okay, what am I going to do, just not apply to my dream major? Do it behind her back again? Lose her as a best friend? It almost feels like now, with her solidly saying they just broke up because they broke up, there's not *that* much of a barrier to working with Holden.

But Corrine isn't selfish. She's never been selfish. This is the girl who did my homework for a week during my worst bout of mono sophomore year. The same girl who punched Harvey Becker in sixth grade after he made fun of me for constantly carrying a red lunch tray—the indicator that I had insufficient funds for lunch and had to get a special (and by special I mean tasteless) lunch. It led her to starting a revolution at the school, where they stopped giving out different-colored trays because it was bad enough having a whole different meal and, as she said, it was "discriminatory" and helped "bullies target lower-income students" for things that were out of their control, i.e., their parents' money.

"Yeah." She sounds like she's convincing herself, too. "Who would I be to tell you what to do anyway? And this is your *dream*."

"Thank you. Can you stop avoiding me now?" I link my arm through hers and direct us toward Coach Hartl, who has come out of her office with two huge boxes stacked atop each other in her arms. Macy, still attempting to suck up for her first game no-show, rushes forward to help. I should be more like Macy, probably.

"I really did have things to do today." Corrine starts ticking things off on her fingers. "The chess club is running out of full sets of chess pieces and the boards are cracked down the middle, the environmental club is coming under fire because apparently Vinny didn't recycle our fundraiser banner, and the student council keeps hounding me about taking over Nicolette's duties, but I keep telling them I don't have any more free time between all the clubs and cheerleading and work."

I'm woefully lazy in comparison. "What about this past weekend? You didn't answer any texts, not even in the group chat."

"Neither did you."

"Touché. I'm going apartment hunting with my mom on Saturday. It went fucking terrible the last time, so . . . do you want to come?" I laugh a little. "I mean, do you even have time?"

"I'm free in the afternoon. After homework and chores. I still can't believe you're moving." Her brows practically meet in the middle. "What about the murals?"

"Right?" I face her, eyes wide. "That's what I said. My mom's acting like it's not a big deal, though."

"Did she even give you a say?"

I raise an eyebrow. "Do you think we'd be looking for somewhere else to live if she did?"

"That's true, and you're probably the only other person I know who can strong-arm people into things as well as me." She sighs, almost dreamily. "Well, you did your best, then."

Did I? Is there more I could do to change my mom's mind?

"Circle up, team," Coach Hartl says, dropping the boxes. "Cold weather gear is here."

Heat fills my gut. I never turned in my money for the gear because, well, I didn't have the money. I sincerely debated handing over Monopoly money to Coach Hartl with hopes that she would think it was funny enough that I could just slide by on it. My grandma used to say that I'd need to be charming in life to get things I wanted, but I'm not sure that's what she meant.

She begins calling girls' names and handing out their matching red-and-black track jackets and pants, a total of seventy-eight dollars each. I guess I'll just be cold.

Kayla stands next to me and nudges my arm. "Did you get enough money?" she whispers.

I debate just laughing hysterically, but that would only draw attention to me and my lack of cute cold weather gear. Corrine steps forward to get hers.

"I didn't have it and I couldn't ask my mom for it," I say. "Not after she had to pay for my uniform to get altered." Because society punishes fat people for being fat. Like a tiny bit of extra fabric really costs over fifty dollars more. My mom didn't say a word, though, because of course she wouldn't. She just coughed up the money, quite literally because some moments we're running on financial fumes, and then told me how cute I looked in my uniform. The uniform I now own because I had to get it taken out to fit my stomach, thighs, and big boobs.

"I wish you would have said something. I still have extra cash from working at the grocery store this summer." She leaves my side to collect her gear from Coach Hartl when she has to call "Kayla!" twice.

I send her a sad smile when she comes back. "Thanks, but I can't start a new I Owe This Person Lots of Money list."

"Sinclair," Coach Hartl says.

I was really hoping to avoid everyone realizing I'm the only one without the new clothes, hoping to avoid my monetary woes being put on blast.

"Yeah?" I ask, drawing the attention of all the girls in front of me.

"Do you need a formal invitation to come collect your stuff or will this do?" She stares at me like I'm wasting her time. She holds a jacket and pants in her hand, extended for me to grab.

I hesitate, wondering if she thought it was a mistake that I didn't order and ordered for me, and now she's expecting payment. Kayla pushes me forward and I grab them.

"Thanks," I say, staring at the clothes in my hands. The red perfectly matches our uniforms, but the black is a little diluted.

Corrine shifts beside me, but when I look at her, she avoids my gaze. Because she paid for these. I didn't even mention that I couldn't afford them. She just knew, which is awful in so many ways, but also really fucking sweet.

"Thank you," I say quietly. Guilt heats in my gut. "I'll pay you back."

She shrugs. "Sure, if you want. It's not a big deal, though."

But it is for me. Corrine does stuff like this because she's thinking of me, because she loves me and cares about me, and I do things like lie and sneak behind her back. Not anymore.

Thank god this will be over in two weeks.

TEN

"Oh my god," Corrine breathes, placing her hand on the wall. "Exposed brick."

Of the four apartments we've checked out so far, this one is my favorite solely because it's a town house. It has two floors and the bedrooms aren't much different in size. If you asked Corrine, though, she'd say it has great opportunities for natural light and a charm she can't put her finger on. She's practically a middle-aged woman.

My mom laughs from the modest kitchen—the smallest we've seen so far, but I'm more likely to use the microwave than the oven anyway. "While that's nice, what do you think of the rest of it?"

"Since it's just the two of you, it feels like enough space." Corrine walks the few feet from the dining room to the living room. "And since Saine will be gone soon, I guess it just matters what you think of it."

"Excuse you. I get a say." We meet my mother near the

wooden stairs to the second floor.

"Then say," Corrine says, taking the stairs two at a time.

"What do you think?" my mom asks, following Corrine at a much slower pace. She watches me over her shoulder. "It's not bad."

"I guess I don't understand how we could afford this, but not our house." The first step creaks when I put my full weight on it. I thought having a second floor would be cool until I realized that coming in and out quietly would be nearly impossible.

"We could afford this *plus* more." She wiggles her eyebrows. "You could maybe get a car."

"A car would be cool." I speed up. "I'd pay you back for it, though."

"The closets are huge!" Corrine calls from one of the bedrooms. "The bathroom is tragic—only one sink—but it's a shower and tub combo for whatever suits your mood, so I'll forgive it."

I take a spin around the bathroom. My mom and I shared a similar size with my grandma. But there's no storage space in here besides behind the vanity and under the sink.

"Where's the closet?"

"The hallway," Corrine says, charging out of the closest bedroom and into the next one.

"Do you already know the layout of the whole apartment?" I ask, entering the room after her. "What's the square footage—" Without even seeing the other room, I know this is the smaller one. The one that would be mine.

"Balcony!" she says with a huge grin on her face. She gestures to the sliding door and the balcony beyond, like I hadn't seen it despite all the light flowing inside through it.

My mom comes up behind me, leaning against the door frame. "It's nice, right?"

The room has a built-in bookshelf. I'm not much of a reader these days, but it's so pretty that I might become one. At the very least, I could use it to store my embarrassingly large collection of DVDs—I know the world has moved beyond, but it's hard to switch formats when I already own them and don't have the money to replace them. The carpet, like in the rest of the house, is a cream color. Not too dark, not too light. The perfect shade. My mom told me before I made any comments today that she checked with all the landlords and they all approved of me painting the walls if we painted them this sad, boring white color when we moved out.

Just as Corrine said, the closet is huge. A shelf sits a few inches atop the rod and a unit of drawers stands below. It's definitely enough storage for me, and the rest of the room has enough space for my desk.

Corrine opens the sliding door and steps onto the balcony to check out the view.

My phone starts vibrating in my hand.

My mom asks, "What do you think?" but the caller ID on the screen stops me from answering her. It's Holden. We don't have plans to do anything documentary-related for a few days. I needed some time for things to go back to normal with Corrine, to let her get acclimated to me spending time with him—and to figure out some leading questions for my future interviews for the Give Holden Heart Crusade.

"I, uh, I think I have to take this." I start moving out of the room, but then look back to Corrine, the sun highlighting her face as she smiles to herself.

I turn away and answer, heading into the hall. "Hello?"

"Saine Sinclair."

I lower my voice. "What's up?"

"Are you free today? For photos?"

"No." I enter the master bedroom and close the door quietly. "Why can't you use Taj again?"

I hate being in front of the camera, any camera. Selfies don't count because technically I'm in front of the camera and behind the camera. I have the control I need to make sure I feel good about how I look as a result. I've been tagged in too many cheerleading candids with open mouths, double chins, and half-closed eyes. Plus, the less time I actually have to spend with Holden, the better it will be for my relationship with Corrine, and probably my sanity.

"I've used him for like three assignments already and Mr. Anderson said he's tired of seeing his smug face." Yeah, that sounds like Mr. Anderson. He's the type of teacher that throws paper at students who seem like they're not paying attention. "He said it seems like Taj likes having his picture taken too much and I need someone who will give me a harder time."

"That's a *problem*?" I walk to the window and pull the blinds open. The sun slips inside, warming my skin.

"Yeah," he says with a laugh. "I need someone more vulnerable."

"Let me get this straight. You can't use a camera-confident guy, so you want a vulnerable girl. To take pictures of. One on one?" My traitorous heart, the one that still has fragmented pieces from his birthday party, starts hammering. I don't do vulnerable. I don't do anything that puts me in a position like I was when the bottle stopped in my direction and everyone stared, but Holden stared *in horror.* I was exposed, and even though no one knew my feelings for him, it felt like they were laid out bare. No thanks.

"Well, when you say it like that . . ." He pauses. "Still yes. Plus, it doesn't have to be one on one. I know Mara really wants to see you. She has a ton of questions about Rose and apparently I'm not an appropriate person to ask."

"So, you're being your little sister's wingman?"

"Essentially."

"Tell her I'm sorry, but I can't today."

"She'll be disappointed."

"With you as a brother, I can't see why," I reply sickly sweet.

"I know you meant that sarcastically, but it was really nice of you to say."

"Bye."

"You can't put this off forever."

I can certainly try. The line goes dead.

When I open the door, Corrine and my mom are standing on the other side, trying and failing to not look like the guilty, guilty eavesdroppers they are. My stomach drops at the expression on Corrine's face. I don't even know how to process it. It's too many emotions at once, too fast.

"I didn't know you and Holden were friends again," my mom says, giving me space to exit the room.

"We're not," I'm quick to say. "He's just helping me with my documentary and I'm helping him with an assignment." Eventually. Maybe. Hopefully not.

"Oh." She frowns, but goes down the stairs.

"How did you know it was Holden?"

"Corrine said."

I glance at her now and she shrugs. "I guessed," she says. "Kayla isn't one for phone calls."

"So," my mom drawls. "What are your thoughts on this place?"

"I like it." I originally say it because I'm eager to change the subject, but I realize, pretty quickly, that I do like it. It's cozy and fresh and I could see myself enjoying it. Once I get over the trauma of leaving our house now, I guess. It's just weird to think we would live in a place that I have no memories of my grandma in. There are only two bedrooms. No space for her to have art lessons. No sign of her on the walls, no spots of dried paint on the carpet, no lingering pockets of air coated in her perfume.

"I like it, too," Corrine says. She points at the corner of the living room. "That lamp you guys have, the one with the mason jars, would look amazing right there. It would capture the light during the day and really brighten up the space at night." She glances at the ceiling. "Since apparently there are only two tiny overhead lights in this room."

"Maybe we could install some sconces?" my mom asks.

"Now you're speaking my language."

"Is this it, then? Is this The One?" My mom turns to me with a huge smile on her face and I know—I *know*—she needs to move out of my grandma's house, needs to have new walls she can paint how she wants, needs to not feel like my grandma just left the room she stepped into every time she enters any room, but hearing her ask the question, say The One out loud, causes me to panic, stiffen, makes all my certainty evacuate from my mind. It's too soon, too real, too final. And, suddenly, this place is awful. We'd be erasing my grandma.

"There aren't enough windows." There are actually zero windows on the bottom floor. Two sliding doors, one off the dining room and one off the living room, but no windows except for the master bedroom. "And, I don't know, won't it get cold with the brick wall? This is an end unit and I bet the wind just whips right through it."

"Through a brick wall?" Corrine asks, blinking once, twice.

"No insulation?" I shrug. "And the kitchen is small. The appliances are old. The bathroom has no closet, so every time I need a freaking tampon, I'll have to walk to get one."

"Heaven forbid you have to do that," my mom says with an amused smirk. She thinks I'm being difficult to be funny. "You could put your tampons under the sink. Next to the toilet. Isn't that a novel idea?"

"The cable hookup is on the wall that gets the most sunlight, so, like, we'll have a glare on our TV unless we have the blinds closed all the time. And with the blinds closed, we'll just have these shitty lights and then our super bright floor lamp. And I don't like having a balcony off my room. Someone could easily get in."

"It would be harder for someone to break in here than it would be at Grandma's," my mom says slowly, her brows dropping low on her face, her mouth slipping into a frown. "I thought you liked it?"

"I guess I don't after all."

"Okay . . . We'll look at the next place, then." My mom wraps an arm around Corrine's shoulders and they head for the door. "How's everything going with you, baby? Still holding the record for the busiest teenager in the world? How did you make time to deem us unworthy peasants with your presence?"

"Well, I had to reschedule a meeting with the president. . . ."

My mom dismisses the comment with a wave. "Just cancel. Nothing good comes from politicians."

I linger behind, taking in the space. It's really not that bad, but it's not home. It would never be home.

ELEVEN

"Do you think Corrine is mad at us?" Kayla asks without looking up from her lyric notebook.

"What makes you think that?" I ask, my arms folded on the table and my head propped on them. "The fact that she gave us the worst bake sale jobs?"

Our table overflows with the kind of baked goods nobody wants. We have the bland table with nuts, oatmeal, and raisins while Sasha and Carmen are so busy selling out of chocolate chip cookies, brownies, and chocolate-covered pretzel sticks, they can't even sit down. Why did anyone spend time making what's on our table? I'll eat practically anything, but nothing here looks appealing.

"Basically."

"I'm not mad at you guys," Corrine says, sweeping behind our table and grabbing the clipboard from between our chairs. I swear her ears got injected with the Captain America super-soldier serum. "I just assumed you would be able to sell the unsellable stuff." She pinches my cheek. "Because you guys are just so darn cute."

Kayla slams her notebook closed when Corrine turns in her direction. "Why do we even have unsellable stuff if it's, you know, unsellable?"

"Because there's bound to be someone out there who wants oatmeal raisin cookies. Look." She pulls some folded bills from the waistline of her cheerleading skirt and hands it to me. "I'll take three, please."

"You are a conundrum of a person," I say, taking her cash and handing over the cookies. She places one in front of Kayla and then one in front of me with a smile.

"Cheers." She raises the cookie like a glass and then rushes over to the popular table.

"She's definitely mad at us," Kayla says, staring at the cookie. "Or maybe *you*. *You* did this to us."

"Hey, Kayla," Juniper says, stopping in front of us wearing a Nope. T-shirt—white tee, black Times New Roman font. "Hi, Saine. I'll take two cookies, please."

"Why?" I ask. "These are, like, cookies for people with digestion problems. The good ones are over there."

Kayla swats my arm, smiling at Juniper. "Two dollars."

"It's *four* dollars—"

"*Two* dollars. Friends and family discount." Kayla smiles wide, showing off her slightly crooked canines.

Juniper hands the cash to Kayla, who tucks it into our very unsecure envelope with Corrine's money. CHHS only has one metal lockbox for fundraisers and it's been lost ever since someone stole the environmental club's money.

"Hey, do you guys take credit?" Devon Miles Smith wraps an arm around Juniper's waist.

"Where do you think you are right now, Buns?" Kayla asks, referring to the bakery we've made a bad habit of stopping at before and after school some days. "Cash only."

He glances at our table with a sneer. "Never mind anyway. These cookies are shit."

"But I got us some already," Juniper says, raising the cookies in her hand. "Oatmeal raisin are good!"

"Maybe if your taste buds have all died." He practically shoves away from her. "Do you have any more cash? I want to get something actually good."

He wanders off without waiting for her answer. Kayla glares at his back.

"Do you guys think I could have my cash back?" Juniper asks the floor. She sets the cookies back on the table. "Please?"

"Do *not* buy that asshole anything, Juniper." I hand her back her cash. "Keep the cookies. Oatmeal raisin are pretty good if you're in the mood for them."

She offers a tight smile and then meets Devon Miles Smart-ass in line for the other table. I take Kayla's and my cookies and fill the empty spots with them.

"Why are we friends with him?" Kayla asks, flipping open her notebook and writing.

"You tell me." I lean back in the chair, adjusting my uniform around my waist. "You're in a band with him. I wouldn't even know him if it weren't for you."

"I didn't know any other people who play the guitar. If you happen to just pull one out of your luscious booty, let me know."

"You know I only pull out one per decade, don't be greedy." I watch her scribble away, the cafeteria nearly muting itself with its sounds. "Finish your song yet?"

"I've finished several."

"You didn't let me see," I sing.

"Maybe if you came to a show," she sings back, on key.

I bark out a laugh. "I know that's a joke."

She sighs. "I can't show my bandmates the songs."

"I'm not in your band." I turn in my seat. "You can show me. You've literally seen me at my worst. There's nothing you could do or say that would be more embarrassing than what happened last year."

One day during junior year, I walked around with my dress accidentally tucked into my period undies the whole way from the stairwell to the front exit of the school. She had to literally tackle me to cover up the embarrassment.

She glances at Devon Miles Smith and Juniper, and I follow her gaze. They're arguing, arms flailing. It's infuriating to watch. Why be with someone who makes you angry, who treats you like shit?

Angling toward me, she lowers her voice. "If anyone in the band read my songs, it'd just be, you know, really obvious." She glances at Devon Miles Smith again. "It might break up the band and we have something good."

I stare at her for a second. Two. Three. "Wait."

"Don't say anything."

"*Wait.*"

"Saine Sinclair."

"*Devon?* Since when do you like guys?"

"*No.* Not Devon."

"So then . . ." I glance back at our friends. They've reached the front of the popular table and Devon Miles Smith seems to be figuring out what he can buy with Juniper's money. "Juniper."

Kayla smacks my arm. "Quiet."

"Oh no." I look between Juniper and Kayla. "Oh *no.*"

"I know!" She shuts her notebook again. "I'm so in love, it's gross. The day we shot the music video was the best day because I got to just be around her all day and Devon was barely around, but, you know, that doesn't stop him from taking credit for the music video *and*, somehow, his girlfriend's hotness."

I rub Kayla's arm and she falls forward, her forehead on my shoulder.

"But even if they broke up, then there would be hurt feelings, and it doesn't change the fact that I'm still in a band with him and I still don't know any other guitarists *and* he writes the majority of our songs." She sighs, her breath tickling my neck, and straightens. "He doesn't even like her, Saine. He just likes having a girlfriend."

"Maybe we can convince her to break up with him?" I shrug. "And then when she does, she can convince him that it's *his* idea?"

"I don't know. I don't want to overstep . . ." She watches Juniper and Devon Miles Smith sit down at our regular lunch table, still arguing. Actually, is it even an argument if he's doing most of the dramatic hand gestures and mouth moving?

"We'll figure something out." I squeeze her shoulder.

"I want to see smiles!" Corrine says, rushing by. "Paint those smiles on like a deranged killer clown!"

"Oh my *god*, Corrine." I burst into laughter as she disappears into the hallway beyond the cafeteria.

Kayla shakes her head. "It should be illegal for a girl to tell another girl to smile."

"Yeah, but when she says it like that, I'm guaranteed to do it even if I don't want to."

Holden

Today 4:17 PM

Announcement at 5

4:17 PM

Lemme know if you need a ride over

4:17 PM

Why do you assume everything
will be done at your house?

4:20 PM

I'm the star

4:21 PM

Playing ball with Taj. Assuming you don't need a ride. BYE.

4:21 PM

TWELVE

My mom has the car, because it's hers and it's a weeknight and she has to go to work, so I walk to Holden's with my equipment slung on both shoulders. By the time I reach his house, my fingers are numb from the cold and I've thought about turning back home to get gloves at least three times. Holden and Taj are playing basketball in the driveway when I walk up.

"Saine Sinclair," Taj greets me, breathless, his hair wind-blown. "Watch this!"

He throws the basketball into the hoop and it bounces down the driveway, past me. I watch it roll into the road.

"What was supposed to happen?"

"Really, you're gonna play me like that?" He chases after the ball. "I made it in the hoop."

"Sorry. I'm all out of participation trophies. Would a high five suffice?"

He dribbles the ball back to us. "No," he says, looking down his nose at me. "It would *not* suffice."

Holden, cheeks splotchy and red, takes the camera bag from my shoulder. "It was a good game, dude."

"Who won?" I ask, tracking him to his front door.

"Me," they both say.

They stop and face each other, nearly identical glares in place. "Me," they say again at the same time.

"Don't listen to him," Taj says, pushing past him and opening the door. "I let him win."

"So you admit it! I won!" Holden lets me go first and the two of them follow, the sound of playful slapping filling the foyer.

"Is Mara here?" I shrug out of my jacket and hang it up.

"No, Taylor's home for fall break or something so Mara's spending the week at her mom's."

"Does she see her mom a lot?" The one good thing about a father who skipped town is that I don't have to split my time between him and my mom; it seems like it would be hard.

Taj bounds into the kitchen and opens the refrigerator, pulling out the half-empty jug of milk. He moves to a cabinet and frees a bowl, then finds cereal and a spoon.

"Yeah, but her mom works as some kind of trainer for office jobs, so she travels a lot. She'll be gone for like a week, then back a week. Repeat." Holden checks his phone. "We've got three minutes. I'll go get my computer."

He leaves Taj and me across from each other at the dining room table. I unpack my camera while he slurps up his cereal.

"Can I interview you?"

Slurp. "About what?"

"Holden. This competition." I hit record.

"Oh yeah, for the VR stuff."

"Yeah. That. You're going to New York with us next weekend, aren't you?"

"No, he just said that if his mom asks, I'm going to New York with him. My parents wouldn't let me."

I frown, heat pooling in my stomach. "So you're *not* going?"

"No," he says slowly, like I'm not understanding and, well, I'm not. "I'm not going, but you are. His mom would freak out if she knew he was going with just you, so he says he's going with me."

I'm freaking out knowing he's going with just me. Things were different when there was a third person.

"It's dead!" Holden says, running into the dining room. His socks slip on the hardwood floor. "My laptop." He sets it down next to me and unfurls his charger from around his arm, plugging it into the wall and then the laptop. It does that classic Mac power noise and slowly comes to life.

When's an appropriate time to ask what is going on with New York? Later, probably? Probably. But telling my brain that doesn't stop the creeping panic. How would I explain to Corrine that Holden and I are going to one of my favorite places together? That just seems like rubbing it in her face, because she's told me she'd go to New York with me if I wanted her to, and I've never invited her. I prefer to be alone there. But even though this is for the documentary and the contest, it feels personal, even to me.

"What time is it?" Holden asks.

"I don't know. After five," Taj says, putting his bowl in the dishwasher.

Holden groans.

"It'll still be there when you get to the site." I film him hammering the keys to the beat of the URL and watch the Vice and Virtual site load. The announcement video for the last challenge fades in from white.

This last challenge, the one that has been shrouded in secrecy, will be wild. It's the biggest and most physically intensive one yet, kind of like *American Ninja Warrior*, designed to be the real-world version of *Fantastic Lorenzo's Planet*, which is an old-school-like "run and jump to avoid obstacles, collect coins, beat the clock" kind of game. Less skill, more muscle, and it's all about speed.

Taj meets my eyes, looks into the camera, and then smiles. "I know just how to help you prepare."

"Mara is going to be so mad she's not here right now," I say, tracking the camera over Holden's backyard, which Taj transformed into a really shitty and much smaller version of the type of challenge Holden will see in New York.

The floodlights cast the entire yard into light, even the parts that dare creep into shadows with the setting sun, and we're all bundled in our jackets as we take in the scene.

"We can keep it up for Mar-Mar," Taj says. "Your parents will be cool, right?"

"I don't know," Holden says, stepping forward to closely inspect the makeshift stairs to the trampoline made out of an overturned wheelbarrow and a deck box. "Maybe if Mara promises to wear a helmet."

"As she should. Safety first." Taj opens his arms wide, puffing his chest toward his obstacle course. "Well? What are you waiting for?"

"Maybe I should get a helmet, too." Holden disappears into the garage.

I set my phone up on the tripod and frame the obstacle course. Then I press record on my rented camera and make Taj stand a few feet in front of it. It's a shame that my phone takes better-quality video than the camera my mom and grandma bought me, but at least I always have it on my person.

"Tell me your name, age, and if you consent to this interview."

"Taj Chakrabarti. I'm seventeen years old and I consent to this interview." He grins. "And you're watching *Ridiculousness*."

He takes a running leap onto his shoddy stairs, nearly slips off the wheelbarrow, and bounces onto the trampoline. When he's midair he jumps onto the swing, attached to the large fauxwood playset, and crosses it without touching the ground.

"No helmet needed!" he yells over his shoulder as Holden comes out of the garage door, frowning at the black helmet in his hands. It has band stickers all over it and a crack down the side.

"Apparently this is the last helmet I owned."

"I remember this." I film the helmet in his hands. "You're so lucky it was the helmet that cracked and not your skull."

When we were around Mara's age, we both begged our parents

for longboards. We took them to the park every day after school for a week, until the last day, when Holden picked up too much speed, catapulted over the track, and smashed his head against the concrete floor of the pavilion by the slides. I never touched my board again. I didn't even take it home with me.

I run my finger over the gash in it. "I wouldn't do anything that required a helmet for a long time after that wipeout."

"Or ever." He takes the helmet back, tucking it under his arm. "Taj!"

Taj appears on the other side of the yard, his dark brown hair blowing behind him as he charges toward us. "I won!"

"If you're the only one playing, by your own admission, you also lost." I smile at him when his grin drops. "Interview? Holden," I say, gesturing to the obstacle course. "Give it a whirl, if you dare."

"Tell my mom I love her," he says resignedly, taking off for the obstacle course.

"Taj," I say, getting a close-up, "what do you think of what Holden's doing?"

He shrugs, brushing back his hair. "I don't really know. He was just like, 'I'm gonna do this contest to win VR glasses' and I was like, 'Okay, dude.'"

"There wasn't a deeper conversation?"

"Not really," he says, adjusting his weight to one foot. "Why would there be?"

Because I need there to be one. "Did you know that it was a series of challenges he had to get through?"

"Yeah, kinda."

I feel myself growing irritated. "Can you use full sentences, please? What did he say?"

"He just said he had to play some games. I thought he meant video games." He looks over his shoulder at Holden, working his way across the playset. "This is cool, too. I'm happy to help."

"Did he say why he wanted to do it?"

"To win? I think he should sell the headset for major cash. Maybe he's going to. I don't really know."

I run with this. "Do you think he needs the money? From selling the headset?"

He scratches his neck. "For sure. He hates taking money from his mom and if he could sell this thing, he'd be looking at getting over a thousand dollars."

"He probably wants that money for college, right?"

"I don't think anyone wants to spend their money on college, but, you know, they *need* to. And art school is hella expensive. So unnecessary."

"Holden's pretty talented." I've seen his photos. It would so obviously be a lie to pretend he's not.

"Yeah, for sure. He has this wild list of all the photography-related scholarships he can go for. He's just waiting for the day to press send."

"Has he said anything about funds being tight?"

"Well, he's always talking about how the minivan is on its last legs. And how expensive his stepsister's tuition is, and she's at, like, a *state* school." He tucks his hands into his jacket pockets and rocks back on his feet. He doesn't look at me when he says, "I know love is great and all, but can you imagine knowing you're signing up to spend double the amount of money on kids than you planned to? Yikes."

"Holden probably feels like he should contribute, right?" That's how I feel, at least. And this money angle, maybe it's not totally fictional.

"Well, he babysits Mar-Mar. Mara, his little stepsister," he clarifies to my camera.

"She's old enough to take care of herself, though. And that time spent babysitting her could be spent working a job that paid him."

"You got me there!" he laughs. "I guess this is the easiest way for him to make a lot of cash fast. I mean, how long did it take you to make a thousand dollars at your job?"

I'm not even sure I *have* made a thousand dollars yet. A thousand dollars for a VR headset. For a month's rent.

"Why don't you tell me about the first time you met Holden. Or why you wanted to be his friend?"

He thinks for a minute as Holden rounds the obstacle course another time, having fallen off the playset. "We met in sixth grade. We had the same shoes on."

"What kind of shoes?" *And did he really base a friendship off having the same shoes?*

"Black Converse."

Did he really base a friendship off having the same shoes that everyone has at least once in their life?

"Taj?"

"Yes, Saine?"

"You're friends with everyone, huh?" I ask with a kind smile.

He grins. "What can I say? I am a very friendly guy."

"And Holden?"

"Yeah, he is too. He's, like, overly kind to people, even the ones who don't deserve it sometimes. Everyone likes him; he's a good dude."

Taj's comments about money are helpful—I should be happy I got them on camera. It's not enough, though. I need more. There's got to be *more* here. And I'll just keep faking it until I make it.

THIRTEEN

On Sunday morning, I run through a light drizzle and several deceptive puddles that look like an inch of water but end up leading to Wonderland or somewhere while on my way to the PSH film department. My shoes squelch as I buzz past the library, the campus reminding me of a ghost town because everyone is still in bed with hangovers or doing whatever they do as Almost Real Adults who don't have classes on the weekend. Maybe they're running through the rain to get to their jobs two minutes late, too.

I pound down the stairs to the little hallway of classrooms and sound booths, and settle behind the desk for another dull day. I avoid falling asleep by learning to make an origami frog, and then I keep myself entertained by folding another frog and making them play leap frog over each other.

"I need to get in the lab," Victor says, jogging down the stairs.

"Good morning to you, too. Couldn't you have used the library?"

He looks at my frogs before swiftly panning to the graveyard of misshapen and half-formed frogs on the floor behind me. "Because you're so busy here?"

I grab my keys and unlock the first classroom on the right. He slips past, flicking the light switch, and the room full of Macs comes to life. Once I have all my footage, I'll have to see about sneaking in here during or after my shifts to work because my computer is struggling to run Adobe Premiere at this point.

He settles in front of one and raises an eyebrow. "Started cutting your documentary yet? The deadline will sneak up on you."

If those words came from anyone else, they'd probably sound polite—concerned or helpful, even. Coming from Victor, though, I know exactly how they're meant: as condescending and taunting. He doesn't even get anything out of my failure— if I *do* fail. Ever since I found out he wanted this job and I took it from him thanks to Professor Michaels, he's been out to get me in one way or another.

"Yes."

"And how's it going?" He clicks a few things on his computer and then meets my eyes again. "We wrapped my project last night so I'm going to finish in the next week probably. Expecting an A."

"Only a week? Really? Glad you have so much free time. I guess a lack of friends will do that for you."

He smirks, smoothing down his weirdly formal long-sleeved button-down. "I take it things aren't going well."

"I didn't say that."

"You didn't say anything, which kind of says a lot."

"It's not like you really give me time to get a word in. You ask a question and then proceed to talk about yourself, but I know narcissists can't help it."

His smirk flickers, but then returns full force because he's right. I'm not saying a lot. Things aren't going well.

"I don't want to talk to you about my documentary." I cross my arms. He continues waiting. "You're just using me to make yourself feel better about your probably mediocre short film."

His smirk gets smirkier and I want to smack it off his strangely symmetrical and smooth face. It's like he's been Photoshopped for an Old Navy ad. He's just missing his white girlfriend wrapped in a too-big scarf on his arm.

I don't know what happens, but it's like the longer he stays silent, the more I itch to talk. To spill my guts. What kind of mind games is he playing here? Am I so used to him talking talking talking that I don't know how to handle the silence—

"My original subject quit." Well, *shit*. "It worked out, though, because that's, like, built-in tension, and a plot twist, and I happen to know a classmate who was doing the contest, so."

"So, you found a better story?"

"Excuse me?"

"The last one was about unrequited love and going after your dreams. Does your new subject offer something more?"

My whole body slumps. "You said that I was aiding a stalker before."

"Your documentary contains multitudes," he says, shrugging. "Or, it *did*."

"This one has a financial struggle."

"And how does a video game contest fix that?"

"He's going to sell the headset for a shit ton of money. It's a prototype, not out for a year." I spent so much time last night trying to manipulate the footage into a story of a struggle with money for college that the lie slips right out, and I believe it. But I am not having another my-story-has-no-heart stress spiral, especially in front of this smug douchebag. "Sorry. I have to watch the desk. Bye."

And then I leave him there with his mouth hanging open in a half-surprised, half-stunned silence.

The rental desk, the computer lab, the sound booths—et cetera, et cetera—close at twelve thirty on Sundays, so Victor has two minutes to get his ass out before I confront him.

About half an hour ago, Professor Michaels and Dr. Lee headed to the annex where the communications staff's new offices are located, but other than that, I haven't seen anyone since Victor. It's almost always just Victor.

One minute to go . . .

And someone walks in. I spin in my chair to berate whoever had the balls to come rent something with one minute to spare, but stop in my tracks.

Holden leans against the desk, his hair messy and his T-shirt a little rumpled under his jacket like he just woke up even though it's midday. "Hey."

I momentarily glitch because Holden plus PSH film department does not compute.

"Hi." I blink. "What are you doing here? Are you here for me?"

He points toward the other end of the hallway. "My dad and I have lunch plans."

My cheeks heat, but he does me a favor by not pointing out how conceited I'd have to be to think he'd be here for me instead of his dad. I wish I could stuff the stupid question back into my mouth. The embarrassment transports me back to the early days of my crush on Holden, when I was eleven and worked up the guts to ask him "Do you like anyone in our class?" and he responded with a laugh and "Don't be stupid." To this day, I still don't know how to take that, but the memory makes me sick.

I eye his appearance with more scrutiny, ready to take the focus off me. "He must be so honored that you deemed him worthy enough of rolling out of bed before one."

He smiles. "I had a late night."

"*Sure.*"

"I did."

"And what were you doing, party animal? Playing checkers with Mara?" I prop my chin in my palm. "Organizing your closet? Memorizing the dictionary?"

"You got me. Did you know antidisestablishmentarianism *isn't* the longest word in the dictionary?"

I frown. "Bless you."

"What?"

"That was a sneeze? Mid-sentence? Was it not?"

He rolls his eyes, drumming his fingers against the counter. "So, when's your shift over? Can you do photos later?"

I push out of my chair. "No, I have volunteer hours for cheerleading."

"Saine," he sighs with such familiarity, such *exhaustion*. "I'm putting in all this work for you and I haven't even gotten five minutes for photos."

"We'll figure out a time and place soon," I say offhandedly. I round the desk. "Hey, Victor! Time's up!"

Victor meets me at the lab door with his bag over his shoulder and his jacket over his arm. "I'm going. I'm going." He pauses down the hall when he sees Holden leaning against the desk.

Holden waves at him, uncertain. "Hi?"

"Hi." Victor glances over his shoulder at me. "Friend of yours or someone you're holding hostage with your terrible sense of humor?"

"Uh." I look to Holden. "Not sure. Holden?"

"Both?"

"This is my documentary subject." I gesture to Holden, then to Victor. "Holden, this is Victor. He was just leaving to be a nuisance elsewhere."

Victor offers his hand and Holden accepts it. "Nice to meet you. So," he says with a deep exhale, "video games, huh?"

"Goodbye, Victor." I physically separate their hands, standing between them. Defending my documentary more than I'm defending Holden. If this were a battle of muscle and not a battle of wits, I'd have to let Holden handle it himself. He towers over my five-three frame at like five foot one hundred (read: five ten).

Holden shrugs. "I like video games."

"Are you any good?"

"I said *goodbye, Victor.*" I try to shoo him away, but he just leans against the desk on my free side. He needs to get out of here before he reveals my story editing so far. Plus, it just feels weird for this world to collide with that world. These two should never meet.

Victor locks eyes with me so I know his question is for me alone. "What are you up to next weekend?"

"Filming."

"With me," Holden adds, drawing Victor's attention. "In New York."

"New York. *Expensive place.*" Victor tilts his head to the side thoughtfully. "Just the two of you?"

"Apparently." Holden still hasn't told me himself that Taj isn't going along and I'm kind of afraid to broach the subject myself.

Victor opens his mouth to say something else, but Holden's dad and Dr. Lee appear from the annex and cut him off.

"Hey, Holden." His dad wraps him into a one-armed hug and I wonder how long it's been since they saw each other last. I wonder if there are warm fuzzies between them, or static electricity. "You've met Dr. Lee, right?"

She smiles, her charcoal curls bouncing in a nonexistent breeze. "He was about half the size he is now."

Holden shakes her hand. "Nice to see you again."

Dr. Lee nods at Victor. "Hello, Victor."

"Hi." He puts his jacket on. "I was just headed to the library."

"Oh, can I join you?" she asks, putting the hood of her raincoat up.

They disappear into the stairwell, taking all of Victor's prodding questions with them, and leave me with two of the Michaels guys. Something that hasn't happened in several years.

"Are you ready?" Professor Michaels asks Holden.

"Yeah."

I grab my jacket and bag from behind the desk, taking my time so it doesn't seem like I'm joining them, which, apparently, would not be a problem, if you ask Professor Michaels.

"Did you want to come along, Saine?" He pushes his glasses up his nose. "We're getting food and taking it to Trev—"

"She's busy," Holden says. "She has volunteering to do."

I slip my arms into my jacket. "He's right." But the quick rejection still stings. I don't know if it's me or his dad or Trevor, but Holden's trying to keep something to himself and I hate not knowing.

"Oh, that's too bad." Professor Michaels frowns. "I guess not for whoever you're helping, though. I'll see you soon."

"Tell Trevor I say hi, please."

Holden nods, his shoulders stiff as he turns to the stairs. "Sure. Bye, Saine."

FOURTEEN

It's a Halloween—or, okay, the weekend before Halloween—miracle that the Cedar Heights Hawks actually win a game. Now, before you get too excited, the other team only scored twice, so it was still a supremely sad and pathetic game no matter the outcome.

But we won, so I'm debating going to Andrea Christie's house to hang with everyone and watch Andrea get into a fight with her ex-girlfriend Jenny over a skirt they both swear is theirs and not the other girl's, when Holden texts that he's going to the gym to "train" and that no one is ever there on Saturdays at ten thirty so if I want to film, this is my chance.

I *do* need more footage, so the drama will have to wait. There's always more to look forward to.

Maybe Holden will be distracted and exhausted into honesty. A girl can hope, at least. That's what I remind myself as I pull into the parking lot off the Carlisle Pike and head inside the creepily empty gym. The worker behind the front desk doesn't even look up from his phone when he says hello to me, still clad in my cheerleading uniform, so I just walk in and find Holden sprinting full speed on a treadmill. He's wearing compression pants with shorts over them and an old-school Queen T-shirt soaking up his sweat. I haven't seen him move like this since we were kids playing flashlight tag in the summer.

I stand on the treadmill next to him, feeling so weird and invasive and like I'm going to get kicked out if I don't start breaking a sweat of my own, and start recording.

"Why didn't you join the cross-country team if you can run like this?"

He glances in my direction, his face red. "I did. Freshman year. Had to make friends somehow."

It's a subtle dig, but I don't recall him marching up to me to break the awkward ice that first time we passed each other in the hall. I only remember wishing he had.

"Are you still on the team?"

"No."

"Why did you quit?"

"Someone has to look after Mara."

"Your parents are pretty well off." My mom once snapped at me as a child for loudly telling her that my one friend was loaded, said it was rude to comment on that, but it's not like I was telling her how poor they were. Like, *boohoo, you're rich and you feel awkward about it*. "Couldn't they just hire a babysitter? Or she could watch herself these days."

Say no. Say you're wearing that shirt until it's threadbare and gray because you can't part with ten dollars to buy a new one. Say your parents are putting away what they would pay a babysitter into a huge account where everyone's college tuition is going to come from.

"I offered," he huffs. Not the answer I wanted, but I could work with it. "Yearbook was a better fit anyway, considering what I want to do after college."

The digital numbers on his treadmill reach three miles and he lowers the speed to something I'd still be running full-force on, but he's speed-walking.

"When did you plan on telling me that Taj isn't going to New York?" I zoom into his soaked face. I look a hot mess when I'm red and sweaty, but he looks . . . I don't know. Different. Like, different from how he's looked before. He looks kind of *real*.

He licks his lips, tries to even out his breathing as he takes the treadmill down a few more notches. "I thought it was obvious he wasn't going from the start."

"And what was supposed to make it obvious? The fact that you said he was going and your mom thinks he's going?"

He grins to himself. "I don't know. Why would Taj go?"

"He's your best friend. I guess I could have assumed he wasn't going had I known he doesn't even know why you're doing this contest."

He raises an eyebrow, mouth a tight line, as he stops the treadmill altogether. He pulls his shirt up to wipe his face, exposing his flat stomach and the trail of hair leading into his gym shorts. I look away. "There's not much to tell," he says into the fabric before dropping it. "Like I told your friend—I like video games."

"Okay, he is not my friend. Just so we're clear." I film him getting a paper towel and cleaning spray to wipe down the treadmill, knowing all of this will end up on the cutting room floor, but it's better to have an abundance of film rather than not enough. "Can I stay in your hotel room so I don't have to pay for my own, then?"

He pauses, balls up the paper towel, and throws it into the trash can. "I thought you were staying with your dad?"

"You know what they say about making assumptions."

"It's not an assumption. You told my mom you were staying with your dad."

"You told your mom Taj was going."

He waves away my comment.

"I don't talk to my dad," I say simply.

He frowns, heading to the free weights. "Why not? Corrine said you go to New York a lot."

"He doesn't call me or anything, he just expects me to show up and, I don't know, not burst into a flame of awkwardness over the fact that we haven't had a relationship in years." I follow. "I just go to New York to be alone without being alone. But this isn't about that. This is about me wanting to claim the free bed in your room since Taj is apparently a nonissue."

"What was your plan if Taj was going?" He starts lifting, but his form is all wrong. I wouldn't know if Coach Hartl hadn't insisted that all bases do weight training twice a week during practice.

I put my hand on his lower back, surprisingly not grossed out by the wetness there, and push. "Stand straight."

He stops. Looks at me over his shoulder even though he's standing in front of a full-length mirror. Adjusts. His arms grow tight, release. "What was your plan?"

"My plan was to sleep on the floor."

He stops again, laughing. "Oh, come on. Your plan would be to *say* you'd sleep on the floor, but then you would have wormed your way into my bed, and *I* would have ended up on the floor."

I step in front of him, point the camera right in his face. "You say that like I wouldn't have shared." My cheeks heat at the admission, but he ignores it.

"You didn't used to when we were kids," he says.

"Well, you had cooties."

"That didn't stop you from sleeping in my cooties-infested bed."

"Beds are cootie-free zones. Only human boys are incubators for them."

"Now that's a documentary I'd watch."

I fix his form again. "Are you saying you're not going to watch this one?"

He winces, setting down the weights. "Fuck no. You think I want to see my sweaty face in 1080p?"

It's a relief to hear. I won't have to recut the documentary to exclude the financial hardship plot if he's not going to watch. "You certainly like your face otherwise. Your Instagram is seventy-five percent selfies."

He narrows his eyes. "You don't follow me on Instagram."

"Yes, I do." I freeze.

"No . . ." A corner of his lips turns up. "Do you creep on me?"

"No! How do you know I don't follow you unless you're constantly checking?"

He bites his lip, holding back a smile.

"*You* creep on *my* stuff, too," I say, lowering the camera.

"So you admit it. You've been checking on me."

"Look." I exhale a laugh. "It was mostly to see what pictures you were posting with Corrine, but then it became a habit."

And it was so so so so hard not to like any pictures. I would have died if I accidentally liked a picture and got caught stalking through all the years of photos he's posted since we stopped being friends. The other twenty-five percent that isn't his face are beautiful photos he's taken: still lifes, portraits, live-action shots from shows. There was, for a brief blip of high school life, a time when a lot of the photos were of Corrine. We both had a habit of using her for our creative endeavors.

"Why wouldn't you just follow me?" he asks.

"Why didn't you follow me?"

We stare at each other for a moment. He pulls his phone from his pocket, unwinding his earbuds from around it, and swipes and taps.

"Problem solved," he says.

My stomach does a weird flip. It can't be excitement or anything. I mean, it's Holden. I've seen him cry over dropping a Fudgsicle. He's not someone to get excited over. It's probably just guilt that it's a semipublic reflection of our . . . friendship? Is that what this is?

"I don't follow for follow," I say with a shrug. "Sorry."

He shakes his head and moves on to the room where guys who stan the gym get really hyped, bouncing off platforms and whipping ropes around to hide how fragile their masculinity is. He jumps onto a platform and off it. Repeat repeat repeat.

"Do you know anything about your competition?" I ask. "The other players?"

"I didn't really get to know them before the competitions because at the first one I was watching Mara, and then at the second I was watching your friendship with Corrine implode." I glare at him. "I pretty much only know the names that are on the website. The fun facts and submissions posted there."

"From their names, who do you think is going to be the hardest to beat?"

He laughs. "Uh. Lada. That's like Russian or something. I don't think I stand a chance against Lada."

"Maybe Lada sees your name on the website and thinks the same thing."

"No, she probably sees my name and says, 'Oh, he's that kid who cried until they disqualified the other guy.'"

"You didn't cry."

He leans in and whispers, his breath dancing across my nose, "On the inside, I did."

"And what's your fun fact on the site?"

He raises an eyebrow. "You didn't check? Wouldn't that have been part of your documentary homework? Documentary 101?"

"I did check." But I want to hear him say it. "Use a full sentence."

Sighing, he mumbles, "I know every word to Carly Rae Jepsen's 'Call Me Maybe.'"

I hold back my laughter as best as I can. "When was the last time you even listened to that? My eighth birthday party?"

"Yeah, probably, but since I know it by heart, it pops into my head all the time. When I'm taking tests, when I'm driving, when I'm trying to fall asleep; it's just *I threw a wish in the well, don't ask me, I'll never tell—*"

"Stop. Don't. It'll get stuck in my head, too."

"*I looked to you as it fell, and now you're in my way,*" he finishes with passion, mussing up my hair.

I pull away and fix my hair, eyeing the piece of equipment he's moved to now. "Don't you think this workout is just going to make you sore?"

"You think soreness will last a week?"

"Depends how frequently you work out. How frequently do you work out, Holden Michaels?"

"You really need to improve your internet stalking because I post gym selfies all the time." He flexes jokingly, but it's not a joke. Because there's a muscle there. It's not huge or rippling or whatever, but it's enough to make me realize that, even when he's not flexing, there's some definition in his arms, it's just kind of hidden by his T-shirt sleeves.

"Huh." I lean in a little closer, widening my eyes. "I guess if I had a magnifying glass or something—"

"You're *so* funny," he says, lightly pushing me away.

We wrap up around eleven thirty and head into the parking lot together, the autumn chill cooling our heated skin.

"Hold on a second," he says, lifting one long finger to pause me by my car—tonight was one of those random nights my mom didn't have to work. He runs to the minivan, parked a few spaces away, and comes back while I deposit my camera onto the passenger seat.

"It turns out they don't make the old light-up shoes in my preferred style, so—" He shrugs. "This'll have to do. Just know it's the thought that counts."

I accept what he offers me: a bag of Hershey's Kisses, cool to the touch from sitting out in the cold. Just like when we were kids.

"I'll text you about New York." He smiles down at me, proud of himself for rendering me speechless. "Night, Saine."

And then he leaves me standing there, the bag crushed in my nearly shaking hand, a bunch of emotions swirling in my gut that I dare not feel, dare not even *look* at, for fear that I'll fall apart in this empty parking lot.

FIFTEEN

"I'm with the band" is an actual thing I have said multiple times in my life.

It gets Corrine and me through the door of Chapman's, the area's most popular all-ages music venue, during sound check of Nope.'s Monday-night show. Weeknight shows tend to draw in weak numbers even when the top-billed act is locally popular, so we're not expecting more than twenty-five people tonight, but we still set up the merch table as if the crowd would boast a hundred.

Juniper walks into the cold, echoing room a few minutes after Corrine and I have started laying out T-shirts, Devon Miles Smith hot on her heels and talking a mile a minute. If her scowl is any indication, their relationship is going *great*. Devon Miles Smith pulls her into an embrace, slaps his lips against hers, and jumps onto the stage, his guitar case smacking against his back.

"About time," Kayla says into the microphone.

"Juniper drives like a grandma," he says under his breath but still loud enough to be heard in this nearly empty room. I flash back to my own grandma, who got pulled over numerous times for speeding.

Juniper rolls her eyes, sliding behind the table. "He's mad because I wouldn't run a red light."

"Last time I checked, Devon," Kayla says loudly, "you were capable of driving yourself in that nice Toyota Corolla your parents bought you this summer." Her eyes flick toward Juniper before she turns around to address her bandmates: Alexa Polizzi on bass and Hayley Schwab on drums. "Now that we're all here, we can stop wasting Danny's time."

Danny, the Chapman's employee who runs the sound booth, currently has his worn-out Pumas propped up in the booth, his phone playing some video on his lap. He used to be a drummer in a band, Snot-Nosed Brat, but, for obvious reasons, their jazz-punk fusion never took off.

"Are you okay, Juniper?" I ask, rubbing her back.

She folds a Nope. T-shirt and nods, eyes cast down. "I'm fine."

Corrine goes to her other side, boxing her in. "He's an ass-hole, no offense. I know we're friends with him or whatever, but it's always been more because he's your boyfriend and Kayla's guitarist."

"Yeah. Not because we like him." I pull the T-shirt from Juniper's hands because, at this rate, she's going to etch perma-nent wrinkles into it. "We like you, though."

"We love you," Corrine says, randomly pulling a pack of

tissues from the pocket in her corduroy jumper she recently thrifted. Juniper takes one.

"You deserve better."

Juniper's face pinches, tears collecting at her waterline. "I need a minute."

She scurries off to the bathroom, leaving Corrine and me to exchange guilty glances. I don't know if Kayla told Corrine about her crush, but it's kind of nice being on the same page without having to discuss it. There's no doubt: Devon Miles Smith is an asshole to Juniper and she deserves better. If she happens to break up with him and get with Kayla, well, I see no problem with that. There are other guitarists and songwriters in the world, no matter how scared Kayla is to search.

Danny gets Nope.'s feedback under control and they play through half a song, Kayla giving her all even when no one's watching, her long hair swinging wildly around her as she tests the microphone out from all spots on the tiny stage.

"Should we go check on her?" Corrine asks, sitting down in the rickety folding chair behind the merch table.

"No, I think we should let her have a moment. He was probably bitching at her the whole ride." I take the much sturdier seat next to her. "Has Logan texted you yet?"

She clamps her hand over her mouth to stop from squealing. "Yes! He said he's probably coming to the show."

"You didn't tell me!" I stifle the part of me that wonders if she didn't tell me so we'd be even. But a bigger part of me knows that Corrine isn't that petty.

"I assumed you knew since he got my number from you.

He's not entirely sure he'll make it, but . . ." She tries to play it off with a long shrug, but I know her hopes are higher than her shoulders.

"He'll totally be here. He practically sprained a thumb trying to type your number into his phone."

She bites back a smile. "We'll see." Her fingers stretch toward her jeans pocket, but she doesn't pull her phone out. "How's your documentary going? You don't really talk about it."

"I thought maybe that would be weird." I cross my arms, my fingers sliding against the faux leather of my jacket. Once the show starts, it'll warm up to a nauseating degree in here.

She tilts her head to the side, considering. "I think it's weirder that you're not talking about it. Filming is like your favorite thing to do. . . ."

"It's going well. I think. I don't know, it's probably total trash. Holden won't really open up about anything." I sigh. "I would have given anything for him to share less as a kid, but now, when I need him to just spew an unconscious stream of thought, he's not into it. It's like he's keeping me at a distance."

Corrine quirks a brow. "Join the club." I think it's a dig at me until she laughs. "He wasn't the 'sharing is caring' type when we dated."

"You didn't like that?"

She doesn't acknowledge my question, even though I don't mean it in a negative way. "Do you realize that neither of you really talk about when you were friends?"

"It was a long time ago."

"Not really. What, five years? And I dated him last year. It could have come up at any time during our relationship, but it barely did. It was almost like I was the one who introduced you two."

"You kind of were." Holden and I have only had one class together, way back in sophomore year, and spoke about two words the entire semester, neither of them particularly friendly. He met Corrine at the thrift shop last year on his search for cameras and they started flirting, and I was like "Oh yeah, Holden, we were friends before middle school," and that was about it. I wasn't going to wax poetic about how we were annoyingly inseparable best friends until the bottle pointed to me and he refused to kiss me. It's kind of a weird thing to throw into your friend's face when she's falling in love with the guy. I let her have her moment; what's so wrong with that?

She offers a sympathetic smile. "I know I'm not, like, the poster child for talking about feelings because it makes me itchy, but . . . I don't know. I feel like he didn't exist before I knew him." She scrunches her face. "Does that make sense?"

"Yeah. Like he wasn't, I don't know, fully fleshed out."

"Yes. Exactly."

I think of how his family didn't even know he had a girlfriend. How there wasn't even a whisper that his parents divorced. "I guess that's just who he is now. He's whoever the people around him need him to be and nothing more." I bite my lip. "He didn't used to be like that."

So, what happened?

A silence falls over us as the band finishes sound check.

"What's next?" she asks. "Are you almost finished filming?"

It's the question I have been dreading answering, even if she never got around to asking. Because of course I have to tell her. It doesn't matter that they broke up, that he didn't cheat and I said I wouldn't lie, and that means no hiding things or not telling her things—especially when I know she'd want to know and would feel hurt for not knowing if she did eventually find out. But I hadn't figured out a way to casually be like "So, yeah, I'm going to New York with Holden and we're going to stay in the same hotel room, but it's cool because we'll have separate beds."

Because, after thinking about it more and more, it's not cool. It doesn't matter how far apart the beds are, or why we're going, because Corrine isn't comfortable with me working with Holden no matter what she says or who she starts to date. This is the uncomfortable eighth-grade "I bought this shirt after Corrine showed me hers and now she's mad, but saying she's not" experience all over, but with a person she knows intimately instead of a shirt we can both own and regret purchasing a year later.

"We should be wrapping soon, actually." I reach for my necklace. My hand drops. "The final event is this weekend."

She turns in her seat toward me. "What happens at this one?"

"It's a huge obstacle course designed like *Fantastic Lorenzo's Planet*." I don't wait to see if the name registers for her because we played the game in middle school at sleepovers. "It should be pretty cool. Five players go in and one comes out."

"So it's like the Hunger Games?"

"No. I just mean only one person wins."

She nods. "Where is it? Maybe I'll go with you to keep you company. Help you film."

My gut clenches. "It's at the Javits Center, in New York."

Her face falls. "Oh."

"Yeah."

The city is three to four hours away depending on mode of travel and traffic and, if you're taking the train like Holden and I will be, how many stops along the way. We could do the train rides and the event in one day if the event weren't starting at eight o'clock at night on Saturday. The last train leaving Penn Station for Harrisburg leaves during what will be the equivalent of exit interviews with the Vice and Virtual web series team.

Hence, staying the night.

"The event starts at eight o'clock. In the evening." Maybe if I lay this out piece by piece, she can assume the rest and I won't have to say it. "We're taking a train up on Saturday and then coming home Sunday morning."

Her eyes flick to mine for a brief second. "So, is the event, like, all night?" She's jumping through hoops to not be right, just like I'm jumping through hoops to not tell her.

"No, it's only a few hours for everything. His mom got a hotel room so we don't have to be out all night."

"Oh, so she's going?"

"No." Guilt fizzles in my stomach. I could throw up. *Where's Juniper?* Let's go back to getting her to break up with Devon Miles Smith. "It'll just be the two of us. At one point, I was told Taj was going, but he's not."

Corrine stares at me for a second. Blinks once. Twice. "One hotel room?"

"Yes." No point in dancing around it now. "Two beds."

"You could probably stay with your dad."

"I barely know my dad."

She worries her bottom lip. "Are you guys . . . friends again?"

"No."

Her eyes search mine for a lie before she clears her throat and stands. "I think I'm going to check on Juniper."

"Corrine," I say, standing too. "Are you okay?"

"Would it really matter if I wasn't?" She doesn't snap at me. Though I feel like I deserve it. "It's fine. You said there's nothing going on; you're not even friends. You're just making a documentary and he's just doing a contest."

"Right." *But is she?* It kind of feels like Holden and I might be friends again. Maybe. The Hershey's Kisses certainly felt like a peace offering, a chocolaty one I have resisted digging into so far because it'll feel slightly more real if I let it.

She points to the bathroom Juniper disappeared into, making her escape, but at that moment, right when the band is loading their stuff off the stage to make way for the next band, Turtlenecks, Juniper storms out, determination on her face, and marches up to Devon Miles Smith. She pokes him in the chest.

"You're a dick," she says. The rest of her speech fades as she lowers her voice so only he, and a wide-eyed Kayla, can hear.

Kayla slowly backs away until she's standing next to me. We watch as Juniper gestures wildly and Devon Miles Smith stands there with his mouth open wide, catching flies because he's trash.

"Tell him, Juniper!" Kayla calls across the room.

Juniper stops scolding him to give Kayla a thumbs-up.

"Yeah!" I lean into Kayla and whisper, "I have no clue what she's saying, but I support her." Out of the corner of my eye, I see Corrine put her phone against her ear and walk outside. My gut clenches. "Do you support *me*?"

Kayla raises an eyebrow. "I mean, I don't support you no matter *what*. Like, don't suddenly become a racist or something. What do you need support for?"

I sigh. "I'm going to New York with Holden this weekend. We have to stay overnight. We're going to be in the same hotel room—*but separate beds*—and, I don't know, is it wrong?"

She looks at the door Corrine slipped through. "I don't really think there's winning with this. It's probably just best to finish it and move on."

"I don't want to hurt her, but *she* broke up with *him*. Why does it feel like she still has feelings? Even with the whole Logan thing."

She shrugs. "I think it's complicated. You were friends with him, she dated him, he's not supposed to be in either of your lives right now, but he is. It's messy. Feelings are messy." She watches Juniper take a big breath and start in on Devon Miles Smith again.

"I'm so in love," she says under her breath.

"What?" Devon Miles Smith asks Juniper, his eyes wide and jaw dropped.

"You heard me," she says louder. She jumps onto the stage and grabs the microphone from the singer of Turtlenecks, a late-twenties guy with thick-rimmed glasses and dyed-gray hair. "You treat me badly and I deserve better. We're done."

She hops off the stage and walks out, the only evidence she was there the stunned faces of everyone and the round of applause Kayla and I break into in her absence. In time to catch the last second of Juniper's show, Corrine waltzes inside with Logan's hand wrapped around hers and a huge smile on her face.

It doesn't reach her eyes, though. Not that anyone besides me could tell.

SIXTEEN

It could be said that Holden is hard to get information out of on a regular day. But, during the three-and-some-change-hour train ride, he is *impossible* to get information out of. He's tense and quiet and moody. Barely speaks four words to me. When I jokingly tell him how cool he'll look wearing a helmet with the GoPro attached while competing, he turns a little green. I thought that was something people just say. But he legit turns green.

By the end of hour two, I've had it with the silence and the way he keeps jiggling his leg. I pull the bag of Hershey's Kisses from my backpack and place five Kisses on the fold-down tray in front of him. Then I go back to watching *Nightmare Next Door.*

The Kisses sit there for all of twenty seconds before he picks one up and unwraps it. He doesn't offer any words, but when he runs out, I replenish them five at a time until the bag is gone and the train ride ends in Penn Station, aka a literal hellmouth.

Holden finally speaks once we're being shifted up the stairs by the exiting crowd. "How do we get out of here?"

I direct him through the overwhelming station with my hand on his elbow, until we're on the corner of West Thirty-Third and Eighth. The event will be held at the Javits in a few hours, so we're going to drop off our things at the hotel first. It's just a matter of getting there. Holden fumbles with his phone, trying to order an Uber, but I lightly push it away.

"We can just walk." The hotel is only a few blocks from here and we don't have more than three bags between us, so I take off and hope Holden follows.

"So your dad hasn't asked you to come visit?" He hides his frown from me by watching the cars zigzag down the street next to us. In the distance, a chorus of car horns start honking.

"Well, we're not really on speaking terms." When you move nearly four hours away from your child, speaking terms becomes a phrase and not a real tangible thing. "He mostly just sends money with the implication that I should visit him."

"Are you just trolling him by coming here, then?"

I sidestep a puddle that stinks of garbage. "He doesn't know."

"My question still stands."

I shrug. "I told you; I like the city."

"Have you ever come with someone else before?"

"No, this is the first time." I fling my arm out to stop him from continuing across the next street. Cabs and bikers zoom past, and a pigeon dares to waddle through filthy standing water before taking off into the air when a truck drives too close. "I already know you'll taint the experience."

"Maybe this will be the best trip and now you'll only visit with other people."

I smile grimly. "What does optimism feel like, Holden?"

He smirks down at me. "Like eating cake for breakfast."

"I do love cake."

Our hotel looms into view, squished between buildings that seem tall just for the sake of being tall. Holden retrieves the key cards from the front desk with little to no issue and we use the elevator to go the whole way to the twenty-third floor, where I realize I might have a moderate fear of heights, and we find our tiny room. With its dirty window overlooking the city, loud AC unit, and . . . one king-sized bed.

Holden frowns. "This isn't right."

My heart starts pounding to the rhythm of "We Will Rock You" by Queen. Their greatest hits album was stuck in the minivan's CD player on the drive to the train station.

It's definitely not right. Even though the bed looks like it could fit three average-sized adults comfortably, this bed is just one bed and not two like I had assumed, like I had told Corrine. This is not acceptable.

"Did your mom really book a room with one bed for you and Taj?"

"This was the recommended hotel for the competition. This might just be what was left." He drops his bag next to the bed with a sigh. "I'll sleep on the floor."

"Don't. That's gross." I look at the compacted carpet. It's designed in a way that makes it impossible to tell how dirty it is.

"You were going to do it."

"Yeah, when I thought I was crashing your hotel reservation.

Now that I'm taking Taj's spot, there's room for both of us."
Logically, I know I should be accepting his offer to sleep on
the floor. I know I know I know. "Your cooties would die of
exhaustion before crossing from your side to mine on a bed this
big."

"You assume my cooties are as nonathletic as you assume
me to be?"

"I call it like I see it." I smile, trying to slow down my racing
heart. There's nothing to panic about. I didn't technically lie
to Corrine. This change of plans was beyond my control. Do
I even need to mention it to her? It'll just unnecessarily cause
tension between us, upset her. But the thought of her never
knowing, or, *worse*, finding out . . . I don't know if she'll buy
that I avoided telling her something to spare her feelings for a
second time, even if it's true.

Holden flops backward on the bed, his arms spread out. "I
call this side, then."

That settles that. No sleeping on the floor now. It would just
make things awkward.

I set my bags down on the other side of the bed and pull
out the cameras, checking for charged batteries, cleaning the
lenses, and packing my backpack with other things I might
need: the lavalier mic, the battery charger, extra SD cards, a
portable charger for my phone, ibuprofen, hand lotion, a comb,
lipstick, two protein bars. My typical emergency bag—at least,
when I'm not with Corrine. When we're together, she's the
mom friend.

After Holden takes a few shots out of the dirty window,
we head outside for food and exploring. I film everything and

Holden takes photos—sometimes even photos of me, and I'm not that mad about it because my face is usually behind my camera or I'm looking at shops or leading the way—and I show him some of my favorite tourist-y spots: the High Line, the very terrible subway, the Hudson River, this restaurant near the Javits Center called Friedman's with what is sometimes a city view and other times a view of six trash bags and construction workers taking up space on the sidewalk. He eases up over time, lets me direct him, answers more questions. When I'm thinking that maybe I will bring someone with me the next time, the worst thing happens.

Holden gets violently sick in the first bathroom he can reach at the Javits Center. Maybe half a bag of Hershey's Kisses, followed by a bowl of macaroni and cheese, followed by a dollar slice of pizza was not the best combination of food while nervous and about to run an obstacle course. Who would have thought?

My mom, probably. Definitely my grandma. Corrine and Kayla. Anyone else, really.

"I'll be fine," Holden calls from inside the men's room.

He throws up again, not fine. I wince at the sound of his gagging, but continue to record our conversation even when viewers will probably only be able to hear me.

"I'm going to get someone," I say, half turning away from the bathroom entrance.

I hear him spit. "Who?"

"I don't know. Maybe they can postpone until you feel better."

"No!" He flushes and then I hear water rushing into a sink. "No. I'm fine."

He comes out a few seconds later, shaky, pale, and sweaty. I can't find an angle to make him look healthy. "I'm fine."

"Is this just nerves?" I ask, wanting to squeeze his arm in, I don't know, comfort? Or maybe to cling on to my one last hope of finishing this documentary.

"I'm fine," he says again. I'm worried it's all he knows how to say.

I suppose, if I'm being completely honest, I'm not ready for our time together to be over. If Holden *lost*—or in this case, couldn't compete—then maybe I wouldn't have to stop filming with him right away. Maybe I could do an extended act three, showing all the ways Holden is saving up for the headset next year or some scheme he (read: I) put in place to get him the headset from the winner. I could come up with a hundred ideas if I had to, in order to extend my time with him.

But if he somehow pulls this off, really is fine and rallies himself for one more miracle feat, my documentary is over; our time to be friends again is over. *Ugh*, and my submission will have the most boring and predictable ending. White guy wins again. We all know this story.

I can't let that happen.

He throws up again, twice, during his pre-event interview and the employee we dealt with during that douchebag's cheating in the last event decides that Holden's not fit to compete. I'm ecstatic, and *panicking*. This is the plot twist I wanted, for my documentary *and* my personal life, but I don't know how to deal with it immediately. What's the best course of action?

"No," Holden and I say at the same time. I can barely catch my breath enough to say it. It comes out like a squawk. My thoughts fly a million miles an hour.

"I'm fine," Holden says again. "I can run the course and I can win." He tries to smile, but even his pale lips are shaking.

"No, you can't," I say too quickly. I'm supposed to be on his side, but no, he can't compete! "I mean, you're not doing well," I add in a caring voice.

"We can't risk you hurting yourself or hurting someone else, or getting anyone sick. . . ." The woman appears to be debating all the things that could go wrong, a slight disgusted sneer on her face as she takes in Holden's appearance. "I'm sorry, but you're not competing."

Maybe *Holden's* not.

I angle the camera at her face. The words are out before I can even frame the shot. "What if I did it in his place?" It's the only way I'd have control over the narrative. Yes, I'll do the run for him and I'll throw it. He loses in an unforeseen plot twist that shocks the crowd and Admissions, and then we spend some more time together as we mold the proper ending.

"I don't know . . ." Her expression twists at the same time my gut does. "I'll have to consult some people."

"Look, I know we've made a bunch of problems, but he's come all this way, gotten this far, and he deserves some kind of chance. It's not his fault. He can't help that he's sick. He *just* got sick; he was great all day until now."

I meet her eyes, and I hate what I'm about to do, but this documentary *will* have an ending, a good one. "If you don't make this work, I will upload this video and let everyone know that Vice and Virtue practically spat on a nearly dying kid's last hope at winning this contest."

Beside me, Holden tenses like he's going to hurl again.

The lady's face goes tight, her lips pursed. "I'll be right back. Don't move."

"You don't have to do this," he says, but he doesn't even sound like he means it.

"I do," I say, and it's not a lie. "You can't, so I will."

She comes back with a man who hands me a badge like Holden's, sans photo, and a snug lime-green T-shirt with the company's logo on it. Holden and I do a two-minute interview together for the web series, to explain what's going on, and then we're led to where the other contestants are waiting for the event to start. We don't leave the room until five minutes before the contest, so any hope I had of filming the crowd and the course beforehand are squashed. I get as many interviews from other players as I can manage, though—something I missed out on at the other events—but most of them don't want to talk and are skeptical of my intentions, with the exception of . . . Lada of the intimidating name fame. She's the only one who doesn't treat me like a dirty cheater.

Lada is not a Russian bodybuilder like I had in mind. She's a petite blonde wearing tie-dyed Nikes and leggings, her eyeliner sharp and perfect. She chews gum, blowing bubbles, until half-way through the interview when she realizes what she's doing mid-sentence and spits it into a trash can four feet away, barely glancing at her target, which she hits, before diving back into the interview. She wants to win the VR headset so she can shove it in her older brothers' faces—all six of them—that video games aren't just for "basement-dwelling, sexist guys."

I know it before I even finish recording: I want Lada to win. At least she's not just in it for the headset. She has something to prove. She has motivation, stakes.

I picture it now, the bittersweet ending: we started with Yvette, but then, plot twist, we have Holden. Everyone will think what I thought about his privilege, but then feel for him because of his financial struggle and his adorable family. They'll cheer when we get the other contestant disqualified for assault! But the real kicker will be him getting sick before the very last contest, one he has a chance of winning. They'll bite their nails as the documentarian has to step in. She doesn't have training, so why would she win? The defeat crushes Holden and the audience because, by now, they've grown to love him. I'll convince Holden to put in a few applications for jobs, to save up money for the headset next year, maybe Repairisburg to bring things full circle. *Shit, my mind is unparalleled.*

The contestants and I are ushered upstairs to the main exhibit hall in the center. Loud music plays throughout the room, but the crowd can still be heard chanting "Vir-tu-al, vir-tu-al," over and over from their positions on every side of the three-dimensional course. There are five lanes of obstacles laid out before us, each identical and completely separate from one another. So while we're competing against each other, we won't have to *deal* with each other. The first one to the end can grab the mystery box, designed like the power boost boxes in *Fantastic Lorenzo's Planet*. It symbolizes the headset prototype we'll win.

The music stops when a young Black man in a slate-gray button-down rolled up at the sleeves steps forward. He brings a microphone to his mouth, and only then do I recognize him from the website and all the articles I read. He's grown a beard since his commonly used headshot was taken. James Heath, CEO of Vice and Virtual, addresses the crowd:

"Thank you for being here tonight. I hope that the contestants all have someone in the crowd to cheer them on," he says with a smile, taking in each contestant one by one and not even noticing there's an extra player in Holden's lane. "I know the trip from Pennsylvania to New York is not an easy one to make sometimes, so if you *don't* have someone here, let me lend you my enthusiastic staff." The crowd unleashes an uproar. "I'd like to thank all two hundred of them for not only being here tonight, on the weekend—" A rumble of laughter echoes throughout the room. "They are getting paid—don't worry— but they're also making sure this event flourishes. It meant a lot to me to be able to shine a light on my home state and the businesses that helped me get where I am today. Now, you may have noticed that I was absent from the first two events. I have to apologize for that. I have been extremely busy working on the latest version of the headset, but I also wanted to get things in place here, at the Vice and Virtual headquarters, because I'll be giving the winner not only the prototype but an exclusive, private tour of where this company does its fine work."

Applause rings around the room and I join in half-heartedly, my heart thumping in my throat. Aside from having to tell Corrine the truth about my documentary, the only time I can recall being this nervous was cheerleading tryouts. Corrine failed to mention to me beforehand that everyone makes the team. She said she wanted me to bring my A game.

"I paid them to clap at that."

Everyone laughs.

"And to laugh."

Everyone laughs again.

"But in all seriousness, I'm so excited to get this going. The participants have been explained the rules and once we've crowned our winner, the tracks will be available for anyone's use—one at a time—and for photos."

He hands the microphone to Chrissy Lo and she instructs the players to take their places. I fix the GoPro onto my helmet while Holden starts recording on my camera behind me. He's green again. This documentary is going to have so many shitty shots. But at least he's familiar with a camera.

Chrissy Lo counts down from five and then the four players on my left, ready before their lanes, tense. I explode forward when she cries *Go!* and give this my almost-all.

I jump over platforms with gusto, dodge spinning objects in my way without falling off the balance beam I'm running over, slide down tunnels like a little kid at a public park, stomp a box open to the beat of the loud music so I can retrieve a key that opens a door, and—holy shit—I'm at the end. The mystery box sits innocently in a large, empty space that every door opens into. The crowd doesn't have access to this area, so no one will know who actually gets to the box first. But it's me, even though I tried not to be first. It's *Holden*.

I can't breathe. I rush forward to snag the box before remembering that I don't want to win, Holden can't win, there needs to be an upset—a reason to keep filming, to find a better ending than Holden doing the contest and winning the contest. Another door opens next to me and Lada charges. I could just grab the box and end this. But there's nothing interesting about easy. Even considering the ups and downs, Holden is just some kid who wants a VR headset for free. What kind of story is that, even with the fake one I manipulated into life behind his back?

Now's my chance. Really, it's been decided since he first got sick. Practically since he sat silent on the train for hours. But his absence from the contest isn't the plot twist. The plot twist is that he was the one who trained, but I was the one who had to compete. And I lost. That's the moral of this story: life isn't fair.

I cross my arms and step away from the box, clearly indicating it's hers. She lunges for it and a siren goes off.

SEVENTEEN

The look of devastation on Holden's face when I exit the obstacle course empty-handed doesn't need to be recorded for me to remember it forever. It's burned into my memory and tainted with guilt.

But because this is a documentary, it *was* recorded, and I'm awful.

"I don't understand," he says, flustered, as we walk back to the hotel after a web series interview, the night thick around us but the sounds and colors still vivid with life. "You were right there. I saw you go in first."

"I told you. I tripped and someone else got there before me." I rub at my elbow like a lying liar lying about fake injuries I lied about. "I'm so sorry, Holden." At least that's only, like, fifty percent of a lie.

His face screws up for a moment and then he exhales loudly. He's still a little pale, but he's no longer sweating or throwing up. He's just completely bothered. By me. By losing. By the competition's end. By the people who threaten to jostle him as he walks along the sidewalk without a care in the world whether he's in their way.

He doesn't tell me he forgives me, or that it's not my fault, and I worry that he knows.

"Hey." I grab on to his upper arm and stop him. "Why don't we get some food in you? You're running on empty."

"I just want to go and suffocate myself in the uncomfortable hotel bed."

"Don't joke about that." I tighten my grip and pull him, so he has to face me fully. "Can your stomach handle some food? Not that crap we had before. Like, a sandwich? Fries?"

I swear I feel the vibrations of his stomach growling all the way up his arm when he says, "No."

I sigh. "Come on. My treat."

He's not enthused, but he doesn't put up a fight when I drag him to the closest food establishment, force an overpriced grilled cheese sandwich in his mouth, and recount my lies over and over, step by step, as he tries to understand how I could have possibly lost his last shot at winning.

We're both exhausted and miserable when we get back to the hotel room. So much so that it's not even that awkward to change and slide into opposite sides of the bed, kind of like an old married couple who don't hate each other but certainly don't like each other. An entire person could fit between us, but with the way we both lie there in the dark silently, it feels more like a wall.

I've almost worked myself into relaxation, a few deep breaths from sleep, when Holden says my name. I stir.

"Saine," he says again.

I blink sleep from my eyes, even though I can barely see anything in the darkness. "Yeah?"

"I'm sorry."

"Why are you sorry?" I turn toward him.

"I didn't mean to make you feel like it was your fault or anything. I appreciate you doing that for me." He rolls on his side to face me, his frown etched in moonlight through the sheer curtains on the window. "You had a lot riding on this, too. I'm sorry."

I mean, I'll still have a documentary at the end of this. "You don't have to apologize, really—"

He sucks in a breath. "Fuck. This is so stupid." He sounds choked up, clogged, stuffy, like . . . like he's about to cry. "So embarrassing."

I'm glad he can't see me in the dark room, because my cringe isn't exactly understanding. It's just a dumb toy. Why is he crying about it? There's nothing wrong with crying, but . . . over this?

"Holden." I reach across the expanse of bed between us and wrap my hand around his wrist. It feels more intimate than it should, under the blankets. "Hey. It's okay. You can save up and buy the device when it goes on sale next year."

He coughs out a sob. "I can't afford to spend that kind of money, not with college next year. And it was—it was supposed to be—for—*Trevor*."

I want to understand, but I still honestly don't. I scoot a little closer and prop myself up on my supposed injured elbow. "What's going on? Talk to me."

After a moment so long and heavy with silence, I'm surprised when he speaks. "Trevor's in the hospital," he whispers.

"*What?*" I spin to turn on the lamp by the bed. He can't just say something like that and not immediately explain.

"He's been hospitalized for almost a year and I wanted to get him this dumb VR headset because all he can do is play video games basically. I figured it would be the only way he could see something besides the same four walls of his hospital room." He swipes a tear from his face, staring up at the ceiling. "He has leukemia—the doctors are optimistic, but it's touch and go. I just—I just wanted to make it suck a little less, make him feel like he wasn't as trapped as he really is, make him forget how he drew the shitty straw."

The itch of tears attacks my eyes. I am the worst possible person in the entire world. Trevor, little baby Trevor who accidentally bought thirty-six hypoallergenic pillows online with his mom's credit card, has cancer.

"Why didn't you tell me this before? I've been asking why you were doing this and you never told me this." Fuck. If I had just *known* . . .

"Because I didn't want sympathy or pity. I just wanted the headset." He sits up so we're face-to-face. "And now I have all those things except the headset, right?"

I reach out to grab his shoulder but let my hand fall short. "There has to be another way we can get that thing." I cross my legs and scoot even closer. "Or we could buy a different one."

He wipes his nose with the back of his hand, his eyes red and watery. "I don't have the money. I can't touch my college funds, my parents can't afford to buy it with the medical bills, and college, and all these kids, and—and—it's just. I fucked up. I got confident after the second game and told him what I was doing. And then tonight, I got too nervous because it's all too big and I've been spending less time with him lately for this and I have nothing to show for it. It wasn't even worth it. He's going to be so disappointed. I shouldn't have gotten his hopes up."

My fingers graze his T-shirt sleeve before I realize I'm pulling him into a hug.

I haven't been pressed against him like this since puberty. The new addition of my chest makes it feels awkward, but my head still fits in the crook of his neck like it was made for me. I rub his back as he clings to mine with tense, desperate fingers.

"We'll figure something out," I mumble into his shoulder. I'll figure something out. Some way to get everything: a perfect ending to my documentary, something for Trevor . . . more time with Holden. I didn't know all the facts and it doesn't make me a bad person for intentionally losing. Especially when I'm dedicated to fixing this.

His hands slide down my back and connect at the dip in my spine. "You don't have to help me. I'm sorry I'm the worst documentary subject ever."

"I'm the worst." The truth gets caught in my throat. I choke out a laugh. "I should have, I don't know, pried harder, to get you to tell me what was really going on. I *knew* you were hiding something."

We fall into a silence that turns more awkward each second that passes after I realize I'm practically sitting in his lap. I don't pull away, though, and neither does he.

"Saine?"

"Yeah?" I'm prepared to back away, to laugh off the weirdness with him, but he surprises me and makes me feel the full force of my shittiness in one blow.

"I missed you."

I keep my breathing even. Don't tense. "I missed you, too."

We finally break away.

He sighs heavily, scrubbing at his eyes with the backs of his hands. "So, this is why I was being weird. I just—I didn't want to get emotional on camera and I didn't want to build this whole thing up in case I failed. And not many people even know about Trevor; I didn't want to exploit him on camera like that."

"It might be better if you talked about it. I know I feel better about—you know, I just feel better when I talk." There's no need to bring up my grandma. And her *death*. Not when he's worried about if Trevor will make it. I mean, *cancer*. Fuck. "What can we do? For him? What does he like?"

I'm realizing for the first time that I don't know teenage Trevor. He wasn't even nine years old the last time I saw him. I just know the little brother who let me dress him up as a cat;

the kid who stole his mother's romance novels for me to read to him before Holden tattled on us; the boy who was always singing and dancing, even without music.

Holden laughs, a fond smile gracing his lips. "He, um, well, he loves watching bands on YouTube, like, all day. Like, live performances. He's obsessed with Freddie Mercury and Billie Joe Armstrong, the guy from Green Day. He has this weird theory about how lead singers would make the most terrifying dictators because of their abilities to control crowds." He laughs to himself. "My submission for the contest was the type of game I'd want to make for him. It's the perfect blend of his two favorite things."

I think of the live music experience Holden designed, the crowd-surfing, playing on the stage to the thousands in the crowd. Maybe we could make that happen somehow. Maybe Holden won't ever have to know I sabotaged this. Maybe we can still be friends. I pull my camera out from the bag next to the bed. I give him a questioning look, he nods, and I press record.

He looks at the camera and then to me, relaxing. "Trevor wants to be in a band."

I zoom into his hands. He's wringing them in his lap. "Yeah, I could have guessed that from how he was as a kid."

"Yeah. Wants to be in a band, but can't sing or play an instrument, can't leave his fucking hospital room." His smile slides off his face, leaving blankness. "This was the one thing I could do for him and I ruined it."

"This was *not* the only thing you could do for him." I make him meet my eyes, force him to believe me just like I'm forcing myself to believe it. "I'm serious. We'll figure something out and it'll be way better than that overpriced hunk of prototype junk. It'll be like—oh my *god*."

"What?" He straightens, watching me with wide eyes.

"We should make the headset." The idea was right there all this time; why did we even waste a moment wallowing? Oh my god, this solves everything. My documentary is *overflowing* with heart now. I'm giddy at the thought of the admissions team crying by the time my documentary fades to black. I picture them wiping their eyes dry and sharing glances that say "we don't even need to deliberate; this girl is *in*."

He laughs, the tension escaping from his body. "Stop. You got me excited."

"No, I'm serious." I wave away his next words. "Like, obviously they'll look terrible because we'll just have to put together a bunch of things and, last time I checked, neither of us were rocket scientists, but, like, we could film stuff for him. First-person-perspective type stuff."

His eyes roam over my face, his mouth slowly slowly slowly forming a disagreement. But then he says, "Okay." He nods to himself. "Okay. We could film stuff he's missing out on. It's not a video game, but it's been so long since he was allowed out to do normal kid stuff that this might be okay. It's something."

"I happen to know a great local band whose show we could film."

He grins. "Yeah. And we could do other things, like—"

"Sneak out of the house!"

"Go to a party."

"And," I say, not getting my hopes up yet, "maybe I can still film for my documentary? We'd get Trevor's approval, of course—I mean, after the fact. This could be a surprise for him." The final act of the documentary will turn into a behind-the-scenes type thing, but watching first-person footage being filmed and then interviews about/with Trevor could totally seal the deal on this thing.

He nods, a grin wide on his face.

My smile matches his now. *This is the heart! This is it!* Things will be okay for both of us and what I did was the right thing in the end—this would mean so much more to someone than just winning or buying a headset. And if the doctors are optimistic, then I will be, too. It's not like I'm using him.

"When we're done and you see how happy Trevor is, you'll forget all about tonight."

His blue eyes meet mine and a shiver goes down my back. "Not all of it, hopefully."

Corrine

Hey how did it go

12:37 AM

Holden got sick and I tried to do the contest for him

12:37 AM

We didn't win

12:38 AM

I'm sorry

12:38 AM

So the documentary is over now?

12:38 AM

I don't think so

12:40 AM

Apparently he wanted the VR glasses for his brother

12:40 AM

Oh

12:41 AM

Yeah he's sick but I guess he hasn't really told people

12:45 AM

He's kind of stuck at the hospital so we might try to MAKE VR glasses for him, I don't know

12:45 AM

Oh that sounds nice

12:48 AM

Let me know if I can help somehow

12:48 AM

Will definitely need help THANK YOU

12:48 AM

EIGHTEEN

Visiting Trevor is the obvious next step in making this documentary—and the VR headset—and yet, Holden is still being a total weirdo about it. He even told Trevor ahead of time that he didn't get the headset, so it's not like I'm about to witness a fight or tears.

"What are you so nervous about?" I practically have to drag him toward the pediatric wing a few days post–New York.

"You're the first person I've told that's not family. It's a big deal."

"What about Taj?" *And, shit, will you be mad to know I told Corrine, who didn't even know Trevor existed?*

"Well, yeah. Of course Taj knows. He had a blast playing dumb for your interviews."

That explains a lot.

"Corrine didn't know." I flick my eyes to his.

He stops walking. "You told Corrine? There was a reason I didn't tell her."

"And what was that reason?" I continue walking and am so fucking relieved when he stomps grumpily along with me . . . like a toddler, but okay. "I was trying to be open and honest with her about this whole thing and that included telling her about Trevor. I kind of thought she'd know already, having been your girlfriend."

"I bet she feels *great* knowing you knew before her for that reason exactly." He falls in step with me as we swing around the corner and approach the main desk.

"I mean, I *did* know Trevor before I knew her, so it doesn't seem that weird that I'd know this, right?"

He sighs. "Don't tell anyone else, okay? You can do the documentary about me trying to help him, but you have to leave him out of it unless he agrees. And you promise only the Temple people will see it."

"Of course. Who would I even tell?"

"I thought that before and look who you told. So, just don't tell anyone else. Please." He works tension from his shoulders. "I bet Corrine will have an Edible Arrangement waiting for me in first period sooner or later. You know how she spends money when she feels uncomfortable and sad."

"Suncomfortable. It's how I ended up with my cold weather gear for cheerleading this year." I grab the hem of my jacket and do a quick twirl to show it off. "It's her love language."

We stop at the desk and wait for the nurse/employee/whoever she is and whatever her job title is to finish her paperwork and acknowledge us standing there bickering quietly.

Holden looks off into the distance, a squint in his long-lashed eyes. "What if he's mad that I told you without asking him first?" His eyes grow wide. "What if Corrine's already over-stepped and gotten *him* an Edible Arrangement?"

"You're the only person who would be upset about an Edible Arrangement. You know they're super expensive and delicious, right?"

"*Holden*," the girl at the desk says, putting aside her clipboard and smiling. She's around our age and devastatingly pretty, with deep brown eyes and freckles scattered across her nose and cheeks. A lanyard around her neck reads "Volunteer." "*Hi*. Did you forget your badge?"

"No," he says, reaching into his pocket and freeing his own lanyard. "I need one for my friend, though."

She notices me for the first time and I try not to laugh at how shocked she is to see another person besides Holden in the world. I guess if I didn't know him, I'd be enamored or swoon or whatever. Like, I can see how he'd be distracting if he were perhaps someone other than Holden.

"Hi," she practically chirps, pulling a blank name tag from nowhere. "Name?"

"I'll spell it for you. S–A–I–N–E."

"Interesting. How is that pronounced, if you don't mind me asking?"

"Like insane without the 'in.'" I smile stiffly, realizing a moment too late that I could have just . . . said my name. I have enough practice with this in school. I suppose there was a part of me that wanted to set her off-balance, though.

She shakes to her senses. She finishes writing my name and

pushes the badge over the counter toward me. I stick it onto my boob with more fervor than necessary.

Once equipped, we head in the direction of Trevor's room and I make sure we're out of earshot of *Libby*—according to her name tag—before saying, "*Holden*, hiiiiiii! That's the girl, right?"

"What girl?"

I nudge him in the ribs, but he grabs my elbow easily in his large grip. "The girl you were buying a necklace for." I tug free of him. *The girl Corrine thinks you had the hots for when you were dating.* But that's not right, no. She wouldn't have known about Libby if she didn't know about Trevor.

"Why can't you like girls with normal names?" I ask. "You could buy her a key chain with her name on it or something and save yourself the money and credit card debt."

"Apparently I only like girls with weird names," he says. He nods at the open doorway in front of us. "This is it."

I take a step forward, but he waits.

"What is it now?" I ask.

"I just—you have to understand, he's going to look—"

"Sick? Older?"

"Yeah."

"I won't run screaming from the room or make any comments or anything." I cross my arms. "I'm not that much of a bitch."

He places his hands on my shoulders. "I know."

I shrug under his grip, not wanting him to know that his comment at the second contest bothered me as much as it did.

"I mean, I *am* a bitch sometimes."

"I am too, though." This is as much of an apology for our nastiness in the past as we're going to get.

I jab my thumb toward the room. "Let's go?"

Inside, two voices sing along to some song I don't know, played at a volume that is probably too loud for a hospital, but, hey, it's the kids' ward and it's the afternoon. A Black girl with a massive head of curls sits on the end of the lone hospital bed in the room, her hands in latex gloves and her mouth covered with a mask. Trevor, or at least a stretched-out, older, thinner version of him, sits on the other end of the bed, a laptop on his knees. His own curls are completely missing, buzzed down like the sides of Holden's head. He's officially not a baby-faced baby anymore.

Holden points at a box of gloves and masks next to the door. I put them on as Trevor and his friend look over.

"Hey, guys. Is that the Reading performance again?" Holden asks, donning his own protective gear.

Trevor smiles, and if the years have been unkind to every other part of him, at least they allowed his grin to stay as bright as ever. "Hey, you actually got it right." He angles the computer toward us and it shows a YouTube video of Green Day playing in, Holden guessed it, Reading. The quality is pretty shit; most likely the video was uploaded back in the Potato Era—480p max, but probably 360p.

"I was about to tell him no just because he always guesses that and is always wrong, but," the friend looks to Holden, "I'm impressed."

"Thanks, Ant." Holden gestures to me. "Trev, you remember—"

"Saine Sinclair! I'd know her anywhere. She's the reason I grew so tall."

"Uh, what?" This girl, *Ant*, looks as confused as I feel.

"She used to water my head so I'd grow like a Chia Pet." He pats his buzzed head. "I'm six foot now. Taller than Holden."

I step farther into the room. "I must have added too much MiracleGro that one time."

Trevor points to the armchair by his bed. It looks worn in and comfortable, not like the other chairs I've seen in hospitals. This is a chair belonging to someone who has been here too long. I sit and introduce myself to Ant.

She waves, her visitors badge crinkling on her shirt. "Antonia."

"Call her Ant," Holden says, dragging another well-worn chair next to mine. His hand brushes against my arm when he sits. "She loves being called Ant."

"Just because I tolerate it doesn't mean I love it." She sends an unimpressed side-eye in his direction.

"What were you guys doing?" I ask, settling in.

"Just listening to music." Ant leans against the meal tray attached to the bed. "Figuring out what to do tonight."

"What are your options?"

"We could watch Netflix," Trevor says, ticking it off on his finger. "Or . . . yeah, that's pretty much it."

He really does need the headset. I bat away the guilt filling my gut and scream at it: I'M WORKING ON IT.

"We could play *Lorenzo* if you wanted to shake things up," Holden offers. I wonder if he'll ever see that game the same way after I totally flubbed his win.

"I don't want to get you kicked out again," Trevor says confidently.

"Crying or screaming?" Ant asks.

"Both," Trevor says.

If it weren't for the precautions, for the sickly, off-white hospital walls around us, I wouldn't know anything was up. Sure, Trevor looks a bit ill, but other than that, this is an older brother getting taunted by his little brother and his friend. We could be in the Michaelses' basement—Holden's new room—and throwing pizza rolls at each other and I wouldn't think twice about it. This must be one of Trevor's better days.

"I did not cry. I really had something in my eye." I can tell by his squint that he's smiling. "Seriously."

"He *did* have Libby flush his eyes, so maybe he's telling the truth," Trevor says.

"Or he's just selling the lie," I add. "Libby seems like she wouldn't care either way."

"Don't help them harass me," Holden says, lightly pushing me.

"Fine. Maybe *they* can help *me* harass you."

"What did you have in mind?" Trevor asks, fluffing his pillow.

"Honestly, anything would be more entertaining than rewatching our YouTube history for the four hundredth time," Ant says.

"I don't know if Holden told you," I say, pulling my camera out of my bag, "but I'm making a documentary about him."

"About Holden?" Trevor points at Holden. "This Holden? Holden Michaels?"

"*Why?*" Ant asks, her face scrunched up.

"He's just, you know, so *interesting*," I joke.

Trevor narrows his eyes. "Lying liar."

It's not until he says it that I remember where I even got the stupid phrase from. I got it from a child—this child. That tracks.

Holden's jaw drops. "I *am* interesting."

"Not *that* interesting. Few people are." Trevor crosses his arms. "What do you need from us?"

"I'll interview you guys. Just ask questions about him and stuff." Since the headset is going to be a surprise, I have to tip-toe around interviewing Trevor about himself.

Trevor straightens, instantly looking uncomfortable. "I don't know."

Ant grabs his foot through the blanket. "You don't have to if you don't want to."

"I'm not really feeling up for that." He kind of cringes. "I'm sorry."

"Trev," I say lightly, "that's totally cool. You don't have to do it at all if you don't want to."

It does pose a problem, though. I know I told Holden that it was cool to leave Trevor out, but the documentary would be seriously lacking in substance—and it might not even make sense. It definitely would lack that tearjerker moment I'm hoping for at the end: Holden delivering the headset to Trevor and Trevor seeing all the hard work his brother put into it for him. Getting into the contest, nearly losing, *me losing*, and then trying to make this perfect experience. Everyone needs to play their roles precisely how I need them.

He seems to relax a little. Holden, on the other hand, looks tense. I can already hear his voice telling me that I'm pushing Trevor too far—and I haven't even tried to push him yet.

"Ant?" I ask, looking at her.

"I'm down." She glances at Trevor. "Is that okay?"

Trevor nods. "Maybe another time for me?"

"Sure thing. We'll be right back." I stand and Ant follows suit.

"We can start a game." Holden moves to the TV and turns on a gaming console that I don't know the name of because it changes every year. An Xbox Whatever 1234.

Out in the hall, I line Ant up next to a terrible Majestic and Inspiring Lion poster, ask her a few questions about Holden, but then turn the conversation in the direction I was hoping I could as soon as I saw her with Trevor.

"When was the last time Trevor left the hospital?"

She chews on her lip. "Um, probably not since he was admitted for extended care. It's been, *wow*, I don't know, seven months? Maybe longer?"

"Can you keep a secret from him?"

"No."

I bark out a laugh. "I appreciate the honesty."

"I mean . . ." She tilts her head to the side, her curls bouncing around her chubby cheeks. "What's the secret?"

"You know that Holden was trying to win that VR head-set prototype, right?" Ant nods, so I continue. "Well, since he didn't get it, Holden and I are making something for Trevor so he can feel like—like he's not always in the hospital. We're trying to make our own VR headset, and we need help from his friends."

Her eyes light up. "How can I help?"

"How about you text me the next time you and any of his other friends get together?" I give her my phone number. "We want to know what you guys like to do and we want to include people he'd be happy or surprised to see."

She smiles. "When would you be giving it to him?"

"Before the end of December." If I recall, Trevor's birthday is December twelfth anyway. It'll make a great gift *and* give me time to piece together the glasses and documentary. My deadline is just four days after. It'll be a tight squeeze adding the reveal, but if I have all the other footage filmed and edited, it'll be more of an insert job than an edit.

"A birthday present?"

"You're reading my mind, Ant." I pause, debating if I want to ask. "And maybe, if you want, you could mention to Trevor about me interviewing him? Kind of strange to not have an interview from one of his siblings, but I'd understand if he doesn't want to be on camera or doesn't feel up to it."

She smiles. "I think I could get him to agree."

We wrap up the interview at the same time Holden starts screaming in shocked anger. Libby rushes to the room to quiet him, warning that she doesn't want to have to kick him out again for disturbing the other kids. Ant and I watch as they go head to head and then play each other, and then the winners of each game—Trevor and Ant, because they spend more time playing this game—battle each other. Ant doesn't award Trevor any pity points and totally decimates him, shaking her hands in the air like the sore winner she is.

Holden thinks I'm in the bathroom.

If he were paying more attention, he'd wonder why the hell I need my camera for that. But he's not paying attention; instead he's consistently getting his ass handed to him by freshmen in a game of something-or-other.

I approach the circular desk where Libby shuffles paperwork, humming to some song on the radio behind her.

"Hi, Libby." I offer a smile that she reluctantly returns.

"Can I help you?"

"Actually, yeah. I was hoping I could speak to Trevor's doctor?"

She stiffens, halfway out of her seat. "Is he okay?"

"Oh my god, he's fine. I'm sorry. He's totally fine. I just had a question for them, if they're not busy."

Libby settles back into her seat and flips through some stapled sheets of paper. "I mean, they're doctors, so they're kind of always busy, but . . . let me see. Dr. Elmore isn't on duty yet, but Dr. Solomon's shift ends in a few minutes. I can see if she's got a second."

"Please. I'll wait." I backtrack to a stiff seat in the waiting room and keep my eyes on the hallway leading to Trevor's room. Holden agreed to be the gatekeeper of the Trevor information, so the last thing I need is him finding out I'm digging into things myself.

Dr. Solomon arrives a moment later, her Avengers scrubs under her long white jacket the first thing I notice. She stops at the desk, but Libby points at me.

I stand and offer my hand. I mean to introduce myself, but what comes out is, "Is that the standard-issue uniform?"

She looks down at her clothes, a piece of prematurely gray hair falling across her forehead. "My scrubs? Unfortunately not. If they were, I wouldn't have had to pay so much for them."

"I'm Saine Sinclair. I'm a friend of Trevor Michaels." I hold up my camera. "I'm making a documentary and was hoping you had five minutes for an interview?"

She glances uneasily at the camera. "I'm sorry, but I can't give out specific information about a patient. It violates HIPAA—you know, patient confidentiality."

I feel my chance slipping between my fingers. "Is there a way we can just speak vaguely about the type of leukemia he has? No specifics about Trevor himself?"

"Possibly." She brushes aside that stray hair. "What are your questions?"

After getting her to say on film who she is and that she consents, I fire them off and she gives me textbook answers, no emotions, just things I could Google myself if I couldn't fall asleep and needed to bore myself. It's frustrating, but probably the best I'm going to get. As we're wrapping up, I do something

I'm not supposed to. It's against the unspoken code of documentarians, morally gray as fuck, and I know I shouldn't do it—but if only the Temple University admissions department is going to see it . . .

"Okay, thank you." I pretend to hit the record button, so she thinks I've stopped, and I fold my arms across my chest, the camera angled at her face as best as I can manage, even though I'll most likely use this as a voiceover. "Off the record"—a downright lie—"is Trevor going to be okay?"

"It changes day by day." She smiles weakly. "It's hard to watch sometimes, but the good days make it worth it, and there seem to be more good than bad lately."

"Is there . . . I mean, just tell it to me straight. Is there a chance he could die?" I'm looking for the logical answer. The *Well, duh, it's a statistical fact that everyone dies* answer. I'm the worst, but she is the best.

"Everyone dies eventually." She sets a hand gently on my elbow. "His chances are probably higher than yours, but it doesn't mean we give up hope. We're all really hopeful for Trevor. He's a fighter and things are looking better each day."

With a squeeze, she lets go. "If you'll excuse me, I need to go. I hope your documentary turns out well."

Once she's rounded the corner and her footsteps retreat down the hall, I finish recording, feeling only a little guilty. She said he'll most likely be okay and I refuse to believe anything else, but stories about overcoming cancer play well; there are built-in stakes. I can work with this—at least I'm not faking the story anymore.

Nope. and friends

Today 11:41 AM

Kayla

Heeeeyyyyy

11:41 AM

DMS

Thanks for the reminder

11:41 AM

DMS has left the group chat.

Ew. Bye bitch

11:45 AM

Corrine

Good riddance, honestly

11:46 AM

Juniper

Should I have left the chat instead?

11:47 AM

Corrine

NO

11:47 AM

Juniper

But all of you were friends with him first . . .

11:48 AM

                                        Now we're finally free.

                                                    11:49 AM

Kayla

Well. Not quite. But we'll figure it out. Will I see you guys at
Blackout tomorrow night?

11:50 AM

Juniper

Thanks :)

11:51 AM

I'll definitely be there! I've never gone

11:51 AM

Corrine

You are in for an experience, Juniper

11:52 AM

NINETEEN

I'm kind of in a funk, which happens sometimes when I'm doing a lot of work on the computer, but I have a ton of footage to sort through after spending five hours with Ant and her friends while they bowled and played pool. By the end of my editing, I'm having to constantly remind myself of what I'm working on, the headset footage or the documentary. I think the Blackout party—a big bonfire in the woods with lots of music, dancing, and strobe lights—might be just the thing to help break me out of this funk, but, at the same time, I don't want to force myself to be social. Don't want to put a smile on my face when my eyes sting from too much artificial light.

But . . . between the contest, the documentary, and the headset footage, I've been spending a lot of time separated from my friends.

I save my file, add a copy to my external hard drive, and then reluctantly start putting together an outfit for the party. I'm sure I'll feel fine once I get there. It's just one of those things where the dread of doing the activity is much worse than the actual activity. Like putting on a bra just for the sole purpose of going to Neato Burrito for takeout.

Despite the chill, I throw on a black dress with sheer black tights and black ankle boots and, I don't know, maybe I'm over-killing it with all the black, so I line my mouth in red to balance it out.

Bagel rockets into my room from the hallway and leaps onto the stool by my bed and then onto the mattress to bark once at my window.

Okay, so that's, like, not terrifying at all.

"What's wrong with you?" I glance out the window, but it's after eight o'clock and the pitch-black darkness stares back at me.

He barks once more and then rolls onto his side, exposing his belly to the window, like a little bitch recognizing his alpha. Something hits the glass and I jump, my heart hammering in my chest. Holden stands outside my window, a smirk on his face and his elbow against the window.

"Can you give me a hand? Both of mine are full." He shifts to show me a six-pack of alcoholic root beer and a pizza box.

I unlock the window and push it up, but stop him when he tries to hand me the items, my heart racing a little. "What are you doing here?" I could probably use my mom's anti-fun health agenda to stop whatever is happening right now.

He looks between the drinks and food. "Delivery?"

"I'm going out." I resist the urge to immediately let him in, even though I used to do just that when we were kids. How would Corrine feel if she knew her ex-boyfriend was sneak-ing through my window with beer? It wouldn't even matter that he wasn't invited. Wouldn't matter that Heart Emoji Logan Heart Emoji would be at Blackout tonight to distract her. "To a party."

"But I'm bringing a party to you."

I accept the pizza and lay it on my bed next to Bagel. "A lot of help you are," I mumble at him, poking him in the stomach.

Holden climbs into my bedroom, his long legs getting tangled in my curtains. "I remember this being much easier when I was smaller."

"That's because it was." I take the drinks from him so he can free himself. "Again, what are you doing here?"

"Ta-da!" He stands straight, flailing his arms out. "Oh, come on. You didn't actually want to go to Blackout. The people. The anxiety of the cops showing up at any moment to bust it. The noise, the smoke, finding a ride there and back. It's just a hassle and you hate people."

"And what are you, if not people?"

"A goddamn delight."

"What exactly was your plan here?" I watch him take off his jacket, revealing a tight, plain white T-shirt that definitely got the memo about his arms that I hadn't prior to seeing him at the gym. He slings the jacket over my chair and faces me.

"Hang out. I didn't want to go to the party either." He flops onto my bed and finally gives Bagel what he wants by petting him. "Who's my good boy, Bagel? Yes, it's you. Bagel Boy. My little Bagel Boy, Seamus. Shame-shame." He lets Bagel lick his cheek.

"Okay, this has to stop if we're going to have a conversation." I pick Bagel up and place him outside my room, shutting the door on his pathetic and adorable face. "Taj was busy?"

"Taj is at the party with Nita."

I smile grimly. "Love your honesty when it comes to my second-best status."

"My twelve-year-old sister also had plans."

I point to the window. "Get out."

He grins, reaching for the pizza box with little effort. He opens it and the smell of melted cheese fills the room. "I come with gifts and you're going to kick me out?"

It only takes a second for me to recognize the additional smell of "The Devil's Dinner," what my mother calls a supreme pizza, because creativity has never been her thing. I haven't had it since before my grandma died because my mom, on the off chance she's down for pizza, only likes cheese—even when I remind her it has vegetables!

I got my terrible taste in food from my grandma, if we're being totally honest.

"Fine, you can stay, but I am going to the party." I grab my phone from my desk and find the group chat blowing up with questions of my whereabouts. Every single one of them asks if I need a ride, so I assume they're waiting for my answer before partaking in some drinking.

"You're gonna leave me here?" He takes a bite, hissing at how hot it is.

"Yeah, see yourself out the window—" I turn from the door to face him. "Why the window, by the way?"

He shrugs, pizza in his mouth. "Your mom has cameras on all the doors." He chews. "Which, what the hell? There's no camera covering the only outside entrance to your room?

What's the point, then? You're unguarded."

"I'll be sure to let her know that you have those concerns as the only person to scope out the house and then break into my bedroom. I'm sure she'll thank you."

"That would be nice since it doesn't seem like you're going to say it." He kicks his shoes off and then twists the cap off one of the beers. "I'll probably just be here when you get back."

I sigh. "If you're waiting for an invite to the party, it's not going to come."

"I'm the one with a car. You'd be lucky to be invited to the party by me."

We duke it out in the Staring Contest Battle Arena. He wins—I remember he always used to win because he has unnaturally wet eyeballs. After the first couple of times we had "playdates" as kids, my mom sat me down and asked if I was bullying him because he always seemed on the verge of crying.

"Fine," I say heavily. "You got me. I don't want to go to the party." I sit on my bed and he turns the pizza box toward me. I pick up a slice and take a bite, kicking off my own shoes. "What am I supposed to tell my friends?"

"Tell them you're staying in tonight and . . ." He stares at the wall. "Is that—" His eyes flick to mine in alarm. "Why is the *Catfish* guy riding a killer whale on your wall?"

"Tilikum."

"Bless you."

I narrow my eyes. "Don't steal my bit. It's not nearly as cute when you do it."

He bites his lip playfully. "But it is *somewhat* cute, right?"

I refuse to focus on how the answer to that is an undeniable yes, so I go for the informative response. "It'd be cuter if it wasn't insensitive. Tilikum is a Native American word, and also the name of the infamous captive orca." I try to decipher how it must look to someone who's never seen it before. Yes, my grandma painted Nev Schulman riding Tilikum into the sunset on my bedroom wall. It's really not as weird as it sounds, especially when you take into consideration that the original idea included Gypsy Rose Blanchard and JonBenét Ramsey—but my mom drew the line, saying it was too morbid to wake up to every day and that she refused to raise *that much* of a weirdo. I smile, remembering how my grandma laughed every time she worked on it. "Those two documentaries are what got me interested in film."

"But what's the whale one?"

I fake-choke. "Excuse me? You've never seen *Blackfish*?"

"You have *Catfish* and *Blackfish* on your wall?" He takes a huge bite of his pizza. "What the hell is with the fish?"

"No, don't change the subject." I face him. "You haven't seen it? We're watching it right now and ruining your childhood love of aquariums and zoos."

"I made a mistake coming here, didn't I?"

"Yes, you did." I pull the DVD from its case and prepare to change his life. "And I'll make sure you regret it and learn your lesson."

Afterward, when we're bored of spiked root beer, Holden and I raid my mother's wine fridge. I've had enough to drink that I pay no attention to my constantly buzzing phone, or the time, and this is how we end up playing a drunken version of the

Whisper Challenge, or whatever it's fucking called, where one person wears headphones playing music and the other whispers something that the original person needs to repeat.

Holden's mouth moves but I have no clue what he's saying. I never have any clue what he's saying. I am exceptionally bad at this game and it probably won't hit me until I'm sober that the only reason he's good at it is because he's most likely *not* listening to music during his turns.

"I have no clue, just say it." I rip the headphones off my ears.

"Are you going to the dance?"

I blink, the alcohol mixing in my stomach. "Was that what you were saying or are you asking me?"

"Both. Are you going to the winter formal?" He spins a little in my desk chair.

"That's a big no." I adjust my tights, wishing I had kicked Holden out earlier to change into leggings. But I'm at the point in my drunkenness that I don't care anymore, and he's not going to see anything, so I just shimmy them down and kick them off my feet. "I can't dance. I mean, I can do a dance if it's *choreographed*, but I can't just dance to dance. That feels too, I don't know."

"Vulnerable?"

He knows me. He knows me he knows me he knows me. Too well.

He breaks the eye contact between us and stands up, pushing the chair under my desk, and starts dancing with reckless abandon. I'm embarrassed for him.

"You just gotta feel it," he says, wiggling his shoulders,

sliding his socks across the hardwood. I'm not sure that he would be doing this if he were sober, but then again, I'm still getting to know this new version of him.

"There's no music playing." My cheeks heat and it's uncomfortable to watch him. To see how little he cares that *I* care he's dancing.

"Technically there is, in your headphones, but mostly the music is coming from my heart."

"More likely it's coming from a tumor in your brain; you look ridiculous." It's not until I finish hissing the last *S* in that sentence that I remember his little brother has fucking cancer.

Thankfully, he ignores the darker connotation. "You too could look ridiculous for a low, low price." He offers me his hand.

"How dare you assume my dignity isn't worth more money." I push away his hand. "Seriously. No."

"You went to prom."

"Did you see me dance?" I take a swig of Moscato straight from the green-tinted bottle.

He frowns. "I guess not."

I spent the night pre-car-accident drinking and making out with Monica Carmichael's date—whom she had abandoned after some fight over him losing her cell phone—and trying not to think about how Elijah and I broke up the week before. I danced in a bathroom stall, by myself.

"You're a cheerleader, you have rhythm, we just need to find the right dance for you." He yanks on my arm until I stand and then leads me into the living room. "We need more space."

He deposits me in front of the couch, runs back to my room, and returns with my laptop in his hands. He places it on the coffee table, brings up YouTube, and searches "dance scenes in movies." I'm being generous; what he actually searched had many typos.

We spend the next hour falling into a YouTube hole, finishing my mom's wine, and seeing what dances are the most fun to actually do and not just watch. We land on one from some awful-looking movie called *Napoleon Dynamite* that we only found because we read an article about *Fortnite* dances and their origins.

I doubt I'll remember this in the morning when my head is pounding and my throat feels raw, but that's what the video is for—I'm not sure when I started recording, but I am and it feels fun and like maybe we're actually learning the dance. We run through it a few times, Holden next to me, and when he turns away, I wrap my arms around his stomach and squeeze, my face pressed to his back. His stomach tenses beneath my touch, but then he stops moving, lays his hands over mine, and squeezes back.

TWENTY

I've never used the word *ruckus* before, but there's a ruckus in the house when I get home from school on Tuesday. I catch a whiff of my mother's chocolate-scented candle she burns when she's convincing herself she's being productive or trying to hide a stench, usually while scrubbing her sneakers with a bleach-soaked toothbrush.

"Mom?"

Bagel starts barking from somewhere near the ruckus.

"Mom?"

"In Grandma's room!" More ruckus.

It sounds like something heavy being shifted on the hardwood, items being dropped, the little *plink plink plink* of Bagel's paws as he trails along. I kiss my hand, press it to the living room mural, and then head to my grandma's room. I can't enter because my mom has a tower of haphazardly stacked boxes blocking the way.

"Hello?"

"Hey," my mom says, her face appearing in the crack between boxes and door frame. Her dark hair is pinned back, several strands trying to escape. Our hair is naturally the same color, but before the school year started, I dyed mine a charcoal color. It just felt like a better fit for my mood. "How was school?"

"What are you doing?" My eye catches on the words "DONATE" and "STORAGE" written messily on the boxes in faded black Sharpie. "Donate? What are you donating?"

"Just some of Grandma's things. Art supplies, clothes—"

"You can't get rid of her things." I pull the top box marked "DONATE" from the pile, holding it to my chest. It was one thing to accept we'd one day move out of the house, but we're not also getting rid of her belongings.

"Saine," my mom sighs, pushing the tower of boxes aside carefully. It's taller than her. "She's not coming back for any of it."

"Maybe *I* wanted some of her clothes, or her supplies. She was my grandmother. You can't just claim full responsibility for her things as if she had no other family."

She cocks her head to the side. "The boxes full of donations aren't anything sentimental."

"Maybe to *you*." I set the box on the floor and open it. The first things I see are several unopened boxes of soap, and memories start hitting me at the same speed that the scent does. Painting on Sundays with a record picked at random blasting through the house. Milkshake Mondays on which my grandma would randomly pull me out of school for a "family emergency" and then we'd get several milkshakes between the two of us and sit at a park to enjoy them. Building tents in the living room and staying up all night watching the worst things we could find on Netflix. Trips to the art supplies store in our pajamas. Cooking three-course meals at one in the morning. All the things I've been carefully and gently pushing to the back burner of my metaphorical stove of unhappiness.

"Saine. It's soap and paint."

"I can use both. I'll use all of it. Why would we donate this stuff when you're clipping coupons in your sleep trying to afford it?" I close the box without investigating further. "And what are you putting in storage? Maybe I don't want it in storage. Maybe I have space for it in my room."

I start getting this itchy feeling under my skin seeing her in this room, with boxes and packaging tape. "Don't pack anything else. I want to go through it first."

Most likely I'll just take everything from her room and put it into mine, but at least then it's safe. How would my mom feel knowing that once she died, I just started giving her stuff away or moving it out of my sight so I didn't have to think about her, so I didn't have to be *inconvenienced* with grief?

No. No, this is not acceptable.

Her mouth shrinks into a thin line. "You have until next Monday."

"And then what happens?"

She slides out the gap she made by the door. "Then I pack it all up myself and start painting."

"Painting?" I follow her to the kitchen, where she gathers bread, mayo, mustard, and ham for her sad dinner. "What do you mean by painting?"

My mother was never the artistic type. She likes logical things like books and maps and math. Things that are formulaic and complete and informational. She doesn't art. It's why my grandma and I meshed so well. We are like-minded people. We see past what's there. We feel things harder. We create.

"The walls." She spreads the condiments on the bread. "I'm painting them all white so they're fresh for the photos. Or maybe gray."

"Photos?" I feel like she's speaking a different language than me, like I'm but a mere human being and she's from some distant planet outside my galaxy.

"For the Realtor." She places several layers of ham on the bread before dropping the second piece on top and taking a bite. "For the internet."

"I'm sorry," I say, stepping forward with Corrine's signature Intense Eyes™. "Are you telling me our house is already on the market? We don't have a place to move if the house sells."

The house can't sell. It's not ready. I'm not ready.

"I don't have a lot of spare time, so I'm getting things done one by one when I can. First up is cleaning—which, by the way, means your room, too—and then painting, and during all of that, apartment searching." She looks exhausted just saying her to-do list.

"I think you're getting ahead of yourself." I finally pull my backpack off my shoulders and sit at the table. "How about I take over cleaning?"

"I want it done *this* century."

"Let me do it on my own time, at my own pace, or else you

can do it on your own time, at your own pace, but with me distracting you and secretly going through everything even after you've gone through it, just to double-check." I stare her down. "It'll take twice as long and be seven times as annoying."

She finishes her sandwich, rips a paper towel off the roll, and wipes her mouth. "We'll do it together. At the same time. At the same pace." She raises an eyebrow. "Deal?"

"Deal," I lie.

It doesn't hurt to do some additional packing, to take the things I know she'll want me to get rid of because of Logic, but I'll want to hold on to because Emotions. I'm mature enough to recognize this. I'm just not mature enough to listen to reason, even when I know it's, well, reasonable.

I deliver a burrito to Corrine for her lunch break at the thrift shop and mentally subtract eight dollars from the total I owe her. Because she's under eighteen, if she works five hours or more—which she does three times a week, from four o'clock to nine o'clock—she has to get a thirty-minute, unpaid "lunch" break.

The shop, unoriginally named Thrifty, is owned by two twentysomething ladies who occasionally hold fashion shows, charity food drives, and the best BOGO sales this side of the Susquehanna. They even let Nope. film their video for "Wasted Youth Starter Kit" here after-hours. The cheetah-print chaise lounge with mysterious red stain that Kayla serenaded the camera on sold the day she posted the video. There is absolutely no correlation between these two things, but we like to pretend there is.

Corrine is the only person in the shop when I enter. She's hunched over the checkout counter, her phone bright in front of her face.

"Food!" She rushes around the counter and grabs the bag from my hands.

"You're welcome." I yank the bag back, grab my own burrito, and then let her practically eviscerate the bag trying to get to her own pound of tinfoil-wrapped bliss.

"I didn't say thank you."

"You should have," I say, tossing the empty bag on the counter for our trash. "Your mother would be ashamed of your manners."

"There are worse things she could be ashamed of me for." She positions herself behind the counter and unwraps her burrito, taking a huge bite.

"Are you the only one here?" I settle behind the counter, pulling up a stool.

"Yeah. Marisa's son got sick at gymnastics and she had to pick him up." She shrugs. "It's been dead, so it's fine. Plus, I get paid an extra half an hour now *and* I get a burrito."

"What happens if you need an adult for something?"

She pauses. "I guess I wait until she gets back."

"What if you have your own emergency?"

"Oh my god, Saine, I don't know." She swallows. "But now you're here. You're eighteen. You're an adult."

We stare at each other in silence for a second.

"Or I could call Marisa if I needed to," she says, taking a huge bite.

"Yes. Smart. I like that better."

"How's the documentary? You didn't need to film or something tonight?" She stares at her burrito like it's the only thing in this world. I barely even notice the edge to her voice.

"Not tonight. It's going well, though. It's not a total trash fire." Earlier this week, Holden and I took a drive around town while blasting music through the crackling minivan speakers. We pretended it was summer and put our hands out the windows, letting them ride the airwaves. A GoPro captured both of us in our seats while I filmed the point-of-view footage.

"Of course not. You're brilliant." She smiles. "It's due in December, right?"

"Yes, ma'am." I printed out monthly calendars for November and December, and marked all the milestones I should be hitting by what dates if I want to have this done in time. The clock is ticking.

"Oh good; you have tons of time, then. Even more since you're not hanging out with us or anything . . ." She raises an eyebrow. "We missed you. Or, you know, I did. Kayla and Juniper kind of sidelined me."

I nearly drop my burrito. "Did they hook up?"

"What? No?" Her eyes widen. "Does Kayla like Juniper?"

I rush to cover up the truth. "That's how *you* made it sound."

"I just meant that they were talking band stuff and taking selfies." She narrows her eyes at me. "You know something."

"I know very many things." I throw my balled-up tinfoil into the trash and walk into the aisles. "Like, for example, I know that my mother is basically trying to paint over the blemish that her mother's death left on our life."

I don't have to see her to know she clams up. Corrine wasn't exactly there for me when my grandma died—like, not emotionally. I get it, death isn't the easiest topic to just talk about on a random Thursday over cafeteria tacos, but death makes Corrine uncomfortable to a whole other degree than meeting parents does. She practically shuts down, folds into herself, and disappears into a little sliver of the space-time continuum.

"That was deep," she jokes.

"She's already started packing up her stuff and wants to paint over her murals—I can't let that happen." I drag my fingers over the clothes hanging beside me, but I'm not really seeing them.

"Maybe it's her way of moving on?"

"That doesn't work for me, though, because my way of moving on is not moving on, not yet. She can't *force* me to move on just because she wants to. Like, I don't know, they go hand in hand because we live together, live with all her stuff, in her house. It's only been a few months." My throat feels swollen and the prick in the corner of my eyes makes me pause. *Shit, I want to hug her so bad. Just see her one more time.* The worst part is that if I did see her right now, I'd probably just complain about her daughter to her.

The last minute is the most I've gotten to talk about this with someone other than my mom in a long time, and even though I'm still pissed and distraught, I'm also relieved. It's like a weight has been lifted to just come outright and say *Stop, I'm not ready yet, don't leave me behind.*

She shrugs sheepishly when I finally glance at her. "I'm sorry."

And then my relief *poofs* away. This is about as far as this conversation will go. Once Corrine says she's sorry, that's the wall. We've hit it at full speed and there's nowhere else for her to go, nothing else she can say. "I'm sorry" is the last thing you say to someone when you're sympathizing with them, when you're hoping they'll move on to something less suncomfortable.

I wish I could fucking cry—or not cry, whatever—to my best friend and get more than just a faux-placid response. I wish I could scream at her that it's okay to feel the hard, painful emotions, that she's safe with me and I want to be safe with her. I wanted to scream that at her back when she and Holden broke up, and I extra want to now.

I pluck out a maroon velvet dress on a whim, the last thing that my finger touched, just so I don't have to look at her with disappointment in my eyes. I know she's not, like, a therapist, but it would be nice if I could talk about these things without her completely shutting down and shutting me out.

"That's cute," she says, coming around the counter. I can hear the relief in her voice, like water filling a cup. "Are you going to wear it to the dance?"

I think of Holden and me, drunk in my living room, learning dances. I get a phantom whiff of his cologne or body spray or laundry detergent and think of pressing myself against him. My cheeks heat. When did he start smelling that good? And before he crawled out of my bedroom window before sunrise, he hugged me in a way he never has, his arms wrapped tightly around my waist instead of his hands spread out across my back. It was so familiar and right.

"I don't think I'm going." I slide the dress back into its spot on the rack. It probably wouldn't have fit me anyway. I'm not one-size-fits-all size.

"But the funds are going to be split to help some of my clubs. You have to go."

I side-eye her, knowing I could just give her the ten-dollar admittance fee and call it even, no dressing up or painful high heels necessary. "Says who? Logan, who you'll have ditched me for at the dance anyway?"

"He'll be there, and I agreed to save several dances for him, but we're not going together. I told him I didn't want our first romantic outing to be at a school dance. It's cliché."

"Well, regardless, I wouldn't want to intrude on *that*."

She bites her bloodred lip. "Look, I was hoping I wouldn't have to say this, but you've been bailing on, like, *everything* lately and you need to go to the dance to prove to your friends that you haven't been body-snatched or something."

"You think an alien would come to Earth and pick me of all people to body-snatch?"

"I don't pretend to know the way an alien's mind would work, Saine." She tugs the dress from the rack and places it against my chest. "That color looks great on you and it's super cute and you have to buy it." She snatches it away from me just as I'm about to grab it. "Wait, no. My idea, my money. I'm going to buy it. A super early Christmas present."

I sigh. There's never any use fighting her on something she's set her mind on. "Maybe I should try it on first?"

"Why?" She finds the tag. "It's only five dollars."

She spins toward the register and stops a few feet away,

plucking a T-shirt from the rack that says *Try back tomorrow*.
"Kayla would love this. Right?"

And, just like that, we're done discussing my house/mom/
grandma issues; we're done discussing whether or not I'm
going to the dance or buying the dress. If it makes Corrine's
eyes tickle with tears or make her feel any type of way that she
doesn't want to feel, she's over it.

I kind of think maybe I'm over it, too.

Holden

Today 12:22 AM

Yeah I guess I'm going to the dance

12:22 AM

Sweet. See you there. I'll be the one with the sick dance moves
making everyone jealous.

12:23 AM

TWENTY-ONE

The main perk of being a designated driver is that I don't have to squeeze into a school bathroom stall with three other girls, share a plastic bottle covered in various shades of lipstick, and pretend to like straight vanilla vodka for the sake of getting drunk in order to tolerate a dance I don't even want to be at.

For what will probably end up being at least fifteen minutes, Corrine, Kayla, and Juniper have left me standing against the gym wall while couples grind on each other to songs I think I know the words to, just for an hour's buzz. Other people would look creepy with a camera in a dimly lit school dance, but I think I'd look creepier without it. Just standing here. By myself. Miserable. At least I have purpose this way. And don't look as pathetic as I feel.

I gather B-roll to help set the scene of high school life for Holden in my documentary, but realize quickly that it could also work as headset footage of what Trevor's missing. Assuming Trevor would be a wallflower at dances. I sweep the Technicolor dance floor and zoom into Macy's happy face as she shouts the words of the upbeat song vibrating the room, capture Mr. Nitt and Mr. Roland flirting, and then stop the whole way on the other side of the gym where Devon Miles Smith stands with some other guys, all of them looking completely pissed off to be here. As if it were mandatory for them like Corrine made it for me.

Someone steps in front of my lens—like, super close so all I can see is darkness—and I prepare to yell at whoever it is, but I'm rendered slightly speechless when I see Holden. He's wearing a black button-down shirt rolled up to his elbows, black slacks that were most likely tailored for him for a wedding or a funeral or something considering how well they fit, and shiny black dress shoes with red thread for a pop of color, and his hair is perfectly curly, reflecting some of the blue mood lighting.

He smiles. "Been looking for you."

"Why?" It stops me in my tracks, even though I should have been looking for him. The documentary, the headset, all excusable reasons to have sought him out. And yet, none of those are his excuse.

"To hang out."

My heart starts thumping into overdrive. If Corrine is ever going to leave that bathroom, I know it's going to be now. I'm not doing anything wrong; why do I feel like I've been caught red-handed? "Taj and Mara busy?"

He dips his hands into his pockets and laughs. "Mara is at a sleepover, for your information. And Taj—" He glances over his shoulder. "Taj is attempting to break-dance while Nita pretends not to know him."

"I'm here with Corrine." I don't know why I say it. It's not like he couldn't assume that. Maybe a part of me hopes he'll scurry off, take the hint that we can't be seen together.

"Is she your date?"

"Yeah, jealous? I bet when she was your date, she never forced you to go to dances and then abandoned you for back-washed vodka."

He stares at me, a bemused smile on his face.

"Okay, so she did that," I say with a laugh, "but at least you got something out of it like a make-out session. I'm just going to have bleeding feet." I lift one leg to show him my heels. Black, like his outfit.

"Ditch the shoes. I've seen like twenty girls stumbling out of theirs."

One of the strobe lights flashes over us and it feels like a spotlight catching me mid-something-I-shouldn't-be-doing. I sink back closer to the wall. Unfortunately, Holden follows.

"And what do I do once I've done that?"

He offers me his hand. "Let's dance."

Something explodes in my chest and rains down into my gut. "I told you. I don't dance."

He nods to my camera. "Pretty sure we have footage that disproves that." His eyes widen. "Oh, hey. I forgot. Vice and Virtual emailed me. They want me to do one last interview for their web series. I figured you'd want to be there when I do."

"Where are we going this time?"

"They're just doing a video chat. We can do it at my house."

"Wow, Saine, you pounce quick." Devon Miles Smith joins us.

I narrow my eyes at him. "Excuse me?"

"You guys are going to 'do it at his house'?" He cuts to Holden. "You did date Corrine Baker, right? I know she's talking to Logan now, but wait until the body's cold before screwing her best friend, maybe?"

It's hard to tell in this lighting, but I'm pretty sure Holden's face has lost what little color he had to start.

"Did you want something, Devon Miles Shithead?" I ask, putting my camera back in my bag and pushing it under the table with all our jackets and bags.

"Yeah. Seen Juniper?" He looks around me, searching for her and not giving me the time of day. "I saw you guys walk in together. Where is she?"

Holden glances between us. "I guess I'll, uh, see you later."

"She's in the bathroom," I tell Devon, watching Holden walk away and feeling . . . disappointed? Relieved?

He slicks back his already slicked-back hair. "She's been in the bathroom for like ten minutes."

"If you know everything, why did you ask?" I try to keep track of Holden's progress through the dancing crowd, but lose him when a song makes everyone scream and throw their hands up.

He rolls his eyes. "Can you go in there and get her for me?"

"No. She's busy."

"I'll just text Kayla, then." He pulls out his phone, but I cover it with my hand. "What?"

"What do you want to talk to her about?"

"I want to work things out."

"There's not much to work out. You're an asshole and she's too good for you."

He furrows his brow. "What did I ever do to you?"

"You were a jerk to my friend. That's enough reason for me to not like you." I cross my arms. "I don't care if this makes things awkward; I'm on Juniper's side."

He gestures wildly. "You can't be on Juniper's side *and* Kayla's best friend."

"Why not?"

"Because Kayla is in a band with me. *Kayla* can't be Juniper's friend. She has to pick—"

Something happens in the room and I can't tell immediately what it is; I just know that something is different. I look at the dance floor, trying to figure out what made the energy shift, but it takes about ten seconds for me to realize that the song I'm hearing is the one from that movie, *Napoleon Dynamite*. The dance song.

A squad of goose bumps zooms up my arms and that's when I see him. The fool.

Holden breaks through the confused—but still dancing— crowd and stands on the cusp of our classmates. He shrugs when we lock eyes.

And then he dances. By himself. Without a care in the world.

He dances our dance. To our song. And it's soooooo embarrassing, but I can't leave him hanging, subject to all sorts of glances, laughter, and imitation. Plus, it kind of helps me escape Devon, even though it means dancing in public to a song no one really knows.

I walk away from Devon, ignore him shouting my name, and stop in front of Holden, mid-dance.

"This doesn't count as real dancing," I say with a huff. "That's the only reason I'm here."

"I don't know what you're talking about," he says, swinging his body this way and that way, like an inflatable person outside a car dealership. "I didn't ask the DJ to play this."

"Sure. Because this is just a song they regularly keep in their high school dance playlist."

He bites his lip. "I saved you from Devon, didn't I?"

"Shut up and dance."

After the winter formal, we end up in the parking lot of Sheetz, as most bored people do in central PA. Kayla and Corrine, despite the forty-degree weather, lie on the hood of Kayla's car eating French fries while Juniper argues with Logan about the proper pronunciation of "GIF." Apparently, she has very strong feelings about it. (It's pronounced like the peanut butter, if you ask her—though, I don't recommend it.) Logan doesn't care how it's pronounced, but it's clear he enjoys seeing her passionate side.

I sit in the passenger seat of Kayla's car, door open to let out some music for the small group of us accumulated, and film everyone. A few guys two cars over are, for whatever reason, physically fighting, but not in the way where anyone gets hurt. More cars that were previously filling our school parking lot pull in, and one of them is Holden's beat-up minivan. I watch as he, Nita, and Taj get out and go inside the store. More awkward than our choreographed dancing was the fact that after the song ended, we kind of just . . . parted ways.

My friends are preoccupied and I don't feel like being cold, so I head inside, content in knowing they can't go anywhere without me and the keys I have in my bag. There's maybe only a few more minutes until one of the Sheetz employees comes outside to tell us to stop loitering, so it doesn't seem bad to spend that time not being completely miserable.

I sidle up to Holden as he's debating snacks—protein bars or baked fruit pieces, *really*?—and nudge him. He seems genuinely surprised to see me and I'm genuinely surprised to see that he looks even better under these harsh fluorescent lights than he did in the darkness of our humid gym.

"Fancy seeing you here." I start filming him. "We should have gotten more footage at the dance."

"But the *lighting*," he says in mock agony. You can take the nerd away from the camera but not the camera away from the nerd, or whatever the saying is. "Can we film more tomorrow?"

"Yeah, we're almost done. Let's attack this thing." We texted the other night about what other footage we wanted to get for the VR part, and now that the list is complete, we just have to check off the items one by one. Hanging with friends? Check. High school dance? Semi-check.

He nods. "Balls to the wall."

"Never say that again. The mental image is just—no."

"I hated it as soon as it came out of my mouth." He grabs a few different flavors of protein bars. "Where's your date? Puking?"

"Stuffing her face, actually."

"Ah, the drunken binge *before* the puke."

"I can't wait to hold her hair back later as she tells me how sorry she is." We mean everything we say with care or, in my case, love, so I don't feel too badly about mocking Corrine's former routine with Holden.

"And you thought it was all—what did you say?—make-outs?"

"I dealt with Corrine's puke long before you ever did. Before she ever had a taste of booze, she was just a weak stomach on a roller coaster waiting to be hurled." I walk with him to the checkout counter, my shoe slipping on a squished French fry on the ground.

"Yes, but she never tried to kiss you after."

"Or did she?" But no, even drunk, Corrine's strictly into guys.

He gestures around us. "Did you want anything?"

"No, thanks. Logan bought us all food as a peace offering for stepping on Corrine's feet while dancing." I cringe. "I'm sorry for bringing him up. And for Devon."

He shrugs with a half smile on his face and hands the cashier a few dollars. He pockets the protein bars, and we walk to the small sitting area, passing Nita and Taj somewhere in the aisles. I can hear them over the music playing through the loudspeakers: Nita's arguing for sour cream and onion chips while Taj is arguing for plain chips with French onion dip.

"You realize you still have your camera in my face." He says it like a statement.

"I hadn't, actually." I set the camera down on the table between us, but let it record.

"Too used to viewing the world through your protective lens?" He pulls out a protein bar and rips it open. "Let's see how you like it."

He takes a bite and grabs my camera, chewing with a smile on his face as I reach out to steal it back.

"No—"

"Saine Sinclair," he says in a deeper voice than normal, "tell me your deep, dark, dirty secrets."

"You're bad at this." I try to grab the camera again, but he just leans back in his chair, out of my reach. Damn these short arms of mine.

"Okay, what am I supposed to do?" He watches me through the display screen even though I'm only a few feet in front of him. Is this how detached I look when I film people? I know I definitely don't stare at the display with such a smarmy smile, that's for sure.

"I'm not helping you torture me."

"*Torture* you?" he laughs. "I'm doing no such thing; you're being dramatic."

I cross my arms. "You know I don't like being in front of a camera."

"Yeah." He takes another bite. "Why is that?"

I shrug.

"I know why." He points the camera back at himself. "Vuuuuuulneeeeeeraaaaablllllllle."

Again, I try to steal back the camera, but my fingers barely graze the device. The thought of it falling between both our hands and crashing to pieces on the sticky floor is the only reason I retreat—footage that can be deleted isn't worth the damage fee PSH has. I knew if I was filming tonight there would be terrible lighting conditions, so I definitely couldn't use my own camera. It's Post–Potato Era quality, but it wouldn't have half a chance in hell of recording anything in the school gym.

"What do you want to be when you grow up, Saine?" he asks.

"A filmmaker, obviously. I want to go to Temple and make documentaries."

He raises an eyebrow. "Look at you with your prepared answer. Why?"

"Why what?"

"Why do you want to make documentaries?" He finishes his bar and crumples the wrapper.

"I just . . . do?" The summer between seventh and eighth grade, when I was no longer friends with Holden, and Corrine was at some culty entrepreneur camp, my grandma insisted I watch less *Jersey Shore* on Hulu and more . . . anything else that was somewhat educational. We watched three documentaries that same day and then I kind of spiraled. It was powerful to know one film could shape my entire way of viewing a topic. There's always an angle with a documentary. It's trying to lead you to a very particular conclusion. There's a black–and–whiteness about it that you can't argue with. "Why do you want to be a photographer?"

He flips the camera on himself. "I want to be a photographer because I like capturing people at their most vulnerable and their most confident. I like being the one to show them how beautiful they are both ways. It makes me feel powerful." He turns the camera back to me. "Your turn."

"I don't want to play this game." I hold my hand out, but don't try to take the camera from him this time. He's going to hand it over, or else. "I ask the questions around here."

"I think you want to make movies because you like being in charge. You like the power, too. And I think—"

Heat tumbles in my gut. "I said I don't want to play."

"Ooh, play what?" Kayla comes out of nowhere and plops down on my lap, nuzzling into my hair. "I love you, Saine."

"I love you, too, Kayla," I say evenly. It's not her fault Holden has me on edge.

"Hey, Kayla," Holden says, angling the camera at her.

She straightens, smiling. She's not even buzzed anymore; her general positive vibe is just back in full force after some time with Juniper. "Hi, Holden. What's the game?"

"What do you want to do after you graduate?" he asks. "It's for the digital yearbook."

"I have to go to college, but once that's done, I want to tour the world and make music and change lives." She cups my cheeks. "Saine, will you document my band's success and tour with me so I never have to be without you and your cute little face?"

"Of course," I answer in a muffled voice, the pressure from her hands making it hard to move my jaw.

"There you guys are," Corrine says, dragging Juniper by the arm into the nook. She stops when she sees Holden. He points the camera at her regardless. "Hi. Sorry. Are we interrupting?"

"What do you guys want to do after school?" Kayla asks.

"I want to backpack across Europe!" Juniper says, sliding into the only other free chair at our table. "Mostly because I have no clue. It's ridiculous to think I should."

"Hey, I'm also going to travel the world," Kayla says, leaning so close to her that she nearly slides off my lap. My velvet dress—because, yes, it did fit—doesn't make it easier for her to sit still, so I put my hands on her hips to steady her. "You should come with me."

"What about you, Corrine?" Holden's fingers slide on the zoom button. "What are your plans?"

She glances at me, then him, and back to me. "I don't feel very good, Saine. Can you help me in the bathroom—"

She tosses her fries right there, her vomit nearly hitting my shoes.

"You were so close to the bathroom, Corrine. So close." I don't dare to stare mournfully at the door behind us.

"Screw you," she says weakly, wiping her mouth and smearing her lipstick.

I move Kayla from my lap and grab Corrine's elbow to lead her to the bathroom. "Not with that barf breath."

"Please don't let Logan see," she says. "He didn't see, did he?"

Holden stands, handing the camera to Juniper. "I'll go make sure he stays away until you're cleaned up."

"Thank you," she mews defeatedly.

By the time I'm done cleaning her up, which means washing her face and basically teaching her how to gargle and spit again like some kind of baby—if this isn't a PSA not to drink, or have kids, I don't know what would be—Kayla and Juniper had pretended to host a whole talk show called *When Sheetz Hits the Fan*, for my camera. Holden was nowhere to be found, but true to his word, Logan stayed away. He greets Corrine with a back rub and a water, and offers her a ride home. Despite not wanting their first date to be at a dance, it kind of still ends up like one.

TWENTY-TWO

Kayla and I have gotten ready for football games at Corrine's house countless times, but this is the first time there's been a guy present. My camera is safe in my bag, but it still feels like Logan's got one pointed at me from his spot at Corrine's desk, even though he's barely taken his eyes off her since driving us here from school.

"So, Logan," Kayla says, sitting on Corrine's bed across from him and fixing him with a serious look, "what—"

"Nope," Corrine cuts her off, capping her lipstick. "We're not doing that."

Logan winks at Kayla. "We'll talk later," he whispers.

"I look forward to it," she says, starting one of two big, messy braids. "If you're going to be around Corrine, you must be Friend Approved."

I look up from Corrine's vanity mirror and say, "We're very hard to impress."

"Leave him alone." Corrine shoves gently into my shoulder

and goes back to applying her eyeliner. "I approve of him and that's good enough."

"Actually," Logan starts, grabbing his backpack from the cream-colored floor. "While your approval *is* the only one that matters, I would like theirs."

Kayla gives Corrine a "told you so" look.

"But, to help convince them," Logan says, pulling a clipboard out of his bag, "I have this."

He hands it to Corrine, and I glance over her shoulder. Not very romantic, but who am I to judge someone else's love life? Mine is nonexistent.

"What is this?" Corrine asks. The paper attached to the clipboard has twenty or so names written in a column, all in different handwriting.

"People who approve of me dating you."

Corrine glances between Kayla and me, her cheeks pink, then meets Logan's gaze. "Are we dating? Officially?"

"I want to. I know you're used to collecting signatures to start clubs, so I thought I'd collect some to start this relationship. If you want."

"Oh dear god," Kayla says through laughter. "I've seen some pretty bizarre heterosexual things, but this turned out pretty cute."

Logan waits, desperation in his brown eyes. Corrine stands only to collapse in his lap, arms tight around his broad shoulders. She plants a kiss on his cheek and says something softly into his ear. It feels too intimate to watch, worse than any sex scene that unexpectedly popped up on TV when my mom or grandma were around.

Kayla turns away from them and says, "I want to see this list. I bet there's at least *one* Ben Dover."

Corrine snorts against Logan's neck and stands up, straightening her uniform. He's blushing just as badly as she is, and it's sweet, but it leaves a gnawing, hungry hole in my stomach.

"So, uh," he says with a little laugh. "I look forward to the third degree from you two," he says to Kayla and me as he stands, gathering his bag. "But I have to get to work."

"Where do you work again?" Kayla asks, feigning thought. "Not for any specific reason, but what's the name and address and phone number?"

"She's joking," Corrine says, wrapping her arm around his and guiding him to the door.

He says over his shoulder, Corrine still leading him away, "I work at Purrfect Match—"

"The cat adoption café?" Kayla squeals.

"Yeah."

"No!"

"Yes!" he says imitating her. He pulls at his black T-shirt with a faded graphic of an angelic kitten on it. "Did you think this shirt was ironic?"

"Leave it to Corrine to find a guy with a job that's as close to volunteer work as possible." I smile when she winks at me. "Bye, Logan."

"Have a good game, ladies." He smiles and disappears down the hallway.

After a prolonged minute of silence in which Corrine and Logan were definitely making out, the front door opens and shuts, and then Corrine appears in the door frame, her cheeks the color of her lips.

I finish applying lipstick and join Kayla on the bed. We spread out so Corrine has no room. She lies down across us with a sigh.

"Is it love?" Kayla asks quietly, sweetly, always the hopeless romantic.

Corrine tries to swat her, but hits me in the nose. "It's too early for that."

"You have a boyfrieeeeend," I say in an encouraging way, but deep down I wonder how Holden will feel to know it's official. Will he be upset? But he and she have been old news, and he handled the mess after the dance with so much composure. The gaping hole of sadness fills quickly with hope, and I don't know why.

"I have a boyfriend." She smothers her stupid-wide grin and laughs. "Why am I the only one who has a boyfriend?"

Kayla bursts into laughter. "Because I like girls? Saine, what's your excuse? Any repressed sexual preferences you'd like to share?"

"No, I'm just chronically undateable. Ask Elijah; he couldn't even not-cheat for a few months."

Corrine rolls over, smashing her elbows into my chest, and gets in my face. "That is not true. He's a piece of shit who didn't deserve you and if you'd let me, I would have had Holden *murder* him instead of punching him."

"To this day," Kayla says, "that is still the most memorable thing I've witnessed between classes, and I was around for Mr. Nitt and Mr. Roland's first lovers' spat." She rolls to her side, propping her head in her hand. "Elijah's face did that thing, like, in slow motion, where his face skin ripples? It was amazing. You could see Holden's knuckle imprints for two weeks."

"But seriously." Corrine delivers Intense Eyes™. "Any updates on either of your love lives that I've missed? Saine, are you . . ." Her face snaps to perky in a million frames per second. "Are you interested in anyone?"

"I don't think anyone is interested in me, so it doesn't really matter."

"Is that a yes?"

"No." I try to sit up, but she's still on top of me and traps me, probably intentionally.

"It'd be okay if you were." Her gaze bores into mine.

"Of course it would," Kayla says, probably catching onto how uncomfortable I am. She helps me push Corrine aside as we sit up. "Well, unless it were Elijah."

Corrine nods. "Good exception. And Logan. Obviously." She *hmms* a second. "And those are the only two I can think of."

I stay silent as they speak, waiting for a third name—but we all know it doesn't need to be said aloud. There's a pause that echoes in Corrine's artfully cluttered bedroom.

"Or Juniper," Kayla says quietly. She cuts to me and then Corrine, biting her lip.

Corrine takes a moment and then her face splits into a grin. "Oh my god!"

"I know," Kayla says in a squeal. "I've got it bad." She plays along with the previous conversation and elbows me. "Off-limits."

I laugh along, tension rolling out of my shoulders, and check the time on Corrine's alarm clock—she and my mom could start a club about ancient technology no one needs anymore. "I'll stay away as long as one of you gets us to the game on time."

"Shit," Corrine hisses, sliding off us and pulling her bright white game sneakers out of her closet.

"Oh, please." Kayla stands up and adjusts her skirt. "The game won't start without Corrine; the crowd doesn't know what to do when she's not there."

At the game, I feel like I have a thousand eyes on me as I make sure Holden's hand is secured through the strap on the camera. Everyone's watching. Everyone's seeing me touch him. And that combined with dancing with him at the winter formal is just too much.

"I got it," he says with a laugh that tickles my cheeks. "I just press record and then hold the camera up."

"Don't drop it."

"I won't."

"It's an expensive camera."

"I *know*. I have my own very expensive camera that I can't drop, remember?" Holden secured a good spot at the front of the bleachers, in the third row, and now people are filling in around him. We want to get a good perspective for Trevor's headset and I told him there had to be other people in the shot for it to feel truly immersive.

"Speaking of, who's taking photos tonight?"

"No one. There are only so many sports photos we need in

one yearbook. They all kind of look the same." When I only nod, he narrows his eyes. "Are you mad at me or something?"

"What? No." I feel like a lying liar because I *am* mad, but I know I have no reason to be. He didn't do anything. Corrine didn't even do anything. I'm just . . . mad. "Why?"

"You seem . . ." He looks me over. "Tense?"

"I just can't have anything happen to this camera." I glance over my shoulder and see my team spilling out onto the track, everyone clad in their cold-weather gear. I still haven't paid Corrine back for mine, but I'm working on it. After I'm done working on this. Corrine would agree that school stuff should come first. "I have to go."

He latches onto my arm when I turn away. "Are you hanging out after the game?"

"I'm still on Friend Probation, so I think we're going to Mikki's house."

"Okay, yeah, that's where I was going. Do you want a ride?"

"I've got Kayla." I tug out of his grip. "I'll see you after the game. To get the camera."

"We could film the party, too."

"Okay." I avoid looking over my shoulder, where I know Corrine is pretending she's not staring at us. I can feel her eyes on my back. But she didn't say his name. She had the chance and she didn't. She was hinting at something with all that, right? He's fair game, *right*?

Do I want him to be fair game?

I thunder down the bleacher steps and join my team. Throughout the game—that we win!—I watch Holden in the crowd, the camera placed so stiffly and consistently in front of his eyes that I think he's going to have to see an optometrist and a chiropractor in one day. He does the wave. He shouts *De-fense!* He talks with Taj and Nita, who showed up halfway through. He even, somehow, manages to catch a CHHS Hawks T-shirt from a T-shirt cannon while still filming. I nearly had a heart attack when I saw him attempt it, but he caught my eye with a blinding and triumphant smile afterward, and I couldn't help but smile back.

Mikki's house is a shit show when we arrive. We don't bother to change our clothes, heading to the party in our uniforms, which has always been bad for several reasons: someone is bound to spill something on their uniform or do something they shouldn't while wearing it—like take photos smoking—and because they're just uncomfortable after a while.

Juniper practically tackles Kayla when she walks through the door, her drink sloshing within an inch of Kayla's uniform before hitting the floor. Two seconds at the party and we already had a near-fatal incident.

Corrine nudges me with a shit-eating grin.

"I'm so glad you're here. Devon keeps trying to talk to me," Juniper says. Her eyes widen and she lowers her voice. "He sent me a dick pic today."

Corrine ties her jacket around her waist. "I'm not even surprised," she says with an eye roll. "A wise woman once said, you are what unsolicited pictures you send."

"I don't get it," Juniper says, putting her arm around Kayla's waist. Another nudge from Corrine. "We didn't even get along. Why would he want to go back to that?"

"Probably because he's not getting any action now," Kayla says. She smacks Corrine's shoulder behind Juniper's back. "He talks about his *dry spell* all the time at band practice."

"Like I was even having sex with him!" Juniper says, cheeks pink.

"You weren't?" Corrine asks. I catch her eyes cutting to Kayla's back and resist the urge to roll mine. She is not subtle.

"We did other things, but not *that*. Not . . . you know, the biblical version of it. Sex-sex."

I walk over to Mikki's gray sectional and flop down in the corner. Corrine sits next, practically on top of me, and Kayla takes my other side, with Juniper on her other side. My skirt is folded under my ass weird, but there's not enough space for me to fix it without elbowing someone.

"But, like, how far?" Kayla's eyes drop. "Wait, sorry, it's none of my business."

"I want to know!" Corrine says, angling toward them by throwing her legs over mine. "What's the farthest everyone's gone?"

Juniper mumbles into her cup, "I think I need something stronger than Diet Coke to talk about this."

"There's nothing to be ashamed of," Corrine says. "I've had sex. A lot of sex."

I don't know why, but my first instinct is to push her off me and get myself a very strong, very toxic drink from the kitchen, away from her.

"Maybe she's not ashamed; she just doesn't want to talk about something she feels is private in a public space," I snap.

Corrine looks sharply at me, then softens and directs her gaze on Juniper. "I'm sorry. She's right. I just don't want people to think there's something wrong with girls owning their sexuality."

"Hashtag feminism," Kayla says half-heartedly. She glances at me and I know what she's thinking, plain as day. She agrees with Corrine, but if Juniper feels bad, she's gonna be Team Juniper.

Corrine slides off. "I'm going to get a soda. Do you guys want anything?"

It's hard not to see her embarrassment when I know her face so well. She's fleeing, hoping we forget that she made things uncomfortable and offering something as an apology. It's classic Corrine Annalise Baker.

"Water, please," Kayla says, as the designated driver.

I smile, but it's tight. "Same. Thanks."

"I'll go with you. I need some ice." Juniper slides off the couch, cup in hand. She offers Corrine a smile and rubs her back as they walk away, talking. Somehow Corrine did something wrong and Juniper is the one consoling her. *Sounds about right.*

"I'm going to ask her out," Kayla says, turning toward me, her knee bent into the back of the couch. "Don't tell Corrine—she's already an eight-count away from planning our wedding."

I smother a laugh. "I won't. Is Juniper interested in girls?"

"I have no clue." She frowns, rubbing the end of her braid

against her palm distractedly. "But I have to ask her. I'm in love."

"Love?"

"I said it was bad!"

"What about the band?"

She groans dramatically. "There are other non-terrible guitarists in the world. You were right."

"You guys will find someone to replace him in no time. I'm sure Hayley knows someone from school; she's in a ton of music courses, right?"

"Yeah. But do we kick him out? Let him quit when-slash-if I start dating Juniper?" Her wide eyes bore into mine.

"He's a douche. He sent a dick pic. Kick him out." I grab her hand and squeeze. "Find someone who isn't a dude to play guitar and you guys can finally evolve into your final form."

"Why the hell didn't I think of that? Or Corrine? It was weird that we had a cishet guy in the band to start with."

She shifts a little closer to me and lowers her voice. "But speaking of Corrine. Is everything okay?"

"I think so, why?"

"Just, like, at her house and now . . . She didn't see your face when she brought up sex, but I did." She raises an eyebrow. "Are you and Holden hooking up?"

"Oh my god, *no*. We're just friends." I shake my head a little. "I mean, we're barely friends. We're just working together for now. It'll be over soon."

"Well, he keeps staring at you. Your friend." Her brown eyes flick somewhere over my shoulder, then lock onto mine again.

"I'd probably get that settled before Corrine comes back. Not that there's anything wrong with being *friends*. She did dump him, after all, and she's moved on."

"There's nothing going on between us." But I turn, planting both feet on the floor. "We're supposed to film some party stuff, though." I look behind us, but can't see him anywhere.

"He went into the dining room." She gestures with her head to the adjacent room.

"If they ask, I'm—" I sigh. "I'm working on the documentary. I'll be back, okay? I'm not bailing again."

"I miss you being around, *obviously*, but the Probation mostly came from Corrine." She lowers her voice again. "I think she's jealous? Like, not even of you. She's jealous of *him*. She misses you."

Guilt fizzles in my stomach. "That's weirdly sweet and I'll take it."

"I felt like maybe, earlier, the conversation was headed into a Big Important Moment and it didn't seem like you were ready for it. Or maybe Corrine was wrong?"

"I . . . don't know." I just know I can't talk about it right now. It'll make it real and I don't want to get ahead of myself. "The sooner I get all this done, the sooner I can be around you guys all the time and make you wish that I had another documentary to work on." I take off my jacket and leave it with her, picking my bag up from the floor.

Kayla smiles wide. "The next one can be about Nope."

I find Holden cheering on Mikki, Carlos, and two guys I don't know while they play beer pong. He's having a side conversation with Nita and a junior, Ricardo, so I wait across the table, awkwardly trying to make eye contact. After a minute, it happens.

He nods at me, says something to Nita and Ricardo, and then crosses the room.

"Should we film?"

I gesture to the beer pong table. "How good are you at beer pong?"

He grins and calls "We've got winners!" to the room.

Holden has to drive, so he can't drink. He's also very terrible at beer pong and he can't even blame it on the fact that he's filming with one hand because I was filming for a while and he still sucked. So, that means I am drinking a lot of beer, which I hate and didn't plan on partaking in tonight, for him. Sometime around ten, when my tongue is long past numb, Logan shows up and Corrine wraps her arms around my stomach, nuzzling into my neck. She wishes me—and Holden—good luck as the rest of our friends cheer us on, even though it's very clear we're going to lose. I hate how easy it is to get my hopes up that this could all be normal. Holden and I friends again. Corrine happy and okay with it. Juniper and Kayla twirling around the five square feet of empty space that constitutes a dance floor.

Soon, we accept defeat and force the people around the sound system to listen to Nope.'s first song ever, "Meme, Myself, and I," which failed to take off but holds weird nostalgia for some CHHS students and spurred a hacking prank where students replaced faculty photos on the website with whatever meme was popular that day. I film this part, feeling safer behind the lens, feeling like I have a purpose for dancing. But even if I didn't have the camera, I think seeing Holden's nonchalance would probably put me at ease. He was a follower when he was a kid, but I find myself taking his lead more and more these days. Kayla dances with her eyes closed, so she doesn't see how Juniper looks at her. Juniper's gonna say yes when Kayla asks her out. I'd bet my acceptance to Temple on it.

When the song's over—they played it four times in a row, at Taj's insistence—the whole group of us moves to the kitchen to fill up on refreshments and, even though we all seem to be getting along, Holden ducks away, apparently to take a call. I step toward him and then reverse back to where I was. I have no excuse for following. I have the camera, my friends are here, the drinks are here. I've switched to water but it doesn't do much to settle my stomach. I'd actually like to just pull a Corrine and chuck it up just to get it out of my body.

It's quieter in the kitchen than any other room, so I hear when Holden says, "Mara, put Taylor back on the phone. I can't understand you." I go on high alert, spinning toward him.

"Is Mara okay?" Then something dark and hot fills my gut. "Is Trevor?"

Holden holds up his finger. "What? Okay. It's okay."

"Is she okay?" I ask again, closer. I can hear that annoying childlike lilt to my voice that happens when I drink.

"Yeah," he says into the phone, "that was her." He glances at me. "No, she's not coming—"

He retracts the phone from his ear suddenly, Mara's loud voice reaching me.

"Please!" she wails.

So, it's not really a discussion at that point. When I tell my friends I have to go and that I don't need a ride anymore, Corrine, snug with Logan hanging over her shoulders, nods in understanding. Friend Probation will probably last a little longer still, but maybe some progress was made tonight.

TWENTY-THREE

The drive to Mara's mom's house lasts only a few minutes, which is great because Holden's white-knuckled driving isn't something I'm keen on experiencing for long stretches of time, even when I'm mellow from drinking.

We park in front of a cute rancher with Christmas decorations lighting up the exterior, and Holden knocks on the forest-green door.

A pretty blonde girl with eyes like Mara's behind red glasses greets us. "Thank *god* you're here. She won't stop bouncing off the walls and I don't know what to do."

She lets us inside the house and we follow her down a hallway before she wheels around and looks at me. "I'm Taylor, by the way."

"I'm Saine."

She glances at Holden, drops her voice. "You said she was *cute*."

He stiffens beside me and my cheeks burn. "She *is* cute," he mumbles back.

"You need to learn better descriptive words. This girl is well past cute."

"I can very obviously hear you guys," I say quietly to the gray carpet. I probably should have taken my sneakers off before trampling on it.

Taylor bites back a smile, eyes flicking to Holden before landing on me. "Yes, that was the point."

She leads us to the room at the end of the hall, the only one with the door open, light and music spilling out. Inside, Mara tears her closet apart, throwing shirts and skirts and dresses and brightly colored pants onto her bed to the soundtrack of The Regrettes' latest album.

"Everything sucks!" she screams into her nearly empty closet. She spins toward the door when we fill the frame. "You're here!"

She rushes forward, burying her face into Holden's stomach. "I need your help," she whines, eyes wide and glistening. "Taylor isn't taking this seriously."

"That's because I don't understand," Taylor says with a laugh. "You're not making sense."

Mara whips her head in Taylor's direction. "How hard is it to understand that Rose wants to go to a movie but we're *children* so we can't go alone?"

"Rose wants to go to a movie?" I ask. "In a friendly way or romantic way?"

"See?" Mara cries, gesturing to me. "She just *gets* it!"

Taylor glances at Holden and then shakes her head. "I have work to do. She's your problem now. Just make sure she gets to bed soon."

"Go back to school and stay there until you learn the intricacies of preteen romance in the twenty-first century!" Mara cries after her. "Love has no bedtime!"

"I don't think they teach you that in school." Holden peels her off him and steps inside, making space on her bed to sit. "So, what's the situation here?"

Mara stares at me for a second and then sniffs the air. "You smell weird."

"She's . . ." He hesitates like he's going to come up with some kind of metaphor or whatever, like when I said that Elijah and I were singing partners, but then he just finishes with a shrug, "Drunk."

"Only until I puke." I grab Mara by the shoulder and lead her into her own room. "What's the problem? You're going to the movies?"

"Okay, so." She takes a deep breath and exhales, her whole body deflating momentarily. "I was minding my own business, just, like, watching YouTube videos of domesticated foxes, as one does on a Friday night, when Rose texted me." She shoves her phone an inch from my eyes. "Do you see that? Do you *see* that, Saine?"

"Almost." I pull the phone away from my face and read the text out loud for Holden's sake. "We should go to the movies. Just us." I raise my eyebrows. "Did you tell her how you feel?"

"I texted her two weeks ago! And she finally acknowledged it!" She holds her phone against her heart. "It was *my* idea to go to the movies, but I hadn't thought of the logistics of it." She looks over her shoulder at Holden, pouting. "I'm a child. I can't drive. I have no money."

"I think this was a John Mulaney sketch once." I sit next to Holden on the bed, not bothering to move Mara's clothes. "You have parents, you know? And they have money."

"But, okay, hear me out. They'll want to chaperone and hover around us and it'll be so embarrassing." She gets on her knees in front of us. "Will you please take us?"

I shrug. "I have no car, so you really have to ask him."

She pivots in Holden's direction, holding her clasped hands in front of him. "I'll do the dishes for a week."

"A week? That's all a movie date with barely any supervision is worth?"

She squeezes his knees until he grimaces and pulls her off. "I will hurt you in so many ways if you say no. I know where you sleep," she says. "Please please please please please—"

"Fine." He wards her away even though she only makes to stand. He turns to me. "Does next weekend work for you?"

"Oh, why am I needed?" I glance between them, telling my heart to calm down. It's not, like, a date or something. We'd be *babysitting*.

"Saine, we're only using Holden for the car. You're there for moral support and to make sure he doesn't embarrass me." She snaps in my face. "Keep up, you drunk."

She crosses her arms and delivers such a good I'm Not Mad, I'm Just Disappointed face that I'd think I'm looking at my mom miniaturized. "You didn't strike me as the type to get this sloppy."

I jab my thumb at Holden. "Blame your brother for sucking at beer pong."

"I remember being better," he says quietly, "and I had to be sober to drive."

Mara stares at us. Blinks once. Twice. "Okay, so, next weekend? Friday night?"

I say, "That weekend in general doesn't really work for me, but I can do the weekend after."

Holden glares at me.

"If you want to go next weekend, you should," I tell Mara.

"You have to be there," Mara says, doing something on her phone. "Showtimes aren't up yet for that Friday, though!"

"That's because it's two weeks away." Holden places a hand on her shoulder. "Breathe."

"Tell Rose you'll go see a movie not this Friday, but the next. You don't need to stress about what and what time because there's always something good at some good time on a Friday night, so it'll be good. Good all around."

Holden bites his lip, looking at me. "Are you getting *more* drunk the soberer you should be?"

"I'm tired." I frown. "But I was making sense, wasn't I?"

"I guess," he laughs. His eyes linger on me for a moment longer than necessary and his cheeks pinken.

Mara taps away at her phone and then throws it on her bed. "I need to pick out my outfit. Please help."

Holden's jaw drops. "It's two weeks away."

Mara rolls her eyes in my direction. "He's gonna be useless at this."

"I should have left you here to spiral," he mumbles.

I clap him on the shoulder as I make my way to the door. This is pretty much my only opportunity to talk to Taylor, so . . .

"Where are you going?" Mara asks, already searching through piled clothes.

"She can't go anywhere; I drove and she's drunk. Are you going to throw up?" Holden skeptically calls after me.

"Don't ask after my bodily functions; it's rude." I head for the living room, no intention on stopping at the bathroom and happy that I didn't lie to get away. Taylor looks like she needs a break from schoolwork, so I pull out my phone and approach for an interview about Holden *and* Trevor.

Thirty minutes later, we hit the road, the vibrations in my seat nearly lulling me to sleep.

"Thank you," he says quietly, eyes on the road as we come to a stop sign.

"No problem." I relax my body one limb at a time, melting into the seat. I've never been one to stay awake into the early morning hours if I can help it. "I love Mara. I'd die for her."

"Don't tell her that. She'll take you up on the offer some-time."

"I always wanted a sibling." I let my eyes close heavily. "I think you were the closest thing I had to that."

"Just what I wanted to hear."

I'm not sure why he sounds so bitter about it. Like, am I really that bad? "Well, until Corrine. Then I kind of realized that she and I are like siblings. You and I weren't, after all."

"Yeah?" he asks in a quiet, hopeful voice.

"I wish there was a way to have you both," I mumble, an inch from sleep.

If he says something else, I don't hear it. I hover somewhere in that in-between stage of awake and asleep where I could tip either way until, over a short bit of time, I feel like I'm literally tipping one way. I jerk awake and hit my head on the window.

"What the hell," Holden says to himself. He slows the car, pulling it to the side of the road, but since there's no real shoulder, we're still halfway on it. "Are you okay?"

"Just moderately concussed, don't worry about me." I glance out the back window, making sure there aren't any cars coming. There's no one around, the area barely illuminated by overworked streetlights emitting an orange glow.

"I think I blew a tire." He turns his hazard lights on and unbuckles his seat belt.

"We should get out of the car." The words claw their way up my throat, raw and painful, thinking about how bad things happen when I'm in Holden's car and someone could come speeding around the corner without enough time to stop before ramming into us. "I want out of the car."

I slip out of the passenger door and stumble to the closest bit of grass I can find, because grass means no cars. The cool air feels perfect on my hot, buzzing skin for maybe two minutes, and then the adrenaline ebbs away slowly, leaving me freezing and realizing that my jacket is back at the party. Holden finishes inspecting the van—pathetically flat tire on the front passenger side—and calls his mom.

"What if I mess it up and it falls off while we're driving?"

he asks quietly into the phone, waving on the lone car we see post-accident. He pops the trunk and unearths the spare tire. "No, you don't need to come." He examines this dark, lonely street. "We're fine. I'll call you if I need help."

He hangs up and crouches in front of me. "You're shaking."

"In trembling anticipation of how hot you'll look trying to change this tire."

He laughs, but it doesn't last long. He meets my eyes. "Are you okay?"

"Yeah. It's just cold." And the panic at a potential car accident has my body shutting down. One minute everything can be fine and the next, you could be dead. Why do I ever get in any car? Why do I ever leave my house or take a chance on new foods? Or any foods? I could choke.

I'm losing my grip.

Instead of telling me to get back in the car where it's warm, he shrugs out of his black jacket and throws it over my shoulders. I slip my arms in and wrap it around me, pleased that it stretches a little as opposed to being too tight like Corrine's and Elijah's clothes. It's perfect, warm, and it smells like him. Not like his body wash or deodorant, but like him. A little sweet, a little spicy. Warm, if warm could be a smell.

"Thank you."

"Perfect fit." He grins. "Unlike that time you stole my shoes, by *wearing* them, and face-planted down the stairs."

"I didn't realize how hard it would be to run in clown shoes."

"They weren't clown shoes, and I grew into them."

My eyes fall on his worn sneakers—not the same shoes that

I tried to steal. "What, the shoes?"

"No, my feet." He considers this. "Well, and the shoes."

"You know what they say about people with big feet. . . ."

His cheeks turn from a weather-bitten pink color to splotchy red, like an apple. "What do they say?"

I lean in to his ear and whisper, "They wear clown shoes."

He pulls away, just a little, enough to see me, and laughs. "Okay, I don't think that's the saying—"

He's still so close, so warm, so fucking cheerful and sweet, like, he went to help his little sister with a romantic disaster at the drop of a hat, and I think I'm, I don't know, attracted to him? Is this the alcohol talking? But Corrine was sober before, and it almost felt like she was encouraging it. What am I—

"—doing?" he asks, yanking away from where my lips had met his for the briefest moment, a whisper of an action. He sucks in his bottom lip and stares at me in horror.

"I'm—oh my god. I'm so sorry." I shake my head, my cheeks so hot that they hurt. I place my cold fingers over them. "I don't know—I'm drunk. I'm sorry." I blink at least five times in the span of a second. "That was . . ."

"It's okay." He stands, avoiding looking at me. "I get it."

I dig my nails into the skin under my eyes for a beat. I'm mortified. Fucking mortified. I have never once done something like this. Not with Holden. It's *Holden*. And I'm not that drunk. I can't believe I let something like that happen. With *Holden*. He's got to be so weirded out. He practically jumped away from me, and I can't fight off the flashbacks of his birthday party when the bottle landed on me and his face looked like

Edvard Munch's *The Scream*. I repulsed him. I still repulse him, present tense.

"I'm going to change the tire," he says quietly to the ground. "Did you want to help?"

I swallow roughly, then force out in a light-hearted, that-was-totally-weird-in-a-hilarious-way-right? kind of way, "Not at all."

He gets to work, the only sound between us the *click-click-click* of his hazard lights until he starts jacking the car up and taking off bolts.

I've totally, completely ruined the good thing that was forming between us.

Goose bumps pebble my legs, so I hug my knees to my chest and pull Holden's jacket around me, zipping it up and slipping my hands into the pockets. My fingers brush against something smooth and stiff in his right pocket. I let my fingers get a feel for it before pulling out a black velvet jewelry box. I don't dare to open it because I just know it'll be beautiful and for someone else and it'll make me want to cry more than I already do. It's probably just all my mixed emotions, my adrenaline crashing, the beer leaving my system, I don't know. Something dark and distant pangs in my gut because everyone's moving on and I can't fast-forward to catch up, and I can't rewind to live in the place where everything was once okay—I'm not even sure how far back I'd have to go anymore.

When exactly did my life become such a disaster? Was it when I started working with Holden? Or before then, when Corrine and Holden started dating? Or was it way back in middle school the night of Holden's birthday when I didn't confront him, didn't tell my best friend that he hurt my feelings, that I *had* feelings for him to hurt?

I don't know what I'm feeling toward him now. Things are complicated. If Holden and Corrine had never dated—had never held hands between classes, had never gone thrifting together, had never gotten detention for coordinating make-out sessions when their teachers thought they were using the restrooms—Holden probably wouldn't even be in my life again. Or maybe he would—because, really, why was I holding such a stupid grudge before? It's okay that he didn't like me back—and we'd all be best friends. But that doesn't feel right.

I wipe away an errant tear. I did not give it permission to leave my eye. I force the box back in his pocket and don't touch it again. It'll make some girl really happy and I shouldn't have snooped through his pockets when he was nice enough to give me his jacket. When he was nice enough to tell me that it was okay that I mauled him, when he's so obviously not interested.

The kiss was an unconscious action. I just reacted. I was basically on autopilot, so there's no reason that I should be able to recall how soft his lips were. How they parted when he started asking me what I was doing. Shouldn't remember how they filled my body with the heat I always seem to crave from him.

I reach for my own necklace that is still not around my neck because it's somewhere at Corrine's house, gathering dust.

TWENTY-FOUR

To be honest, I didn't think house parties with live bands were really a thing until tonight. In an old three-story house in the middle of Nowhere, Pennsylvania, about twenty minutes from Millersville University, Nope. continues to slay their set with Zo, temporary guitarist from Turtlenecks and nonbinary ruler of denim vests after Devon Miles Smith quit *this morning*. Apparently, Zo knew how to play most of the songs and covers already, but they learned the rest in about four hours, which, according to Kayla, is more than Devon ever did.

I sing along to "Netflix and Kill," soda in hand and camera bag slung over my shoulder, as Corrine and Juniper dance around me, having some sort of battle to see who can be louder when shouting the words. The song ends and we throw our hands up, screaming our applause as the people around us clap not half-heartedly, but maybe like three-fourths-heartedly. These people would have been fine with some loud Bluetooth speakers, but Hayley, Nope.'s drummer, was roommates with the party's host freshman year. A gig's a gig, even if the band's not getting paid.

Corrine throws her arm around my shoulders and kisses my cheek, leaving a sticky, mouth-shaped lipstick mark behind that she insists on Instagramming.

"I'm so happy you're here," she says. "And Kayla practically shit herself when she saw you showed up. Even if it *was* just to film for your documentary or whatever."

I ignore the jab, mostly because I got amazing footage for the VR headset a few songs ago. Trevor'll feel like a member of Nope. the way Kayla flirted with the camera and made the crowd hype up in my direction. "I hope she changed her pants before the show."

She shrugs jokingly.

"Hey, how are ya?" Kayla asks into the microphone, breathless. The small but polite crowd gives a collective holler.

She flips her long, curly hair over her shoulders and smiles. "I'm so happy we could be here tonight. You know, I applied to Millersville, so maybe I'll see some of you next year." Another cheer. Another smile. The highlighter on her brown skin shimmers in the colored lights set up for the party. "So, for anyone who isn't familiar with us, which could be a lot of you, we are Nope. and Nope. is Alexa on bass." Alexa plays a little ditty when Kayla points to her. "Hayley on drums." Drum solo. "Some of you may know her from class. Me on vocals and general hip-swaying. And, for possibly *tonight only*, which should make this very special, Zo from Turtlenecks killing it on guitar." They do some kind of picking on the strings, but it's barely heard over Juniper's, Corrine's, and my screams.

"So, um . . ." Kayla is breathless again, staring at her feet, slowly picking her words. "That last song was called 'Netflix and Kill,' and this next song is actually brand-new, and I wrote it, and it's called 'Oatmeal Raisin.' I hope you like it."

My jaw drops, but Juniper doesn't seem to experience anything other than excitement. Kayla is finally sharing a song she wrote. That's huge enough, but it's called *Oatmeal Raisin*? And the fact that Kayla admitted to me that her songs were about Juniper?

THIS SONG IS ABOUT JUNIPER, I want to yell. Corrine cuts to me, her eyes full of hearts.

It's a catchy song, not a sad, slow love ballad by any means, and it has everyone dancing, even though no one knows the words. It's not until the bridge, when Kayla starts singing Juniper's name, that our friend stops dancing. My heart is racing watching Kayla, eyes closed tight, singing her heart out and Juniper realizing what's happening.

I mouth, "Oh my god," to Corrine and she mouths back, "Oh my god."

By the time the song ends, Juniper has zombie-walked herself to the front, and stopped right in front of Kayla. Kayla opens her eyes and Juniper leaps into her arms, tackling her. Juniper locks her lips onto Kayla's as the band plays on. Corrine breaks into a huge grin watching them; she can't take her eyes off a happy ending.

I'm happy, I am. But seeing them entwined just makes me think of Holden. Reminds me that we haven't spoken since I threw myself at him last night, except for when I texted him that I was filming at Nope.'s show tonight and he so eloquently said "okay" in response. We're coming to the end of our list of footage to collect and then the documentary will be over, and . . . what will happen to us? What has already happened to us?

The band continues its set, Juniper dancing wildly in the front, never taking her eyes off Kayla. She has a different kind of confidence now. She was a born front woman, but now maybe one day she'll attain creepy dictator status or whatever Trevor says.

After Nope. finishes, a playlist kicks on and the band joins us. Kayla and Juniper pretty much only have eyes for each other, but it's sickeningly cute, so we allow it. Zo tries to explain their technique for learning songs quickly, but it flies over my head. I think Hayley and Alexa somewhat understand, being musicians themselves, but Corrine meets my eyes multiple times like, "What language are they even speaking?"

She grabs my elbow, steers me away from what sounds like a math problem about music, and nods to a corner of the living room. "There's a guy over there that keeps looking at you."

I expect to wonder who it is, but I don't. He meets my eyes instantly, and I know them.

"Victor," I groan. "What the hell is he doing here?"

"You know him?" She raises an eyebrow. "You know a cute college guy and haven't told me?"

"He's a pain in the ass," I say, taking a drink. "I know him from Penn State."

"Wonder what he's doing here." She watches him for a second, and his mouth curves into a smile surrounded by pillowy lips. "You should go talk to him."

"Why would I do that? I'm not a masochist."

She shrugs. "He looks like he's into you."

"Well, I'm not into him."

Intense Eyes™ now. "Are you into someone else?"

My stomach drops. "No? I already said I wasn't. I'm too focused on my Temple app for anything else." This is the conversation with Kayla all over, except it's way more uncomfortable and it feels way worse lying.

Wait, am I lying?

There's nothing going on with Holden. I mean, sure, I kissed him, but he didn't reciprocate, and I was tipsy, and it just seemed fun? I barely made the decision to do it; my body just reacted. It would never happen again, and just because it *did* happen once doesn't mean it meant anything.

"You don't like, I don't know," she says, biting her lip, "someone at school?"

"Just say what's on your mind, Corrine."

She bites her lip harder, and that's when I notice how watery her eyes have gotten. *Great.* This conversation is about to end with no resolution, just to be brought up again, at another uncomfortable time.

I grab her shoulders, refusing to tiptoe around this anymore. "What's wrong?"

A tear leaks out, but her mascara and eyeliner stay in place. The perfect visualization of Corrine Baker. Put together no matter what. "I'm sorry. I just don't believe you."

"You're my best friend. I would tell you if I was having fuzzy feelings for someone."

"Even if it was Holden?" She blinks her eyes dry. "I'm not

mad if so. I guess I've just been . . . jealous?"

Despite the uptick in my heart rate, I tilt my head to the side, brushing her hair from her face. "Of what?"

"I barely see you these days and it's because you're with my ex-boyfriend. We don't talk a lot anymore. It . . . plays games with my head. I'm happy with Logan, but he's my boyfriend, not my best friend."

"You know, *you're* also super busy." Then I realize it sounds like I'm blaming her, and that's the last thing I want to do, not when I kissed her ex-boyfriend, not when she's felt like I abandoned her. "We just need to have some time together. Maybe a spa day?"

She sniffles. "You hate spa days."

"Well, yeah, they're invasive and kind of gross, but I'd do one for you."

"Thank you." She hugs me. "Does that include mani-pedis?"

"Don't push it," I grumble, rubbing her back.

"If you didn't pick at your hangnails, they wouldn't be so bloody every time."

"Now is not the time for this lecture."

"You're right," she says, straightening with a smile. "If you're not interested in someone, then now is the time for you to hook up with that guy you don't like as a power move."

Shit. Something sinks in my gut. "No . . ." I look over my shoulder at Victor and find that he's staring back at me. "I think that would be—"

"A great idea." She crosses her arms. "When was the last time you had an orgasm?"

"Oh my *god*, Corrine." My cheeks heat and I try to play off the conversation, but she stares me down. "I don't know. I don't keep track of that." And if I did, I wouldn't find this to be the time or place to discuss it.

"Clearly it hasn't been recently, then. Don't you masturbate?"

"What's happening, pals?" Kayla slings her arms around Corrine and me.

"Corrine is forcing me to talk about my masturbation habits. Would you care to join?"

Corrine separates herself from us. "What we were actually talking about is how there's a cute guy staring at Saine and she won't go talk to him." She jabs her thumb over her shoulder. "She's not in a relationship, she's not into anyone, there's no reason not to."

Kayla squeezes me tight against her, protective. "If she doesn't want to, what's it matter?"

"I'm in a relationship now. I have to live vicariously through you for weird party hookup stories."

"Why don't *you* just have a weird party hookup?" Kayla asks, nearly slopping her drink on me as someone pushes by us.

"It's not the same if it's with your boyfriend, and I'm not a cheater."

"Fine, fine. I'll take one for the team," I lie like a lying liar. She says she's fine, she says it's okay, but I feel like she's pushing pushing pushing me to prove that I do or do not like Holden. The problem is . . . The problem is that I don't know. I'm scared to look too closely to find out.

I can't hook up with Victor. I don't want to, and who even knows if he wants to hook up with me. I walk over to him anyway, just to get Corrine off my back.

He smirks when I stop in front of him. "You don't go here."

"Neither do you." I take a sip of my drink, only to realize that it's been empty for a while. The sticky remnants of the soda linger at the bottom. "I'm with the band."

"You should ditch the zeroes and get with a hero then."

"Did you expect that line to work?"

"From the way your friends are watching you talk to me, yes, I assumed that's why you came over."

When I look over my shoulder, Corrine and Kayla make a big show of turning around and acting like they weren't watching. I pan back to Victor.

"Want to dance?" he asks.

"I don't dance."

"Okay." He nods, glancing into my empty cup. "Do you want to grab a refill and go upstairs where it's quieter? Get to know each other better off campus?"

"Here's one thing you definitely know about me: I'm in high school."

He laughs. "Yeah, but you're eighteen, right?"

"More romantic words have never been spoken."

"There's where you're wrong." He leans in. "I'm not trying to be romantic, I'm trying to get into your pants."

I stare at him for a second when he pulls away, smirking. Is this what I have to look forward to? If I'm not cheated on, I'm alone and every guy will be a scumbag?

But that's not true. There's another option, one I don't want to admit to knowing. There are people like Holden. People who are sweet and funny, but in like with someone else enough to buy them expensive jewelry like a total romantic sap.

I grab Victor's T-shirt and pull him in close, smashing my lips against his. At no point in the next twenty-three self-loathing minutes in the bedroom upstairs does he turn into Holden. At no point do I enjoy myself. At no point do I forget the thought that has weaseled itself into my mind:

I'm in love with Holden Michaels.

TWENTY-FIVE

I leave the party without my friends, an increasing trend in my behavior, and drive slowly home, my limbs trembling. When I wake up the next morning, I shower, but don't look in the mirror when I get out. I can't stand the thought of seeing myself after what I did last night, after what I *realized* last night.

Avoiding a mirror is a lot easier than avoiding my mess of feelings. I turn my phone on airplane mode, throw on headphones, and go through my grandma's room, boxing anything I look twice at. My mom won't be awake for hours, her room completely black, her own noise-canceling headphones over her ears and playing the calming sound of an ocean lapping against the shore, but I still try to be quiet. Except for my music. I turn my music up loud. It's angry and selfish and raw. Like me.

I place my grandma's jewelry box on my desk next to my computer, the documentary up on the screen, and don't even open it. The necklace I want—the one I *need*—isn't there, but maybe I'll find a replacement. My back aches when I really get to work, but I make some progress . . . in taking things from her room and putting them into mine. Probably not what my mother had in mind, but she'll have to deal for now.

At some point last night, Corrine texted to ask how things went between Victor and me. I told her it was great even though it wasn't. Like with Elijah, my vagueness was most likely enough for her to believe we had sex. Like, as Juniper says, sex-sex. Instead, I bruised my knees trying to give him a blow job, but my mouth was too dry. I faked the orgasm when he enthusiastically went down on me in return to speed things up so I could leave. How was I supposed to enjoy any of that when it felt like there was another person in the room?

Oh, shit. How am I supposed to go back to work after what we did? Maybe I do need to see a therapist—

Someone taps me on the shoulder and I fly a foot in the air, my headphones sliding off and hitting the floor with a disappointing plastic sound.

Holden full-body cringes. "I'm sorry. I didn't know how else to get your attention that wouldn't scare you."

I clutch my chest, my heart sprinting a mile a minute, and I can no longer tell if it's because he scared me or if it's because this is the first time I've seen him since our awkward goodbye post-kiss. "Where did you come from?"

"Your bedroom window. You weren't answering my texts, so I let myself in. What are you doing?" He sits down next to me in the doorway of my grandma's room, which looks like a natural disaster has hit it, his knee knocking mine. He notices the yellowing bruise there. "Ouch, what happened?"

I ignore his question, my heart doing a back handspring in my chest. "Going through my grandma's stuff. My mom wants to get rid of it for when we move."

"Wait. When are you moving?"

"I'm not sure. Soon."

"You didn't say anything." He face slackens. "Where are you going? Far?"

"Sorry to disappoint," I say. "We're staying local, but we don't really have a place yet." I think of The One with a strange fondness. It kind of feels like a new start, a do-over. I definitely want it now.

"Will I still be able to sneak in your window?"

I smile, though I shouldn't. I shouldn't entertain the idea of this continuing, whatever it is to him. It's not fair when it's so much more to me and he has no clue. When I've lied to my best friend about it multiple times. "Probably."

"Keep me in mind."

That won't be a problem.

I tap my temple. "Got it. Make sure the house is convenient for Holden. Top on my list of priorities."

"I get it, you know?" He gestures to my grandma's stuff. "After Trevor moved into the hospital, I couldn't walk past his room, but at the same time, I only wanted to spend time there. He had this rotting banana in his trash can that was stinking up the place, but I refused to let my mom take it out because—because it would be like acknowledging that he wasn't there to do it. That he might not ever come back." He bites his lip. "I used to wander around the house just looking for him, knowing he wasn't there, but kind of feeling like he was just around the corner."

"I know that feeling." It aches in me every day. I nudge him with my shoulder. "I kept soap."

"*Used* soap?"

I scoff. "They were unopened boxes of new soap, not a rotting banana peel."

"I didn't keep the banana peel, I just didn't let anyone throw it out." He pauses, then grins at me. "Now that I've said it out loud, I guess I know why my mom took me to therapy. It wasn't even a banana *he* ate. It was Mara's."

I pause for a moment, debating my words. "Do you go to therapy, like, regularly?"

His eyes cut to mine. "Yeah. Every other Wednesday after school."

"Does it help?" I pick at a hole in my sock instead of looking at him. "You don't have to say if you don't want to. I know it's personal."

His gaze burns a hole in me until I meet his eyes. "Yeah, it helps. Have you ever gone?"

"Once." I bite my lip. "A couple months ago."

"How was it?"

"It was awkward." I laugh a little to myself. "Mostly she did all the talking and then I pretended like I didn't need to be there while desperately wanting to be there."

A small smile breaks out over his lips. A sympathetic one. "Why don't you go more?"

"It's not affordable under my mom's health insurance, so it's just another thing to pay for. I'm fine."

"You can go to therapy even if you're fine. Sometimes it's nice to talk, to be heard."

"I just . . . I don't know, maybe I'm not doing so well with— the whole thing? My grandma, I mean." I shrug. If this were a scene in a movie, it would be cut. There's no need to even be having this conversation because I'm not saying anything.

"That's understandable. She was a huge part of your life and now she's not around."

"And my mom—" My eyes start to water. I blink a few times to stave off the tears. "My mom just wants to move on and I think maybe I want to, too?" I sound like an idiot. "But I feel like that would be betraying my grandma. And if I move on, but then decide I wasn't actually ready to move on . . . I don't know. I don't know what I'm feeling."

"There are ways to do both, you know. You can move on, but still process your emotions about everything. Still grieve. Still live. It's a balance. You'll never be fully okay with her being gone." He squeezes my knee, careful to keep his thumb away from the tender bruise. "A therapist could help you with that."

I nod, not sure what to say. It's an option. It's a possibility.

It feels good to talk about it regardless.

He removes his hand and focuses on the room in front of us. His eyes bounce off different things and I just watch him. His long, dark eyelashes fan his skin, and his mouth breaks into a smile. He latches onto the camera around his neck, drawing my attention to it.

"What's with the camera?" I ask, suddenly aware of the fact

that I'm sitting here with the guy I'm in love with in no makeup and raggedy pajamas.

"My assignment is due in two weeks and you can't keep putting off finishing it. I've helped you, now you help me."

"You're not done helping me. I still need an interview from you. And the V and V follow-up footage."

"Okay, sure." He removes the lens cap. "We'll do those this week."

I cover my face, then let my hands sift through my hair, yanking it from my messy bun. "I have to get changed. Put on makeup."

"No." He latches onto my arm. "No. You look great. Besides, you were all done up in the New York photos, this will be a nice contrast—really show off your versatility."

I know he's lying even without having seen myself today. "Holden."

"Saine. You look fantastic." He stares at me for a second, his face growing serious. Meanwhile, it feels like a clown car full of butterflies just pulled up in my gut and have thrown open the door. "But if you want to change, I'll understand."

His stare grows long and I roll my eyes. "Yeah, of course I want to change. I feel"—I adopt a mocking version of his smug tone—"*vulnerable* this way."

He's a lying liar to say I look fine.

"My mom is here," I say, standing. "Try to be quiet."

He turns his camera on and I panic, thinking he's just going to go for it, but then he aims it into my grandma's room. "Can I take pictures of the murals?"

I blink. "Um, sure?"

"Cool. Maybe we can get a few of you in front of them, too. Personality pictures." He stands, stuffing his face behind the camera. "I'll see you in a second."

Feeling properly dismissed, I go into my room, shutting the door quietly behind me as his shutter clicks away. I sit down in front of my computer and open the webcam. My hair is curly from drying in the messy bun, adding volume that helps distract from the dark circles under my eyes. My lips still have remnants of my bright red lip stain that hasn't worn off. I get up, walk straight to my closet, and put on the first dress I can get my hands on.

Holden enters the room and shakes his head when he sees me. "You really didn't have to change. I was just joking."

"I'm not letting anyone from school see me like that."

"I saw you like that."

"You're, I don't know, you're you. And it's not like I had a say in the matter because you just showed up." I awkwardly stand there. "Where do you want me? Here?"

"Let's start at your desk," he says. "With the documentary up? It's your natural element. It's like your Batcave."

I raise my eyebrow.

"Your Fortress of Solitude?" he tries.

"How has it taken me this long to realize you're a DC guy? We can't be friends anymore." I sit down at my desk, stiff, and stare at him. "Now what?"

"I don't know," he says, shrugging. "Just work?"

I face the computer with a sigh. "This is awkward."

He clicks a few photos and releases a low, rumbly laugh.

"Only because you're making it awkward."

"Says the guy taking pictures of me doing nothing."

"How about you decide what you want to do and then do it? Like, choreograph it?"

"This isn't like dancing."

He stops, looks around my room, and then darts beside my bed, retrieving my camera. He hands it to me and I accept it, frowning. My rental was due back to PSH today. Fuck.

"What do you want me to do with this?" I ask, holding it as if I've never held one before.

"Film me."

"Excuse me?"

"You just smile more when you're behind a camera." He lifts his own. "Film me."

He knows me he knows me he knows me.

"Holden?" My voice cracks. I lower the camera and then chicken out and lift it, partially blocking my face. *Five-six-seven-eight.*

"That won't work, I can't see your face." He lowers his camera and squats in front of me, so I have the high ground sitting on my computer chair. "What's up?"

"I—I, um, I don't know." My hands are shaking, breathing is hard. I keep getting flashes of last night, and the visceral hatred I had for myself threatens to spill out of me. We're almost done with the documentary and the headset and his class assignment and then we're done. We're done. "I . . ."

"What is it?" He puts both of our cameras on the bed and, with a quick glance at my face, places his hands on my bare knees, sending waves of goose bumps up my skin. He stares at me, lips parted in the shade of First Kiss, and I just go for it.

"I know it went horribly the first time and you're not into me like I'm into you, but I really want to kiss you." My words come tumbling out at warp speed.

He clears his throat and his words come out gruff. "I'm into you."

Something clenches inside me. My heart? My stomach? Lungs? I think I'm dying one internal organ at a time, and the process is definitely not slowed down any by his fingers pressing into my skin. "You—no, you aren't."

"Why would you think I'm not? I've been *flirting* with you. Just . . . been waiting for you to get the hint."

I back away so I can see his whole face, because hunched over is really not the way to have a life-changing conversation. "Why didn't you kiss me back, then?"

His mouth drops open. "You were drunk! You said so yourself!"

"Drunk actions are truth actions or whatever!"

"Not always!" His eyes flick to my lips. "I didn't want to take advantage of you or something."

"Well, I'm not drunk now, and you—"

His hand wraps around the back of my head and he pulls me into him, his soft lips smashed against mine. He breaks a breath away. "That wasn't my best, I'm sorry, I was excited—"

I press my lips against his, drawing a startled groan from him. We stand up at the same time, adjusted so his face angles down instead of mine. His skin is smooth under my fingertips and

I slide them over his cheekbones, graze his scalp, trace a chill down his neck. He breaks the kiss and stares at me with wild eyes, his breathing erratic. And then he dives back in, swinging me around so I land back-first on my bed, with him holding his weight over me. The sound must startle Bagel, wherever he is, because he barks and rushes into the room. Holden pulls away.

"Shhh, Bagel. Quiet." He ushers him out of the room and shuts the door. He turns back to me, his cheeks red. "Should we stop?"

"Do you want to?"

"No. Do you?"

"You're the one who asked!"

In the blink of an eye, Holden's hovering over me again. He kisses my neck, and then my temple, the touches featherlight. "You're so beautiful," he whispers. "It's devastating."

I don't know what to say. Nothing I could say back would ever sound as sweet, as sincere, so I kiss him instead. His hand trails down my side and latches onto the hem of my dress, sliding it an inch or two higher.

I break away from our kiss, reluctantly, to say the biggest mood killer that absolutely has to be said. "I'm not—I'm not ready to have sex, or anything, besides, like, kissing. Not right now." My cheeks heat and the words fumble out of my mouth in such an embarrassing way that I close my eyes so I can't see his reaction. "I haven't—Elijah and I didn't, well, not with me. You know what I mean?"

"Are you saying you're a virgin?"

"It's not that big of a deal." I crack an eye open. "Is it?"

His own face turns tomato red. "Of course not. We've—we've got time, if we wanted to. I've—I've only done it once, so . . . I get it."

I pull a totally unattractive face of disbelief. "But Corrine said . . ."

"I really don't want to think about her right now." He flops to the empty space next to me. "What did she say? That it was awful?"

"No, she said you guys had a lot of sex."

He raises his eyebrows. "Well, that's not what happened, but I appreciate the lie."

"So, what happened, then?"

"She really wanted to and I wanted to make her happy." He rolls the words around in his mouth. "Neither of us were too happy afterward."

"Not really selling yourself here," I say as a joke, trying desperately to lighten the mood that is so dark and awkward right now.

"I have to be honest," he says. "We had sex, got into a fight, and then she broke up with me."

I sit up, leaving Holden lying on the bed behind me. "I don't understand. She *never* mentioned this."

"Probably because you were the reason we broke up."

I whip around and he breaks into laughter at the sight of the stunned look on my face. "What do you mean? I didn't do anything!"

"No, you didn't do anything." He joins me in sitting. "Sorry, that's not what I meant."

"What did you mean, then?"

"I mean, we had sex and it was awful and I didn't love Corrine. And that was, unfortunately, when she realized it. So, she broke up with me."

I stare at my hands in my lap. "She told me there was another girl."

"There was." When I meet his eyes, his face is serious and perfect. "*You*, Saine."

Even though we were just kissing, even though he admitted to being into me, hearing that he's been into me for *months* feels new and scary and thrilling, my excitement now competing with my guilt. Did I do something to steal Holden from Corrine? If that's the case, why did she seem like she was pushing me to him?

His fingers skim over my arm. "You okay?"

"I just feel . . . a lot." I rest my hand over his, stalling his motion. "She was so nice to me after the breakup, though. And . . . not nice to you."

"Corrine wasn't mean to me. She just—" He shrugs.

"I'd hate me if I were her. I'd hate both of us. And then during the last few months, I'd *loathe* us."

"But it's Corrine. She's mature." His fingers play with mine for a second longer before he brushes a thumb against my bottom lip. It's thrilling to experience something brand-new with someone I've known for years. "I think she was annoyed with me after we broke up because I didn't make a move, you know? Like our breakup was pointless if I wasn't gonna ask you out."

When will my mind stop being blown today?

"Why didn't you?" I ask.

He laughs, startling a bark from Bagel outside the door. "Are you kidding me? Even if that wasn't the biggest dick move, it was still impossible to even get close to you. You were guarding Corrine 24-7 and glaring holes through me."

"I thought you had cheated on her," I mumble. "She said there was another girl and I connected the dots."

"Oh yeah? Do the dots feel connected now?"

"Shut up." I shove him gently.

"Plus, I wasn't ready to admit it . . ." He bites his lip.

"But now?"

He leans in close, his nose grazing mine. "I like you a lot, Saine Sinclair."

His lips brush against mine and I feel that hole in me slowly repairing itself. I'm kissing Holden. *Holden*.

"I like you a lot, Holden Michaels." I can't say the actual words I want to, the ones that rang so loudly in my head last night, but I think he gets it. I think maybe he even feels the same way.

TWENTY-SIX

We break away from each other eventually, our breathing uneven and shallow. I'm staring at his tousled hair and wet lips, thinking maybe I *am* ready when I remember my mother's home. She could have walked in at any moment. She's usually dead to the world once she falls asleep, but this *would* be the day she wakes up and checks on me. The day I'm straddling my best friend's ex-boyfriend.

Oh god.

He watches me for a second with hazy eyes. They grow clearer as the happiness fades from mine.

"Are you okay?" he asks quietly.

"Yeah. You?" I roll off the bed and try to flatten some wrinkles from my dress. I can feel the panic building beneath my skin, feel the buzz up and down my limbs, but I'm holding it off.

Corrine.

I know now that my gut instinct telling me she was pushing me toward Holden was right, and yet . . . I can't escape the fear that she'll never speak to me again. I could lose her. It's one thing for me and Holden to hypothetically be together, but it's another thing entirely for it to be real, especially when I insisted I didn't have feelings for him. What if this was all a test of my loyalty? For her to offer him up on a silver platter and me to say politely and firmly, "No, thank you."

Is being with Holden, however long, worth losing both of my best friends? Because what happens with Holden now? I'd like to date, but then when we break up, he's gone. I can't take losing him again. I can't take that on top of losing Corrine. And even though Kayla is all *She broke up with him*, I'd still be the girl who made a move on Corrine's ex. So, Kayla will probably awkwardly flit between us, Juniper in tow, until the school year is over and we all part ways or until she feels too guilty being my friend.

Holden stares at me.

"What?" I ask.

"Be honest."

"I—I can't right now."

"You can't be honest?"

"Yes." My lip trembles, so I bite down on it.

He stands, laying his hands on my shoulders and squeezing. "Was that yes a lie?"

I shake my head. "No. I just can't talk about it. Not right now. I'm . . . processing."

"Okay. Was this too weird?"

I shake my head again, faster this time. "No. It was more weird that it *wasn't* weird."

He places a hesitant kiss on my lips in response. It's over too soon. "How about pizza, then?"

"What?"

He kisses me again, slow and gentle. "Pizza. Supreme." He leans into my neck and presses his lips there. "And cheese sticks." He bites down.

I laugh. "Are you getting turned on by the thought of food?"

"No, I'm turned on because of you, and I just happen to be really hungry."

"We'll get some delivered, then."

"And then maybe you'll let me in on what you're 'processing'?"

"Maybe."

"Maybe I can help you."

"Maybe," I say with a nod.

I order our food and a salad, no onions, for my mom, and while we wait for the delivery, I work on splicing together some footage while he takes photos. It's the only thing I can think to do to get my mind off the inevitable. Eventually, I tune out the *click-click-click* of the shutter and barely notice when he starts rearranging some furniture in my room so he can get an unobstructed view of the mural. He takes photos of it and it reminds me that very soon, if my mom has her way, the wall will be white and no one will ever see Nev riding Tilikum into the sunset ever again.

I stare at the screen for a moment before leaning back in my chair, my body relaxing. The only other footage I'll need to finish the documentary is Trevor's reaction to the VR headset, which is almost complete, and Holden's interview. And while my excuse to hang out with Holden will vanish, maybe I don't need an excuse other than I Want To now. I'll have to figure out the Corrine thing ASAP—maybe, just *maybe,* she'll be happy about it—and I will, but until then, I'm going to let this go on as it was intended from the start. The time is dwindling away and the deadline is approaching, and I'm surprisingly okay with the near-end result. It doesn't need to be perfect; the whole reason I'm applying is to learn and get better.

Holden collapses onto the bed and caps his lens. "Progress update?"

"Almost done. It doesn't completely suck." I glance at him. "Though it's very amateur. I'm hoping your pretty face makes up for that."

He grins. "All the world's problems would be solved if everyone looked at my face for two seconds?"

"Just two seconds?"

"I figure that's all a mere mortal can take before they just combust with yearning."

"Confident."

"I have reason to be." He sits up on his elbows. "You're into me, so I must not be too disgusting."

"Barf." The doorbell rings and I jolt from my seat, rooting through my bag for my debit card. "I'll be back."

"No!" He reaches forward, flicks the card out of my hand dramatically, and pulls cash from his pocket. "It's on me."

I stare at the spot where my debit card was eaten by the darkness behind my desk. He smiles sheepishly.

"I'll get that while you get the pizza." He drops to his hands and knees, his head disappearing under the desk.

I rush to the front door, not wanting the delivery person to ring the bell again on the off chance it'll wake my mom. Not that she would wake up to anything incriminating now. But when I swing open the door, it's not a delivery person waiting for me. My heart bottoms out. "*Corrine?*"

"You're alive!" She smiles and offers me a pink drink from Starbucks. "I was starting to worry because you weren't answering your phone." She steps inside without being invited in—something that has never been a problem before, mostly because her ex-boyfriend wasn't in my bedroom any other time. Her vintage bell-bottom jeans swish with her steps.

"What are you doing here?" I stop her in the middle of the living room.

She frowns. "I told you, you weren't answering your phone. I thought maybe you choked on your vomit in your sleep or something. I was worried."

I wasn't even drinking last night. "My phone is off." I shake the drink, stirring the smoothie contents. "Thank you. Now's not really a good time, though. My mom is still asleep."

Oh god it feels awful lying without lying I'm so tired of lying to her why can't I just tell her she made it seem like it would be okay and this wasn't planned it might be fine.

Her face falls and she takes a step back. "Oh. Okay. I thought maybe we could do our spa day if you wanted to get out of the house?"

"Do you need help with the food?" Holden's voice echoes down the hallway.

Before I can do anything—though what would I even do?— he appears in the living room and the drink Corrine brought me nearly slips out of my grasp. She tenses up, like she's just another photo Holden's taken to curate his Instagram presence.

"Did I . . . interrupt something?" she asks in a small voice. Pink floods her cheeks as she takes in his disheveled hair. Her eyes cut to mine.

"No." Stop lying stop lying stop lying she CAUGHT YOU!!! "I was working on the documentary." Technically, not a lie, but also not the full truth. "Holden was taking photos." Closer.

She stands there with her mouth in a line, not saying anything until— "What's going on here? And don't lie. You said you weren't lying anymore, Saine."

I stand between them, silent. I should just admit what's going on. What happened. It wasn't planned. She gave me so many opportunities to come clean. I'm spiraling and I think they can both tell, but I can't move toward Corrine without abandoning Holden and what he means to me, and I can't move toward Holden without abandoning Corrine and losing her once and for all. Maybe if I just stay here, stay paused, I can figure out something to say that will make it all better.

"I guess you two have some things to talk about," Holden says, stepping forward. And then, without grabbing so much as his jacket or his very precious camera, he walks out the front door. And I have to choose. I have to choose. *Choose!*

But I don't call for him to wait. I don't speak to Corrine. I stand in my grandma's living room, holding myself together just barely, my shoulders up to my ears and all my muscles tensing.

"Don't lie," Corrine whispers, her eyes shining with unshed tears. "I gave you so many chances to talk about what was going on between you two, and if you were lying the whole time—"

"We, no, there wasn't anything happening—I don't know . . . we hooked up."

"How *long* have you been hooking up?"

"It just happened today."

"Were you going to tell me?"

"Of course!"

She rolls her eyes. "So, no. You weren't."

"I would have, eventually, when I figured out how to say it. When I figured out what was even happening."

"Well, sure, it would be pretty awkward to just start dating Holden and not give me any warning." She tilts her head to the side. "But maybe you would have done that. I feel like I don't know anymore."

"I didn't want to hurt you."

"You did, though. And I don't think you tried very hard not to." She turns toward the door. "I would have been okay with it, for the record. It would have taken some time to get used to it, but I tried to be open and accepting. But instead of owning up to it, you do this behind my back." Her shoulders wobble for a moment and I know she's trying not to cry. "I've been trying, Saine, and it doesn't feel like you have."

I still don't move. I can't choose. I can't pick one. I want them both. I need them both.

She leaves, and takes any hope of things being okay on the cutting room floor.

Nope. and friends

Today 4:52 PM

Corrine has left the group chat.

TWENTY-SEVEN

The next day, Holden catches me after school in the parking lot. Corrine didn't answer my calls or texts all yesterday, and she didn't come to school today despite there being a fundraiser during lunch for one of her clubs. Kayla and Juniper didn't think anything of it, but by the end of the period, they were questioning my silence. I told them I wasn't feeling well, and when I saw Holden across the cafeteria with Taj, I wasn't even lying. I was so wrapped up in what happened with Corrine, I hadn't even thought of Holden's tense exit.

"Hey," he says, pulling me toward the minivan. "You didn't text or anything. How did things go with you and Corrine?"

"They didn't really go . . . at all. Are *we* okay?" I ask.

"As long as I'm not some dirty little secret, yeah." He pauses. "Am I?"

"She knows what happened, but not that we . . ." *Not that what? We're . . . what?*

His fingers brush away a dark strand of my hair that flies

across my vision. "She'll cool down and then you guys can talk. She's probably feeling a lot of unpleasant things, and we know how she feels about . . . feeling feelings."

I can't help but smile a little.

He leans down, his fingers tangling into my hair behind my ear, and plants a soft kiss right at the corner of my mouth. He freezes and glances around, but it's just us and the minivan. "Is this okay?"

"I said you're not a secret." I prop myself up on tiptoes to kiss him, but he pulls away.

"So Kayla and Juniper know? Your mom?"

I drop back down. "Well, no—I'm not sure what there is to know, if you know what I mean."

He nods. "Yeah. We should discuss that."

"I want to talk to Corrine first." I grab his collar and pull him in for a kiss, soft and silent against his lips. "I messed up by not doing that the first time . . . and the second time."

When his brows knit together, I add, "The first time being when we decided to work together and the second time being when she asked if I had feelings for you and I lied."

He smirks. "How long have you liked me?"

I debate playing this cool, but Holden knows me. He knows I'm *not* cool. "Since your twelfth birthday party. Not kissing me was the ultimate neg." It almost doesn't even sting to joke about this.

"It wasn't a neg!" His cheeks go bright red. "I liked you and I didn't want our first kiss to be with an audience of Cheeto-stained idiots."

"Excuse me?" I take a step back to see him fully. "I hated you for years because of that; why wouldn't you have just said?"

He slides open the minivan door and coaxes me inside until I'm on my back in the space between the front and middle seats. "Why didn't *you* say you liked me?" He shuts us in and kisses me sweetly, one arm propping himself above me and the other bringing goose bumps to life on the skin under my shirt. "We could have been doing this," he says with his mouth against my neck.

"As fun as this is," I say, pushing him away with a smile, "we're in the school parking lot, these windows aren't tinted, and my mom needs the car."

He groans in Teenage Boy Angst, but lets me out. He walks me to my car, his hand in mine subtly at our sides, and kisses me before opening my car door.

"Interview tomorrow. My place. After school. Please bring my camera and my jacket."

"Got it, but sorry, the jacket's mine now. It smells like you."

"Fine, you can keep it, but I'm picking you up tomorrow morning for school. Then we can go together to my house after." He kisses me and I can feel the smirk on his lips when he does. "Reintroduce you to my bedroom before the interview—"

I grin. "Do you remember when I said I had to go home?"

"Do you remember when I said you're my favorite person in the world?"

"I *don't*, actually. When did you say that?"

"Oh. Huh. I meant to. Guess I got distracted." He tries to plant another kiss on my neck, his thumb drawing lazy circles on my thigh, but I duck under his arm and into my car.

"See you tomorrow." I shut the door before he has the chance to delay me further. I can't help but feel guilty when I think about how I started the day miserable and ended it in pure bliss, essentially for the same reason: because I can't keep myself away from Holden Michaels.

Ultimately, Trevor hadn't given the okay to be in the documentary—*yet*—so I'm still hiding that he's the heart of the film from Holden. I think in the end it'll be okay since he said he wouldn't be watching it anyway, and I tell myself this over and over when I start to feel bad. This is a lot like keeping Holden a secret from Corrine. It's kind of fine as long as he doesn't know, and the only people who will see the documentary are me and the admissions team at Temple University.

While he's setting up for the video call with Vice and Virtual, I interview Mama Michaels about her kids. She gives me candid answers to questions about Trevor's diagnosis, his prognosis, his likes and dislikes—basically everything I can't get from Trevor or Holden.

"He hadn't told me why he was doing that contest, but I knew." She smiles with watery eyes, the camera capturing it all. "I just know Holden. He's good. I have two great sons."

Wrapping up, I ask, "Where do you see yourself this time next year? Ideally."

I slowly zoom in.

She tilts her head to the side in thought. "Let's see. Holden's away at school, a photography major. Maybe he'll decide to be some kind of photojournalist. I don't really care as long as he's happy. Taylor's halfway to her own degree, Mara's following Trevor around *everywhere* and he's constantly groaning about how he didn't sign up for a younger sibling. And I have to remind him that he did that to Holden."

"But what about you?"

She blinks. "Oh, I don't care much. As long as they're healthy and happy. I'd just want to be around to see it, with Darren."

I offer a small smile behind my camera. "Last question: Who's your favorite kid?"

She bursts into laughter, a single tear leaking out finally. She brushes it away and settles down. "I don't have favorites. I love them all equally."

"Don't lie."

She just winks at the camera, leaving the question unanswered like I hoped she would. It'll make for a good soundbite to play over a little montage of her kids in the final moments of the documentary. I wrap up and head downstairs to Holden's room, where he's set up a tripod for my camera and some semi-professional lighting equipment he either owns or stole from the school's photography lab.

"Is it time?" I attach my camera to the tripod.

"Just about," he says distractedly, tweaking the light behind his laptop a smidge. He checks how he looks in his MacBook screen, the camera displaying his well-lit face bright and crisp. "I still have no clue what they want to ask me that they didn't already. It's not like I won."

I ignore the stab of guilt that gives me. Things have been

better, for the most part, since I threw the contest. Vice and Virtual will get whatever extra footage they need from Holden and I'll get *my* interview, and then the reveal for Trevor and . . . then we're done—minor editing notwithstanding. The thought doesn't fill me with overwhelming, heavy sadness or regret anymore; I feel hopeful. Just because this ends doesn't mean we don't have something else beginning.

God, I'm so glad Yvette bailed.

Vice and Virtual lets Holden into the Zoom and he's greeted by a representative who introduces herself as Charlotte. They do some small talk about the weather and school, how *unfortunate* it was that he couldn't compete in the last contest. Again with the guilt.

"So, Holden," Charlotte says with a glossy smile. "We were reviewing footage for our final episode of the web series—the whole series goes live next week on YouTube—and we found something interesting that we hoped to have you comment on."

I shift out of sight of the camera, watching the screen as Charlotte requests to screen share. Holden glances at me over his shoulder and accepts.

"As you'll see," Charlotte continues, "the girl you had run for you—"

Everything goes in slow motion as a video begins to play.

"It appears she—"

My insides constrict.

"Let someone else—"

Shock. My whole body is in shock. I can't move. I can't even talk.

"Win."

On the screen, it's clear I didn't know I was being filmed by anything other than my GoPro. It's right there, plain as day, me letting Lada take the box and win. I might as well have rolled out a red carpet.

I can't believe I forgot they were filming their own docuseries.

"Holden?" Charlotte asks, her face appearing on the screen before him again. "Would you care to comment?"

For a moment, he doesn't move. All the sound has tunneled down to just the *thud thud thud* of my increasing heart rate. Then he clears his throat and it feels like the oxygen returns to the room.

"I have no comment." He slams the laptop lid down and swivels to me, a dumbass deer in the headlights.

Oh shit. I can't believe I convinced myself that Corrine was the only obstacle in a potential relationship with Holden. Up until now, I was still working on this documentary behind his back—using his little brother to tug on heartstrings, fabricating a financial struggle to make him relatable. All my manipulation comes flashing forward and I'm stunned into paralysis. Why did I do that? Why did I do that to Holden and why am I only really feeling bad, realizing the consequences, now that it's come to light? Now that I have him to lose as something other than a friend? Is it because I lost him before and survived? I don't think I can this time.

Everything I did was to make the documentary better. One tweak here, one lie there, color correction to make it consistent.

It was okay when it was just me and Admissions. It was our secret, a harmless one that wouldn't ever come back to haunt me. I didn't mean for *this* to happen.

"I can explain."

His tone is hard, sharp. "I'm sure you can't."

I reach for his hand, but he pulls away, standing in one swift motion. "Holden. I didn't know. I didn't know why you wanted the headset."

"I'm supposed to forgive you then, because you didn't know? You knew that I wanted them, and you almost had them, but then—what?"

"I just—I panicked. It was about to be over and then I wouldn't get to see you all the time anymore. Look at this whole story we created after you lost. I found the heart *after* the contest."

"Oh, please," he says through gritted teeth. "Don't lie. I know when you're lying, Saine. You've always been a bad actress."

With my heart threatening to hammer its way through my rib cage, I take one steadying breath. "That *is* the truth. Part of it. But there was nothing to your story, because you didn't tell me the truth. I couldn't let you have a happy ending. You didn't earn it and my documentary would have been boring. It was like, in that moment, you getting the prize would mean me *not* getting into Temple."

"Tell me this is a bad joke."

I focus on the ground. "I needed an excuse to be around you, to keep working on the documentary."

"You didn't. You didn't need an excuse. You could have just

303

asked me. I wanted to be your friend again so badly, I wanted you, and you, you did *this*." He attacks the tears shedding from his eyes with careless hands. "You're so selfish. You've always been so selfish. It's always about what you want."

"I didn't know." My voice breaks. "I'm sorry. I didn't think it was a big deal, but as soon as I knew, I tried to fix it."

"Fix it? The only thing you tried to fix was your documentary." He pulls my camera from the tripod and stuffs it into my hands; I nearly drop it. "Good luck finishing now. I'm out."

"You're out?" I track his progress as he tears down the lighting equipment. "What does that mean?"

"It means I'm not filming anymore. And you can't use me and my brother as some plot device to get you into school. I'm *done*."

"It's so much better, the story going this way." I ball my free hand into a fist. "You *earn* the ending. There's nothing exciting about just getting the headset. At least Lada had something she wanted to prove; even when I tried to *make* a plot about a financial struggle with your family, it wasn't special. This plot with Trevor is so compelling—"

"Not everything has to be a fucking story! Sometimes someone just gets something they want without having to jump through unnecessary hoops. Maybe just going for the thing means they've earned it. Stop trying to play the director of my life." He thrusts a hand into his hair. "I can't believe I thought this could work. I can't believe I forgot how you're always looking out for yourself first. To call Trevor a *plot*. And on top of manipulating this thing by losing the contest, you were lying

304

about why I was doing it? For money?"

It hurts. It does. I didn't think making one little decision would end up like this. I didn't know it would affect Trevor. I didn't *know* and it's like he's not hearing me, not caring that it was an accident. He just wants to be mad and that makes me mad.

He points to the door leading to the stairs. "You need to leave."

"Holden."

He turns back to his equipment, throwing the pieces onto his bed. "Go on. Leave."

"Please turn around and talk to me—"

"You're used to doing things behind my back; this won't be any different."

ACT THREE

in which forgiveness is fought for

TWENTY-EIGHT

My grandma isn't here when I get home, but this isn't the first time I've forgotten and had the full force of her death hit me again. She's the first person I want to talk to about this. She'd tell me how I can fix it all. Next on my list of people to talk to would be Corrine, but I can't call her. I can't even talk to Kayla because she didn't know that Holden and I were semi-officially together.

My mom finds me pacing in the living room, reaching for my necklace that I probably will never get back at this rate unless it's suddenly thrown in my face along with some of Corrine's most creative insults.

"What's going on?"

I pan to her, my tearstained, stiff cheeks aching when I open my mouth to speak. "What are you doing home?"

She rushes over, holding me close and rubbing my back. "I had some personal time to take. Tell me what's happening."

"I messed up."

"Back up and explain what happened."

"I fell in love with Corrine's ex-boyfriend," I say.

"Isn't that—wait, that's Holden, isn't it?" She pulls away to look me in the eyes. "Baby, do you like Holden?"

"I love him," I whisper, tears coming fresh. "And I've lost him, and Corrine, and I don't know how to get them back."

"Sit down," she says, gently pulling me to the couch. "Explain."

I exhale. "I sabotaged Holden's chances of getting the VR headset he wanted, and kissed him, and kept stuff from Corrine, and told her I didn't have feelings for him when I knew I did." I bite my lip. "But I swear—I *swear*—I didn't mean any of it in a malicious way, I just wanted a better documentary and more time with him, and it was the perfect excuse. But I also didn't want to hurt Corrine, so I just, I don't know, didn't tell her how deep I dug my grave and now I've come out in China or whatever."

"Grandma always said you were an overachiever."

"It's not funny," I say, leaning my head against her shoulder. "Corrine hasn't spoken to me since Sunday. We've never gone this long without talking; even when she had her devices taken away for back-talking Mrs. Fields in eighth grade, she found a way to message me."

She squeezes me against her. "Love complicates everything. It tells you you're right when you're wrong. It makes you do things you know you shouldn't. It's the most powerful feeling in the world." She sighs, and a loose strand of my hair falls into my eye. "I don't really have any advice for you except groveling.

You messed up, kid. Apologize for it. Over and over again."

I nod, but I hate that answer. It sounds long and painful and like I'm not going to get the outcome I want. Unacceptable.

"But if you love them both, and I think you do, things will be okay eventually. They love you back, and when you love someone, you're more likely to forgive them for the stupid stuff they do."

We sit in silence as my mind spins a million miles an hour. I can't turn in my documentary anymore. It doesn't have an ending, it doesn't have Holden's or Trevor's blessing, and Holden would never forgive me if I turned it in. I have to focus on finishing up the VR edits and putting together the headset, so at least then I have something else to give to Holden when he's not interested in my apologies. I have to keep begging Corrine to forgive me. She needs something tangible, I think, because that's how *she* shows that she's here for me, but I don't know what to do. Not yet.

My mom thinks I need something mind-numbing to do, so I don't spiral. She's right, but I put up a fight the whole car ride to the apartment complex that houses The One.

"What are we doing here?" I'm not in the mood to discuss leaving the only place that feels safe to me right now.

"I wanted to show you our new apartment." She puts the car in park and exits the car.

"What?" I leave the car, slamming the door behind us. "You mean *potential* apartment?"

"Nope." She pulls out a key and opens the front door. "Our

new apartment—townhome, actually. They still have to install some new appliances and put down new carpet, but this is it."

"You made this decision without me? When I said no?" *And more importantly, when I'm feeling lower than dirt, you bring me here to rub it in my face?*

She glances at me over her shoulder. "I'm the adult. I'm the one who'll end up living here longer than you." She walks into the echoing, empty living room. "And I knew you liked it. You just found reasons not to because you didn't want to move. So I made the decision."

"Without me. Against my wishes."

"Guess we know where you get that from," she says quietly.

I ignore her, because if we go down this rabbit hole, I get my stubbornness from her and she gets it from my grandma. "I'm not ready."

"You're never going to be ready unless I force you to be."

It's been no time at all in the grand scheme of things. I'm allowed to grieve, even Holden said so. "Why am I here? I have other things I need to deal with."

"Go to your room."

"Excuse me?"

"Just go," she says, pointing to the stairs.

She follows me up and into "my" room. There's a sheet on the ground, paint cans and brushes on top.

"Let's get to work," she says, offering me a smock stiff with paint splotches—one of my grandma's. I haven't seen it in months. There's a little handprint on the bottom left side from when I "helped" her one day.

"What?"

"We're painting your wall."

"I told you earlier, I'm not in the mood for manual labor." I watch as she throws on her own smock, one I've never seen before. "You might have noticed the complete emotional breakdown I'm having? Maybe?"

"And I said we need something mind-numbing. That sounds like cleaning or painting to me." She starts prying at the lid of the paint can. "I figured you'd prefer painting over cleaning."

"Painting is *not* mind-numbing." I think about all the lectures my grandma gave about freeing your artistic spirit and leaning into your passions. All that fluffy bullshit seems to have skipped over my mom and landed squarely in me.

"Well, this kind is."

I step up next to her as she pops the lid off, revealing bright teal paint, the same color as my three un-muraled walls at home. She pours it into the plastic roller tray and offers me a fresh roller brush.

"Nothing better for an emotional breakdown than the ability to just turn everything off for a moment."

I accept the brush silently.

"Now's the time to tell me if you want something special on it, or some kind of design that requires painter's tape."

I shake my head. Plain walls will have to do; I'm not sure I'd even want the hellscape I'd be stuck with if my mother and I attempted something else. It would definitely never compare to what my grandma could do. Besides, I can't make any decisions right now. My life has turned into one mistake after the other and they're rolling down the hill, picking up each other and speed, until they crash at the bottom and pin me against more of my problems.

"Why are you doing this?" I dip the roller into the paint and start on the opposite side of the wall from her. "And don't give me a sugary answer, please."

"It's a nice, relaxing distraction. It's productive. It's—" She shrugs. "It's really the only thing I could think of to help you right now." She smiles sadly. "Grandma was the one with the answers."

"She was."

"And yet," she says with the hint of a laugh, "I'm not sure she'd even know where to start with all of this. You really did get yourself into a mess with this one."

I replenish the paint. "I just want to be able to have them both. They were both mine before they were anything to each other. It doesn't seem fair that I can't have either now."

"It probably doesn't seem fair to them that they're losing you now, but *you* did that." She dips her roller into the paint. "How would you feel if you were in either of their places?"

I stare at the paint growing in front of me. "Blue." She laughs. "I'd want to punch me. I'd want to punch me right in the ovaries."

"Something tells me neither of them will be doing that, though. *You* have to be the one to make the first move."

"So I need to punch myself in the ovaries?"

"You'll figure it out."

We fall into silence. I watch her methodically paint the

walls, her strokes even and consistent while mine are erratic and patchy, and admire that she's doing this for me. She's packing up my grandma's stuff for me, so I don't have to go through the pain she probably is when she goes through it; she's taking care of picking the place she knows I liked best; she's painting painting painting and working working working. She's doing her best to connect herself to me and my grandma, even when it's a painful connection right now, all to make me feel better when I definitely don't deserve to. I could learn a thing or two from her. Selflessness.

TWENTY-NINE

"This documentary has no ending," I say into the camera.

I take a deep breath. "The ending was supposed to be giving Trevor the VR headset we made," I say, holding up the cheap goggles I bought for holding a smartphone in front of your eyes, "but then you found out that I manipulated your story and, rightfully, you're pretty pissed off. So. This will have to do."

I'm about to turn off the camera, but stop myself. I look into the lens, not feeling the scrutiny of the Temple admissions office, but of Holden. I'm not turning the documentary in. On the very unlikely chance that I got in with it, I couldn't live with that. I'd be doing the thing Holden specifically told me not to by making Trevor a plot device—treating a suffering, sick *friend* of mine as nothing more than the key to my own success. I'd be a terrible documentarian, having manipulated my subjects, having lied, having ignored their revoked consent. I'm more likely to be a reality TV producer at this rate.

"I like being able to filter the world to my liking, so people see me or what I want them to see, the way I want them to see it. And that fear of being exposed as something imperfect is what got me into this mess. If I had just been honest . . . If I had let things unfold the way they were supposed to, I would have a lot less problems in my life.

"I'm always looking for a story, but I ignored my part in this one because, I don't know, I'm not the hero. I'm the villain. And that's hard to acknowledge until everything falls apart. I'm sorry, Holden. I was wrong. And I'll try to make it up to you."

I stop recording, transfer the footage to my computer, and add it to the end of the documentary. I don't want to overthink it, so I just put it on a flash drive with the VR footage for Holden, and then close my laptop.

My mom just left for work, so the car is gone when I need to make my way to Holden's through a gust of flurries. His beat-up minivan isn't outside his house when I knock.

"He's not here," Mara says, trying to close the door in my face.

I slide my foot in to stop it and offer the flash drive. "Will you please just give him this? I finished."

There's hesitation clear in her eyes when she looks at my outstretched hand. "I shouldn't. You should give it to him." She gnaws at her bottom lip. "He's with Taj right now."

I sigh, a huff of cold air filling the space between us, and pocket the drive.

Mara frowns. "Why'd you do it?"

"I was selfish."

The door opens a fraction more. "Are you guys going to be

friends again in time for my date?"

A sharp pang attacks my heart. "I don't think so. I *hope* so, but you're probably going with just Holden."

Her composure splits. "He was only invited because he has the car! I need you there."

"Maybe Taylor can go?"

"She's back at school." Her bottom lip juts out. "When I told her to go back there, I didn't really mean it. Now I don't have her or you. And Holden's a total mope. And I can't hang out with Trevor because I can't get to the hospital on my own and my parents are always busy." She sniffs. "I'm lonely."

I pull her into a tight hug and she exhales so deeply I think maybe I punctured her. "It'll be okay."

"You have to make this right," she says into my embrace. "He was so happy lately and you're, like, the coolest friend he has."

"I'm going to do my best."

"I don't think I can stay friends with you if he's not friends with you."

I want to laugh at this, but she's being serious, so I just squeeze her tighter and then release. "I'll try. I can't lose both of you."

She wipes away a tear and nods. "At least he has a huge, big, monstrous crush on you, so he'll probably be more inclined to forgive you. Don't tell him I told you, though."

I smile. "Good to know."

Before the first bell rings the next day, I find Taj at his locker and politely threaten him into telling me where Holden is. Two minutes later, I walk into the computer lab—also known as Holden's Fortress of Solitude—as he's flitting through several yearbook photos in Photoshop.

He eyes me warily when I enter, but because there's another kid in here, earbuds in his ears, I think maybe I'm safe from any outright yelling Holden's reserved for me.

"I can't tell you to leave because the lab is open to anyone right now, but you should leave," he says, eyes back on his computer, the glow from the screen highlighting the dark circles under his eyes.

I sit down next to him, and it takes me an embarrassing amount of time to calm down. I watch as he tweaks the photos in minor ways, distractingly awed at his work. The photos are stunning to start with, but once he's worked on them for one, two minutes, they come alive, like he knew exactly what he would do with them when he took the photos.

He finally looks my way. "Are you just going to sit there and stare?"

I swallow. "No." I pull the flash drive and headset from my backpack and offer them with a shaky hand. "You don't have to forgive me, and you don't have to watch this, but I'd like you to do both. Mostly the forgiveness part because I just got you back and losing you feels awful."

He ignores me long enough to save his photos and collect his things. "Bye."

"Holden," I say, standing when he stands. "Please. *Please.*"

"If I take that, you're going to feel just a little less guilty about what you did." He looks me up and down. "I'm not feeling generous enough to give you that relief today."

He swings his backpack over his shoulder and turns to leave, but I grab on to his bag, unzip one of the many pockets, and stuff the drive and headset inside. It's his to do with what he wants now, but if I know Holden—and I know Holden—he'll be driven nuts by the thought of this thing in his bag, and he'll watch it. *Please let him watch it.*

I'm met with a sneer when he pans toward me. "Even after everything, you're still just doing whatever you want without thinking about how it makes anyone else feel. Maybe we were meant to stop being friends all those years ago."

"That's not true."

"Did you ever for one second in your selfish life stop to think about what life was like for me when you stopped being my friend?"

The words hit me like a blow to the stomach. "You stopped being *my* friend."

He laughs harshly. "Yeah, keep telling yourself that." He starts counting on his fingers. "I texted you, I invited you to hang out, you were the only person at my birthday party that year who wasn't from my new school—I fucking tried, Saine. Then you just left me, and I had to deal with *so* much on my own. It took forever for me to trust Taj because I thought he was just going to leave me one day when I became too much for him. You left me for no reason."

"I was embarrassed. I thought you didn't like me." I rewind to his birthday party. The bottle lands on me and the horror on his face isn't because I'm disgusting. It's because I'm his best friend and he loves me and he's twelve and doesn't know what to do.

"My brother gets sick, my parents divorce. Do you know how that made me feel?" He cuts me off before I can say anything. "Pretty shitty, Saine! You know what would have made it better? You not running away from me." He scrubs at the side of his face and his voice is weaker this time when he says, "You not making me trust you again just to have you pull the same shit all over."

"I just made some mistakes."

"It's not a mistake when you knew what you were doing was wrong. You *chose* to do what you did. So why should I forgive you this time? You're just going to mess up again and I'm just going to be the dumbass who lets you do it, over and over. I've always been that idiot who followed your lead. Well, I'm not doing that anymore, and I'm not going to forgive you. You have to *earn* it, right? Can't let things be too easy for you just because you want it."

With that, he pivots away from me and out the door just as the bell rings.

THIRTY

The weather copies my mood for the next few days, and that would be great if I were happy or something. But the rain and wind, the sleet, then the snow . . . it's just a little too much for me. It's already dark by 4:30 on Tuesday and I'm heading toward another night of me doing homework and then going to bed with a random nature documentary on before anyone who'd order an early bird special would when the phone rings.

It hasn't rung in so long that I forgot we had a landline. It trills again, muffled.

"That scared the shit out of me," my mom hisses, wide-eyed with her hand clutched to her chest. "Can you get that, please?" She turns back to her lunch bag where she's stuffing celery sticks.

I unearth the phone from a pile of coupons that slide onto the floor and answer. "Hello?"

"Hi, is this the Easy Easel?" a deep voice asks.

I nearly drop the phone. *No.*

"I saw the sign in your yard," it continues. "My son's six and he really needs a creative outlet—"

With my heart hammering, I hang up and throw the phone on the counter, causing the rest of the coupons to slide off. I don't even bother with shoes before throwing open the door and marching outside. The fibers of my sock stick to the bits of ice lingering on our driveway, but I keep pressing forward, the whole way to the sign sitting innocently in our front yard. It's been there so long that I hadn't looked twice at it since my grandma's heart attack. It was just always there. Faded and worn, but there.

I stomp onto the snow, my feet burning from the cold, and try to rip the small wooden sign out.

"Saine? What happened—" My mom stops mid-sentence to gape at me fighting with the sign.

"This stupid piece of shit!" I scream at it. The ground has frozen around it. It refuses to give up my grandma, but if I had to, then it definitely has to. I yank until my fingers are frozen and raw, until it wiggles free and I fall on my ass.

"Hey," my mom says, helping me up, "what's going on? Are you okay?"

My face feels chapped, windblown, and tight. It's not until she pushes away a tear that I realize any managed to leak out in the low temperature.

"Why do we still have this stupid thing up?" I throw the sign into the driveway. It skids a few feet until it hits the tire of our car. "There's no one here to teach lessons."

"I didn't even think about it." She ushers me back inside, her hands on my shoulders. "I'm sorry. Did someone—was someone trying to schedule a lesson?"

"Yeah, but they won't make that mistake again." I wipe away another tear and peel off my socks. The floor, which is usually arctic levels of cold on my bare feet, feels warm enough to thaw me.

I try to break away from my mom to get into warm, dry clothes, but she just holds on to me tighter. "What?"

"We should talk about this."

"I don't want to." I take a breath in. *Five-six-seven-eight.* "I'm fine."

She meets my eyes, and it's unwelcome how much they look like mine. How much they look like my grandma's. "You're very clearly not fine."

I look away. "You have to go to work."

"Screw work."

"Yeah," I laugh bitterly. "Tell that to the power company."

"This is about more than just the phone call."

I sniff, shuffling my foot against the other. "It's been a bad week."

She raises her eyebrows. "It's Tuesday."

"A bad *year.*" I sniff. "I'm mad—really mad, but I don't have any right to be." I shake my head. "I don't know why I'm mad."

"Of course you have a right to be. Awful things have happened and you made some mistakes. You're mad at the world and you're mad at *yourself.*"

"You always have to work," I croak out. "And Grandma is gone. None of my friends like me anymore and, even if they did, they wouldn't for long because I'm depressing to be around and I screw everything up. When you leave, I just go to bed so I don't have to think or replay me messing up over and over again." The devastated, angry looks Holden and Corrine gave me rewind and repeat in my head every night until unconsciousness takes pity on my pathetic self and sweeps me away.

Everything is a jumbled, chaotic mess.

"Hey, look . . ." She pulls her phone from her pocket, one hand still on my shoulder like she thinks I'll run away. "I have to call work and let them know I'll be late. Go change. Into something warm."

I'm so relieved she's not leaving that I do exactly as she says; I might even overkill, with a beanie, gloves, and the faux-fur-lined boots I got two years ago for Christmas.

When I come back out to the living room, my mom sits on the couch with her jacket folded over her lap. "Ready?" she asks, standing up.

I sniff again. "I don't know. Maybe?"

"We're taking a walk." She throws the jacket on and zips it up to her chin.

"Is this where you take me into the woods and murder me so you can save some change on a single-bedroom apartment?"

"Too late for that; the lease has already been signed."

She nudges me out the door with a smile and we head right onto the sidewalk. I don't know where we're going—I just assume we're getting some fresh air—until we turn onto Richard Street and head toward a small cemetery a few blocks away.

I stop.

Over her shoulder, she says to me, "No. Come on. Let's go."

I haven't been here since her funeral, even though her grave is only a few minutes' walk from a place I am every single day. It kind of makes me feel bad. Like, just to consider how lonely I've been. She must be even lonelier.

I'm not someone who believes in heaven or hell, and I know my grandma isn't here anymore, but I still feel ashamed that I haven't come to visit her.

Selfish. How am I any better than Corrine if I avoid things that make me uncomfortable, too? I tiptoed around all the Holden stuff at the beginning because I didn't want the conflict. I didn't visit my grandmother I insisted I missed so much when she's been just a moment away.

We wind our way through the graves and I'm careful not to step on anything that's obviously the final resting site for someone, and stop in front of my grandma's.

There are flowers here. Fresh ones. I glance at my mom, tears welling in my eyes again despite the cold. A wind blows her hair across her face.

"Do you come here?" I ask in a weak voice.

My grandma was well-liked and well-known around town, but someone would have to be pretty close with her to leave flowers. I can't imagine any of her students did, since most of them are too young to fully understand why they weren't going to the Easy Easel anymore.

"Every other Tuesday." *Tuesday. The day she died.* She wipes at her nose. "Hey, Mom."

I face the headstone and whisper, "H-hi." Then I burst into

nervous laughter. "This feels so stupid."

"It helps me," my mom says seriously.

"I need her to talk back." I bite my bottom lip. "To tell me what to do."

"You know who would do a really good job at that?"

I lean against her shoulder, my eyes scanning the smooth stone in front of us. "A *therapist*, I know."

"I could go with you, if you want. Or I could keep doing this. You could come here with me." She lays her head against mine and wraps an arm around my back. "Whatever works for you. We'll make it work for you."

I don't want to argue about money, about how that therapist visit could be groceries for the week. Not when I'm so low. Not when we're in front of my grandma's grave. She would scold the shit out of us if we argued about money in a graveyard.

It sounds like a setup to a joke, and the image of it has me laughing. "Grandma would make me go to therapy."

"It wouldn't even be a choice."

"I . . . I want to talk."

My mom pulls away and nods, her attention on my chilled face. "It doesn't have to be a weekly thing. We'll go at your pace."

"I'm just worried about the—"

"No. Don't." She pushes some hair behind my ear. "That's my job."

"But—"

"The only thing you should worry about is wetting your whistle so you don't get hoarse from talking."

"That's such an embarrassing thing to say, I'm sure even Grandma is cringing." I stop myself from laughing when I realize I'm essentially making a joke that my grandma is dead. I continue to be the worst. But when she sees my face, my mom's small smile falters.

"It's okay, you know?" She breaks eye contact to watch an old man walking through the graves on the other side of the cemetery. "To process this how you want. I'm sorry for trying to make you do it my way."

"I don't think making jokes is really processing it."

"Are you kidding me? Jokes and laughter are the only thing that keep me going every day. *Your* jokes and laughter." She nods toward the flowers on my grandma's grave. "Those flowers? They're petunias." She watches me for a second before laughing. "She fucking hated petunias."

She bends over, hands on her knees as she continues to wheeze. I laugh hesitantly, and when she spots my bewildered face, she laughs harder. "She said they were the Dixie cups of flowers."

Now I join in full force, more because of the absurdity than anything being funny. But it's okay. It feels *nice* to laugh after the days I've had. After the loss we've suffered. Everything with Corrine and Holden will work out in whatever way it needs to, but in the meantime, I'm going to take care of myself and be ready for them if they decide to give me another chance.

THIRTY-ONE

My new—but some could argue *not* improved—extracurricular schedule is a lot to handle all at once: a weekly seven-in-the-morning Jane Austen Appreciation Club meeting, a lunchtime fundraiser for the prom planning committee, and a donation drive for the environmental club, which I joined even though it wasn't in jeopardy of being shut down because I know how much it means to Corrine. I even initiated a new program for basketball season where the cheerleaders take donations before the game in exchange for doing whatever dance the donor requests.

To no one's surprise, I am the only other member of the Jane Austen Appreciation Club because people who like Jane Austen are busy reading Jane Austen and also have Intense opinions about her work that they do not need confirmed by others. This I know all from things Corrine has said in the past. I have not yet read one of Austen's books, but I plan to now that I am automatically the vice president of the club. It was the most urgent on the list of Chopping Block Clubs.

Here we are, sitting in Mademoiselle Desombre's empty French classroom, these uncomfortable desk chairs beneath our thighs, silent. To her credit, Corrine has an Austen book in front of her but I can tell she's not reading it. That's not even what this club is about. I read the information in this huge binder of clubs for the year. We're supposed to *discuss* the books. Again, I haven't read any, so maybe she just knows that we can't talk about them.

I clear my throat. "Corrine?"

"What?" Her tone is clipped, but I note something hopeful in it.

"Can we talk?"

"Would you like to discuss Jane Austen?"

"No?"

"Then no."

I think. *What will make Corrine talk?* "What about Darcy? Mr. Darcy?"

She puts her book down and raises an eyebrow at me. "What about him? How do you know who he is?"

"I have Netflix." I figured it was better than coming in totally unprepared, right? Not like I could really sleep knowing I'd be seeing her in the morning anyway. Seemed like a better use of time than staring at the ceiling imagining every scenario in which Corrine could maim me.

Despite the eye roll, she says, "Continue."

"For all intents and purposes, he was kind of a real asshole for a while, but it wasn't really his intention."

"Are you trying to Darcy your way out of the fact that you lied to me and did things behind my back?"

"*No.* I'm just saying that he wasn't trying to be an asshole, but he was. And he was sorry for it, and he tried to make up for it."

"Is that why you joined all of my clubs?" She turns to face me. We're about six desks away from each other because she took the first seat when you walk into the room and I had taken a back seat, worried about getting caught alone in a classroom before school started. I'm new to the whole club thing. "To make up for what you did?"

"No, I joined your clubs because you were worried about them being shut down, and I know how much you like them and you want them for your college apps." I bite my lip. "And I guess also because I wanted to show you I was sorry."

"Start with the truth next time."

"If everything I said was the truth, how am I supposed to prioritize one truth over the other?"

"I don't know," she says, throwing her hands in the air. "I don't know, Saine."

I move to the desk next to her, cautiously. "How about we talk?"

"We are talking."

I search her eyes. "I don't want to lose you. You're my best friend."

"We need to get a lot out in the open, then."

"You can start." I continue when she glares at me, "I meant you could ask me questions, not that you've been keeping things from me."

She flattens her hair, then flips it over her shoulder. "I would like to know why you didn't just tell me about your feelings for Holden."

I take a deep breath. "It wasn't until the Millersville party that I realized I had them as badly as I did. I didn't want to hurt your feelings or upset you, so I kept anything I might have been feeling to myself. It was hard to even admit it to myself."

"Yeah, you hid it from me, lied to me, and now my feelings are more than hurt, they're, like, *dead* because you could have just told me. If I'm your best friend, how am I not worthy of the truth? Of knowing what's going on with you?"

"I didn't go about it the right way and I'm sorry. I've never . . . done this before."

She avoids my eyes. "What's going on with you guys now?"

"We're like negative nothing." I pick at the corner of the desk. "I fucked things up, separately, with him, and now I think you two could start an I Hate Saine club."

She stares at the Smart Board at the front of the room even though it's blank, like her expression. "That just pisses me off even more."

"I thought you'd feel vindicated or something."

"Why?" Finally, she turns to me, her brows furrowed. "Because I'm that petty? I'm in a really good, fun relationship, but you think I'd be happy that you and Holden went through all that, made me feel the way I did, all for it to result in you two *not* being together? Saine, I *wanted* you guys together," she says with exasperation in her voice.

"Yeah, he mentioned that. . . ."

"We were not a good fit. I broke up with him. I told you it was okay if you had feelings for him. Why would you not just tell me?"

"How was I supposed to tell anyone else if I couldn't even

face the facts in private?" I so badly want to reach out to her, sink my claws into her skin and never let go. I feel her drifting away and all I can do is watch, like that bitch Rose when she let Jack sink in *Titanic*. God*damn* Corrine for making me watch that with her every year on her birthday. It's not romantic. It's sad. "I've liked him for a long time."

"You should have said something the moment I mentioned meeting him last year."

"You would have thought I was so pathetic asking you not to date him. He rejected me when we were kids and I harbored feelings for him that turned so rotten I thought I *hated* him. Like, how do I even explain that?"

"With words. You just did it."

"Oh, and you're so receptive to words?" I hate the bite in my tone, hate what it does to her face, but then she sighs and nods.

"You're right. I'm sorry."

"*I'm* sorry," I say, pointing at myself.

"I guess the situation was a bit . . . complicated." She raps her fingernails against the desk. "Not entirely your fault."

She turns to me with watery eyes. "I lied about having sex. I didn't have a lot of sex. I've had sex once. Please don't tell anyone."

Part of me is jealous that their first times were with each other, even though they've both said it sucked, and first times don't really matter unless you make them matter. Another part of me just feels bad for them both. It should have been fun.

"It's okay," I say softly.

"It's not. You liked him and I rubbed it in your face without even realizing." She wipes at her eyes. "And I guess I did it after

I realized, too. Because even though I said it was okay, I didn't want to lose you to him."

"It's okay," I say again with force. "I forgive you."

"Don't think that you forgiving me for lying means I'll for-give you for lying." She bites her peach-tinted lip.

"Wouldn't dream of it."

She picks at the cover of her book. *Sense and Sensibility*. I wonder if that one's a movie, too. "I guess I do sort of forgive you. Not sure if I trust you, though."

I reach for her hand and squeeze, stalling her from flicking through pages. "I will do anything to build that up again."

She straightens in her seat. "I'm not sure how I would have reacted if our roles were switched. I want to think I'd be more considerate, but . . . I really don't know. I wouldn't have wanted to hurt you either."

We share a small, hopeful smile.

"Can I ask you something completely off topic that has been bothering me for a while? Since we're clearing the air?" I ask.

She blows out a breath, slow, and then meets my eyes. "Yeah. Go for it."

"I don't think you need to prepare yourself that much."

"I think I know what you're going to ask."

"Why did you, like, disappear after my grandma died? I mean, you were physically there and you were so helpful, but, like, emotionally? Why do you . . . just go away when I need you?"

Her voice cracks. "I'm not good with that stuff. You're always the one calming me down and talking sense into me, and I couldn't be that for you. I'm not good at talking. With the breakup happening at the same time, it was just a lot of feelings at once."

A laugh breaks free. "I know you freak out about this stuff, but, like, a hug? A hug would have gone so far. Just saying you were there for me if I needed you? I needed that, even if you were bad at it. I felt like you abandoned me, and then I felt bad for feeling that way because you were going through your own thing and I shouldn't depend on someone else to handle my grief. . . ."

Some of her hair gets caught in an errant tear, a slice of copper against her pink, splotchy cheeks. "I feel really bad about it. I just clam up." She clears her throat. "*Ugh*, I hate crying."

I laugh a little. "I just want you to know that I needed you; our relationship's not one-sided." I wipe my own tears away, knowing I don't look as good as she does when I cry. My makeup definitely doesn't stay intact like hers does. "Our friendship can't be over."

She latches onto my hand. "You can't get rid of me that easily."

Holden

Today 7:35 PM

I'm picking you up from practice

7:35 PM

We're going to the hospital to give Trevor the headset

7:35 PM

THIRTY-TWO

Holden doesn't say anything when I slide into the minivan, tucking my backpack and duffel between my legs, which only makes me more nervous to be in his presence. Not even the soothing smell of the new vanilla air freshener can calm me down. I'm about to just blurt out my feelings like the huge, selfish asshole he says I am when two voices from the back startle me.

"Hi, Saine."

"Hey."

In the second-row captain seats, Mara and Ant sit with smiles on their faces, so big that I'm forced to return one, even though it's more confused than happy.

"Hey." My heart hammers so violently in my chest I'm surprised they can't hear it. If they could, they would for sure make fun of me. Kids are ruthless. I used to respect the No Filter thing, but now I'm hoping their hardware was upgraded to include one because I cannot take it today.

"I'm so excited," Ant says when Holden starts driving. "Trevor's gonna flip out."

"Holden wouldn't let me try the glasses," Mara says dejectedly, a pout on her lips. "But if *you* say I can, then maybe—"

"No," I say lightly. "Trevor first." I glance at Holden. "And if Holden said no, you should respect that. He put a lot of work into the headset, and it's his gift for Trevor."

Mara sinks back into her chair but doesn't fight it. Holden's tense beside me, his knuckles white on the steering wheel. If the muscle twitches on his face are any indication, he's having some kind of internal battle with himself. Probably debating whether or not he should just ditch me on the side of the road. I fucking hate myself for even thinking it—I shouldn't think it—but he still looks so good, even with his dark circles and gnawed lips. What a shame he hates me because I really, really love him.

"So, what's going on with the two of you?" Ant says, leaning forward with a barely concealed smile. I stop looking at Holden immediately. "Are you fighting?"

"No," Holden says, *angrily*.

I smile tightly at Ant. "You heard him."

"Sure." Her brown eyes pan from me to the back of Holden's head. "I totally believe you."

Holden mashes a button on the dash and NPR starts playing, a dull drone in the background.

"Saine was selfish," Mara whispers to Ant after a few seconds.

I stare straight ahead, watching the van devour the road to the hospital. We pass through Camp Hill, the cracked sidewalks outside businesses suddenly very interesting to look at when the alternative is the grumpy face of the guy I betrayed.

"We need to talk after," Holden says quietly, eyes unblinking and forward.

My stomach drops even though I knew this was coming. I couldn't really expect him to just suddenly be okay with me. "Yeah, we do."

When we get to the hospital parking lot, Holden lets us out at the front entrance so he can find a spot. I walk the girls inside and sign us in at the desk like Holden had done with me.

"Hi, Mara," the volunteer—Libby, from before, because of course—greets them. "Hi, Ant."

She looks to me and I see her eyes glaze over. I'm not even worth noting to her, even though I came in with her favorite visitor once.

"Saine," Holden says, coming up behind me and reaching around to sign the list. "Hi, Libby."

"Hi, Holden." Her heart eyes track him the whole time we walk to Trevor's room.

Inside, Trevor is curled up on his bed, the room dark and warm. His mom sits next to him in one of the worn chairs, her yellow scrubs wrinkled. Like her, we don masks and gloves and gather around his bed.

"Hey, guys," she greets us brightly, but exhaustion taints her tone.

Holden's eyes crinkle toward his brother—a smile. "Hey, Trev."

Trevor sits up. "Hey." He glances at each of us for a second. "What's going on?"

"I, um, I had something I wanted to give to you." His hands

shake around the glasses, already attached to his old phone where I had instructed him to transfer the VR footage.

Mara offers Trevor headphones with silver Sharpie flowers crawling up them.

"Holden made you something." I push on Holden's shoulder gently and nod toward the glasses.

He hands them to Trevor. "They're shit."

"Rude," I say, pulling the standing fan closer to Trevor's bed. The first scene is driving shotgun with Holden and I want him to feel the wind whipping through his hair—or lack thereof. "Press play, put the glasses on, and then the headphones."

Trevor does as he's told, curiosity lining his face, and I plug the headphones into the exposed end of the phone. Ant leans her elbows on his bed, watching him as if she'll see what he sees, but not really caring that she won't. Mara sits on Mama Michaels's knee, eyes blinking impatiently for her turn. Her stepmom lays a hand on her shoulder, most likely to stop her from lunging at the device.

It takes about three seconds, but Trevor's mouth splits into a grin. His head starts nodding, and he mouths the words to a Queen song I don't know the name of. Holden wasn't shy about belting it, not for Trevor, not in front of me or the camera. Despite the cold weather and the dead trees, we pretended it was a summer day. And just thinking about that moment makes me want to cry. I have the footage backed up on my computer, but I can't replay that moment. I was there, but it wasn't for me.

Ant holds Trevor's hand as he cycles through the car ride, Nope.'s show, sneaking out of his bedroom window, playing chess with Mara at home, bowling with Ant and friends, the house party, and other things I filmed just in case it would matter, just in case he would care what it's like to watch stupid TV with his stepdad scream-laughing his way through, to sit in the cafeteria with other people who chat too loudly to be having real conversations, to be back in his bedroom. In case he wanted to know what it was like to sit in the crowd at a football game, alone, but surrounded. Together, but an individual. Holden helped with a lot of it, but other times I had just been filming. Things I thought would end up on the cutting room floor for the documentary felt perfect here.

By the end of the reel, which lasts about thirty minutes, he takes the glasses off and wipes at the tears pooled under his eyes. His voice cracks when he tries to speak, but Holden leans in, forcing his thin body into a hug that he reciprocates with full force.

"I'm sorry they're not the real thing."

"No, that was really cool," Trevor croaks out. "Even better."

It's clear there doesn't need to be a larger discussion. Trevor knows what the point of the headset is. He feels it completely.

Mara watches with a smile, then her eyes dart to mine. "Can I try it now?"

Trevor laughs, tearing the headphones from his ears and handing Mara all the equipment. "Have at it."

"Then me," Ant says, helping Mara gear up.

Holden breaks away from his brother, wipes his own eyes, and motions for me to follow him out of the room. As we're disposing of our masks and gloves, Mama Michaels wraps Trevor in a hug and starts asking him tons of questions about what he saw. We wander a little way down the hall, until we end up in the waiting room. It's pretty dead, which I realize now is terrible word choice given my location.

He sits down and I take the chair next to him, shifting a little at the stiffness, but mostly the awkwardness. For a moment, he just watches me. I try not to look away, but his gaze is heavy and it judges me.

"I'm sorry," I blurt out at the same time he says, "So, I watched the documentary." He pauses, giving me time to respond, and the only thing my dumb ass can think to say is: "I thought you didn't want to see your sweaty face in 1080p."

"Turns out I'm still good-looking. Who would have thought?"

Me.

"I'm sorry," I say with a sigh. "Again. I shouldn't have done what I did."

"You shouldn't have, no. And the whole financial struggle . . . How would you like it if someone shined a light on your money problems at home? Especially if they weren't as bad as someone made them out to be?" He jiggles his leg, waiting.

"I'd be furious and embarrassed and ashamed, and you're right to feel that way."

He sniffles. "Despite that, I think the glasses are pretty fucking cool, and I think Trevor really liked them. He has enough video games. This is something just for him."

I clear my throat. "Thank you for letting me be here to see it."

A heartwarming ending and not a camera in sight.

It's just what I deserve.

We end up drenched in painfully awkward silence—my first visit to the gynecologist wasn't even this bad. At least there was small talk to distract from the intimacy. He blows out a breath and then faces me again, pulling his leg up onto the chair.

"You aren't applying to Temple anymore?"

"I don't have a documentary to submit and the deadline is a few days from now." The thought of applying filled me with excitement two weeks ago. Now it's not even dread. It's just hollow. There's a spot in my gut where my Temple application used to sit, and now there's just empty air. I carved that hole there myself.

"Couldn't you submit the glasses or something?"

"That's—no. Those are Trevor's. That's for Trevor, and you." I hadn't even thought about submitting that footage. It would definitely help me stand out. But it's not a documentary and I'm not going to use this family anymore.

He nods to himself. "Okay. Test passed."

"What?" He was testing me to see if I'd run with that idea? He really thinks I learned *nothing* from all this shit.

"I'm still pissed at you," he says matter-of-factly. "So, if you're not submitting the doc so I won't be mad at you, you might as well just do it. Don't throw away your chance at the spot just for forgiveness."

"It wouldn't be right. I'll just hold out hope they have the program next year and transfer in, if I can." If I even want to pursue documentaries after this. If anything would deter me, it would be this whole experience. I'm in no shape to be a director, a storyteller. My grandma would be disappointed. I'm just as bad as *Jersey Shore*.

"I watched the footage. It was good." He meets my eyes. "And those scenes you added . . . you were always filming?"

"It's kind of my default setting, sorry."

"No, it was nice." He zones out over my shoulder for a second. "I think if I were in Trevor's position, I would miss those normal moments more than the fun stuff."

"I'm sorry," I say again, and cringe because it's such a Corrine thing to say over and over again. I've hit my wall. I literally don't know what else to say. I fucked up and I'm so so so so sorry.

"I don't like being mad at my best friend."

My brain screams at my heart to not get its hopes up, and yet it starts racing. I shrug off his words. "Taj?"

"I obviously mean you. But you can't do something like that again. You *can't*." His voice breaks and it echoes so loudly that I feel my heart crack, threatening to shatter.

"I promise I won't. It was so fucking stupid and not worth it. Losing you was not worth it."

He watches me for a moment. "You'll have to make it up to me."

"I'll do anything." The words fly out of my mouth faster than I expect them to and I stumble on the last word. "Anything," I say again.

"I have an incomplete portrait assignment due next week."

"Great, I have a face." I even point at it to emphasize this very obvious fact.

He smirks. "Coming on a little strong, don't you think?"

"That's me: Saine 'coming-on-a-little-strong' Sinclair."

For a moment we just stare at each other. He takes in my face, eyes roaming from top to bottom, while I just wait, nearly holding my breath. It feels like we're on a precipice of something big, something that will define us for years to come, like the spin the bottle game I never expected to dictate my future.

He pulls his phone out of his pocket and holds it up, clearly taking a photo of me. I let him, still waiting.

He smiles at the screen and then shows me. My cheeks are red, my hair is a little frizzy, my eyes are wide with dark circles that are only amplified by the terrible hospital lighting. And yet . . . I think I can see myself the way he sees me right now.

Vulnerable.

And it's not a bad look.

Unknown

Today 3:07 PM

HI IT'S MARA

3:07 PM

I had to physically fight Holden to get your number

3:07 PM

So I assume you won?

3:08 PM

Yeah I started crying so he'd think he accidentally hurt me and then stole his phone when he was getting an ice pack
3:08 PM

Wow, your mind. Unparalleled.
3:08 PM

Thank you. I know. I just wanted to say thanks for going to the movies with Rose and me
3:08 PM

You're welcome. Did you also thank Holden since he paid for it, drove, and looked the other way when you two held hands very adorably over the popcorn?
3:09 PM

Ugh and Holden thought I would be the one annoying YOU.
3:10 PM

THIRTY-THREE

"I thought your big, strong boyfriend was supposed to come help us move this stuff?" Juniper grunts, holding the end of my desk by herself while Kayla and I struggle with the other side.

Yes, we regularly throw human beings into the air at football and basketball games but can barely handle this desk. In our defense, our end of the desk has drawers. Empty drawers, but still, way more wood than her side.

"He said he would stop by when he could. He's watching Mara right now." It would have been helpful to use the minivan to move things like my desk, but babysitting duties call. I used to think that Mara was old enough to watch herself, but now after knowing her, I'm not so sure it would be the safest thing.

Kayla drops her arms, giving the desk's weight to me. I drop it accidentally. "Sorry. Ever since Coach made me a flier permanently, I feel like I have two limp noodles for arms. They're not getting enough exercise."

Juniper sets down her end. "I ask you to carry me all the time and you refuse."

"You're one inch shorter than me so you think you deserve to be carried around everywhere? Who are you, Ariana Grande?"

I groan. "Can we save the marital dispute for after we get the desk up the stairs?"

"Wait, are we really fighting?" Juniper asks, her brows low.

"No, I thought we were just putting off taking the desk upstairs," Kayla says.

Juniper relaxes. "Oh, okay. Same page."

Laughing, I pick up my end again. "Let's go."

"Ugh, *men*. Can't live with them, can't live with them," Juniper grunts.

We carry the desk up the stairs slowly and awkwardly, struggling to maneuver it over the banister to walk it back to my room. But we make it without breaking the desk! And my room is starting to look like a real room, like someone might live in it for more than just a few moments at a time when she's unpacking boxes.

Before she went to work, my mom helped us load the desk into Kayla's car, which was an amazing feat that I did not think could be accomplished. I lost two bucks over it. Kayla, who has a better understanding of the Narnia-wardrobe-like qualities of her car, understandably won that money. My mom also slid the boxes with my bed frame on top of the desk and said something like "Tetris!" afterward. After securing both the mattress and box spring on the top of the car, we were good to go. Juniper had to sit on my lap, but we made it work with Kayla only a little jealous.

Now, Kayla wipes sweat from her forehead. "I'm gonna smack Holden when he gets here."

"At least he's nothing like Devon. He would have shown up after we're done and then asked for Chinese food to compensate him for his time," Juniper says.

"The wooooooooorst," Kayla sings, flopping onto my bed.

A knock on the door startles me. I pull my phone from my pocket but see no texts from Holden saying he's here or on his way or *anything*—like, seriously, where is this kid? I pound down the stairs, dragging Juniper and Kayla with me because like *hell* am I going to open a door by myself with a stranger and the pitch black of winter ready to greet me.

But it's not a stranger. It's Corrine, with a bundle of flat square packages in her hands.

I frown, not because I'm unhappy to see her—I'm actually a little giddy—but because I'm confused. "Hey?" I step back to let her in. "I thought you were working."

She shivers a little, wiping her feet on the doormat outside, and then comes inside. "Marisa let me leave early."

"Hi, Corrine," Juniper says with a smile. "Whatcha got there?"

Kayla rushes forward to help her with the packages, setting them on the long table my mom and I moved in last weekend.

"Just some wall art." She pulls her jacket off and leaves it on a dining room chair. "Obviously not for the exposed brick wall." She blows a kiss to it, acting more normal than she has the last few months. More normal than I deserve, at least. "It's perfect how it is."

I think part of her wants to skip the awkwardness and I'm not mad at that.

Kayla tears into the packages, revealing a bunch of kitschy frames, no doubt courtesy of a Thrifty shopping trip. There are four total, and each one is filled with a gorgeous photo of . . . the murals. My grandma's murals that Holden took photos of before my mom and I bit the bullet and painted over them.

I can't breathe.

"Holden helped me. . . ." She waits for my response. "I hope that's okay."

I pull her into a tight hug, my throat threatening to close and hot tears threatening to spill like a dam. "I love them so much."

"Do you want to hang them around the house?" She squeezes me back. I can't tell if her words are muffled with emotion or just my hair. "Put one in each room?"

"That's such a good idea," Kayla says, showing the photos to Juniper, who has never seen the murals before.

"Is that—"

"Yes. Don't judge me," I say, cutting off Juniper's confused question. I turn back to Corrine. "Will you help me hang them?"

She pulls some Command Strips and a tiny little level from her pocket, always the prepared Girl Scout. "I thought you'd never ask."

After hanging the photos, all four of us manage to set up the security cameras around the apartment, and then we stuff our faces with Neato Burrito, which is close enough that *I can walk! to! it!* It's a school night, so they leave around ten o'clock. Corrine is the last one out, and I stop her with a hand on her arm.

"I have a question. Since we're still kind of clearing the air." I step back so she can come inside and close the door behind her.

"Bring it." She says it with more confidence than is written on her face. Her perfect brows twitch as she tries to keep them from closing in on each other.

"Why haven't you given my necklace back to me?" I reach for the spot it used to hang, making it clear where a necklace should go. "Did you lose it?"

She sighs, hands fidgeting at her sides. "I . . . I meant to give it back. I really appreciated the sentiment behind it, but I just felt, I don't know. I felt bad. I didn't want to remind you of your grandma when it seemed like you were bouncing back, you know? I didn't want to make you sad or remind you that I—that I wasn't there for you."

I fight back a smile. "Look at you opening up so easily."

Her response is practically ripped from her mouth, it comes out so quickly. "Felt like a ceramic knife slicing me from head to toe."

"*Corrine.*"

"I'm sorry," she says through a laugh. "It's true."

I shake my head but pull her into another hug. "Can I get it back?"

She nods against my shoulder. "Yes. You'll have it so soon. Like magic."

We part ways and I fall into bed about half an hour after. Holden's parents probably got home too late for him to come over, but that doesn't explain his lack of texting me back. I'm about to text again when my phone buzzes and his smiling face fills my screen.

I answer instantly. "Hey, is everything okay?"

"Yeah, sorry. Mara instituted a no-phone rule during our back-to-back Avengers rewatch."

"I'm so happy she's introducing you to better comic book movies."

"Hilarious. I'm outside."

"Outside where?"

"Like, right under your balcony."

I jolt upright in bed, terrifying Bagel when I kick the covers off, and stumble to the sliding door leading to the balcony. It's freezing out—below freezing, if we're going to be technical—but I unlock it and throw it to the side. I step onto the faux-wood balcony and lean over the edge, spotting his pale face in the moonlight.

"This is kind of romantic, but we have a front door and my mom's not home."

He shrugs. "I saw the camera."

"That means the camera probably saw you. So, you might as well use the door."

"I was promised you'd keep me in mind when you got a new place. You know, for easy access inside."

"Yeah, well, you're tall." I gauge the distance to the ground. "You could probably get up here."

"Let's find out." He takes a running leap, latching onto the balcony, and pulls himself up to a standing position on the opposite side of the bars. "Not too bad. Definitely can't do that after arm day at the gym."

"Stop trying to convince me that you go the gym and get over here."

He leans in to kiss me and I grip onto his arms.

"Come on. I don't want you to fall."

He climbs over and we go into my bedroom, the lights of the parking lot mingling with moonlight, casting my room in an eerie glow, like time has stopped for a moment. He takes off his shoes and joins me on the bed, Bagel leaving us after giving Holden's hand a cursory lick.

"I can only stay for a little. My mom gets home at eleven and if the minivan isn't in the driveway, she'll call search and rescue." He rubs his hands together, warming them. "Sorry I didn't let you know I wouldn't make it."

I don't go into full Corrine meltdown mode when people don't answer their phones, but I did have a highlight reel of teenage stupidity running full speed in my mind. I'd be impressed with my brain's creativity if it didn't mean I had to witness Holden getting into car accidents in various ways all night.

"I forgive you." It's literally the least I can do after the last few months.

He tucks himself under the blankets even though he can't stay and pulls me closer, one arm under my neck and the other across my waist. He nods at the picture of my grandma's murals hanging on the wall behind my bed. "I see Corrine stopped by."

"Yes. I really love the pictures." I scoot closer to him, even though it's pretty much physically impossible at this point. Not even twelve-year-old lovestruck Saine could have imagined something as sweet as this with Holden. "Thank you for helping her with that."

He nods, his nose brushing against mine. "That wasn't our only collaboration."

I pull back a few inches and raise an eyebrow. "Yeah?"

Grinning, he reaches under the blanket and fights against something for a moment.

"What's happening here? Should I leave you alone to finish . . . ?"

"Got it," he says, revealing his hand above the blanket, a small velvet box in it. The same box I found in his pocket after the flat tire. Has he been carrying that around all this time, waiting for the opportune moment to give it to—me? "This won't look too good on me, so I hope you like it."

He opens the box and I can't resist looking this time, now that I know it wasn't meant for someone else, that it wasn't a gift someone else rejected. It's my *grandma's necklace*. I grab the box, my breath wrestling its way up my windpipe. "Wait. I literally just asked Corrine about this."

I'm so confused, excited, happy, sad that I could throw up. I'm not even jealous that Corrine and Holden orchestrated these two things behind my back, together, because they mean so much to me, my friends and what they did.

"Holden." I pull the necklace out of the box and examine it, making sure it's really mine. "How did you get this? *When* did you get this?"

"I talked to Corrine yesterday. She said something super sappy that only she would say about how it was always supposed to be me and you."

I sit up fully and he helps me put it on, which really means he holds my hair to the side, but it's the thought that counts. I touch the chain around my neck, feel the weight of the charm, the familiarity of it, even after being without it for so long. "I found the box in your pocket a few weeks ago. I thought you had bought that necklace for someone."

"No, I was just carrying the box around. I had to work up the nerve to talk to Corrine about it because I didn't want to upset her more than it already seemed she was with, you know, everything. And then things went to shit. I had thought about buying you that necklace, though. *Before* all of this. But I knew this was the one you really wanted." He sighs, but it's laced with contentment. "I don't want to come between you two. I know she was there for you when you thought I couldn't be."

I kiss him and slowly move us down to the bed. "I think things will be okay."

"I hope so." He slides a sock-covered foot over my bare leg. "How's it feel to be sleeping in a new place?"

"It was weird at first, but now that you're here?" I grip the charm around my neck. "Feels like home."

ACKNOWLEDGMENTS

I expected my second time writing acknowledgments to go much easier than the first—I know who I want to thank and what I want to thank them for, but putting the words down on the page is, ironically enough, extremely difficult. Please don't revoke my Author Card for the bumbling I'm about to do. Thank you:

To my editor, Elizabeth Lynch, who I wish I could clone and gift to all of my author friends so they could experience your kindness, organizational skills, and talent.

To the HarperTeen team, who help things run so smoothly in the background that I never have to stress. Thank you, Mikayla Lawrence, Gwen Morton, Sean Cavanagh, Lisa Calcasola, Aubrey Churchward, Jessica White, and Linda Schmukler.

To my dream team of cover creators, Jessie Gang and Sarah Long: thank you for bringing Saine and Holden to life. I hope we have many more wonderful works of art together in our futures.

To my agent, Bridget Smith, who responds to emails nearly immediately and always has an answer, or will find one, so I don't combust.

To Rachel Lynn Solomon, Sonia Hartl, Carlyn Greenwald, Annette Christie, Andrea Contos, Auriane Desombre, Marisa Kanter, Jennifer Dugan, and Susan Lee, who all live way too far away from me.

To Jenny Howe, Sierra Elmore, Monica Gomez-Hira, Tori Bovalino, Claire Ahn, Samantha Eaton, and Rachael Lippincott, for giving me feedback and friendship.

To my mom and my sister, for inspiring my fictional women-only families.

To my partner, Dylan, for his constant support, love, and humor.

And lastly, to my grandmother, Betty, whose heart and home are painted across these pages.